The Long Way Down

Craig Schaefer

Demimonde Books
Joliet, Illinois

Craig Schaefer / Demimonde Books
2328 E. Lincoln Hwy, #238
New Lenox, IL 60451-9533
www.craigschaeferbooks.com

Publisher's Note: This is a work of fiction. Names, characters, places, and incidents are a product of the author's imagination. Locales and public names are sometimes used for atmospheric purposes. Any resemblance to actual people, living or dead, or to businesses, companies, events, institutions, or locales is completely coincidental.

Cover Design by James T. Egan of Bookfly Design LLC.
Author Photo ©2014 by Karen Forsythe Photography
Book Layout & Design ©2013 - BookDesignTemplates.com

Craig Schaefer / The Long Way Down -- 1st ed.
ISBN 978-0-9903393-1-1

The Daniel Faust Series

1.

"I know what you are," the old man said. The tremor in his voice told me he wasn't so sure. He'd introduced himself as Jud, Jud Pankow from Minnesota. He was a long way from home.

We sat in a booth in the back of Tiki Pete's, a seedy diner four blocks east of the Vegas Strip. I doubted the place would survive a health inspection, but the grimy windows and the backwater street kept the tourist traffic at bay. Besides, I didn't come here for the food.

"Then you know I'm not a private investigator," I told him, "not a licensed one, anyway."

He gripped a coffee-stained manila folder in his thick farmer's hands and clenched his jaw. I sipped my mai tai.

"He killed my little girl, Mr. Faust. He murdered her and he threw her away like a piece of garbage. I don't need any private eye to tell me that."

"The police think otherwise. You want me to prove them wrong?"

"I don't care what anybody thinks," Jud said, "and nothing's going to bring my baby back, proof or no proof. I know that."

"So what do you want from me?"

His rheumy eyes flooded with a pain I couldn't imagine. The folder crinkled in his grip as he whispered just loud enough for me to hear, "I want him *punished*."

I should have sent him away. I didn't know why, but I felt like a roller coaster ratcheting its way up the first peak, inch by inch, heartbeats from a plunge into bad craziness at a hundred miles an hour. All my instincts screamed at me to drop this one and walk.

Looking at him, though, I didn't have the heart. He needed some hope. Hell, he just needed someone to give a damn.

"I don't make promises," I told him and watched his eyes light up.

He fumbled in his pocket and shoved an envelope into my hands. It was stuffed with green, all small bills, rumpled and faded. This wasn't fresh-from-the-bank money. It was the kind of cash that sits in a coffee tin in a kitchen cabinet for years, saved up for a rainy day.

"This," I said, tapping the envelope, "buys you a few days of my time. If I don't think I can help you, you get it back, minus my expenses. Now, is Stacy your...?"

"Granddaughter. Her pa, he was never in the picture, and her ma's got...she's got problems. Don't think she even noticed when Stacy ran away. I watched over the girl best I could. Even sent her money a few times after she left home, when I had an address to send it to. Then she took up with that...that bastard. She wrote to tell me she'd moved in with him, that he'd gotten her a job, a good-paying job..."

He slid the manila folder across the table. On top of the stack inside was a ragged newspaper clipping, torn from the *Vegas Sun*, and the stark headline told the story.

"Porn Star Drowns in Storm Tunnel."

I didn't need to read the article. I'd already seen the story on TV. Even in the middle of the Mojave it rained a few days every year, and we were nestled in a natural basin. There was a network of storm tunnels and drains underneath the city to trap the occasional downpour and keep the water off the streets, which was great for everyone, except the indigents who holed up down there to escape the heat. Sometimes they managed to stumble out ahead of the rain, and sometimes maintenance crews had to fish out the bodies.

Next in the pile was an autopsy report from the Clark County coroner's office. No photo, just a few pages of medical jargon dense enough to make my eyes water. Cause of death was drowning, no surprise there, but I frowned when I read the bit under that.

"Time of death is difficult to estimate, but given the diminished signs of rigor mortis as well as the subject's skin condition, coroner estimates TOD sometime on 3/15."

"The rainstorm was on the seventeenth," I said, flipping back to double-check the date on the newspaper clipping.

"That's right," Jud said.

I looked up at him. "She drowned two days before the storm."

He nodded.

"Either the doc was dead wrong, or there's a criminal case here. Why aren't the cops looking into this?"

"I wasn't even supposed to know." Jud stared at his hands. "They told me they could only give that report out to immediate next of kin. Granddad don't count. On my way out, a young fella pulled me aside and put that copy in my hands. Said I oughta read it real close. Well, I did, and I did some checking. Found out the case was referred to this Detective Holt, so I gave him a call."

"What'd he tell you?"

"Whole lot of nothing. Told me they were working on it, but he's got eighty cases on his desk and yadda yadda. Made it clear my little girl was a lower priority than getting his dishes done."

Her letters home sat under the autopsy report. Longhand on loose-leaf paper, talking about life in the big city. She signed each one "Love, Stacy" and drew the *v* as a tiny heart. I glanced at the dates. The letters came farther and farther apart.

"She never said anything was wrong?"

"I'd have come out to get her myself," he said, his weathered hands clenching into fists, "if I'd only known what she was really doing, what he was making her do."

"Tell me about the guy."

Jud snorted. "Artie Kaufman. Calls himself 'Daddy Warbucks' when he's filming that filth. Turned Stacy into his star performer."

I sipped my mai tai and shook my head.

"Problem there, Mr. Pankow, is you just took away his motive. If Stacy was making money for this guy, why would he kill her?"

"Have you seen the kinds of movies he makes?"

"No," I said, "don't think I have."

"You'd remember if you had. They aren't right, Mr. Faust. The things he does...he's not right."

I tapped the envelope again and thought about my over-due rent. Whether Artie Kaufman was a killer, Jud looked about a heartbeat away from going to see him with a gun in his hand. I didn't want to get involved. I also didn't want the old guy to spend the rest of his life in prison because he did something stupid.

"I have some ground rules." I picked up the envelope. "Are you staying in town?"

"Got a room at the Value Lodge on East Tropicana. Until Friday, anyway. Can't afford to stay longer than that."

"I'd rather you went home tonight, but if you're going to be here, I want you in that hotel room doing absolutely nothing. You don't go within a mile of Kaufman. And if I look into this and find out he's got clean hands, that's the end of it. I want your word."

Jud nodded slowly, and I wondered how much I could trust him to hold to that.

"Next," I said, leaning in and giving him a hard look, "I'll check into Stacy's death, but that's the extent of what I'm offering. If it was murder, and if I find the person responsi-ble, anything that does or does not happen next is at my discretion. You will not be involved. This is for your protec-tion and mine. Understand?"

He chewed that over. Jud was the kind of man who thought out his sentences before he spoke.

"I heard about you. On the computer. Traded mail with a lady named Jenna Rearden. She told me what happened to her ex-husband."

Jenna. That explained it. I was going to have to tell her to stop tossing my name around. I'd done a job for her, all right. I normally don't get my hands that dirty, but the ex in question had been paying visits to their six-year-old daughter's bedroom at night. I took exception to that.

"She said he's locked up in the nuthouse," Jud said, eyeing me cautiously. "Said they have to keep him on happy pills or all he does is scream until his throat gives out. Doctors can't reckon why, neither."

"I told you, I'll look into your granddaughter's death. Past that, I don't make promises."

Jud studied me.

"Jenna Rearden thinks you might be the Devil."

"Yet here you are." I finished my drink. "Lucky for you, I only take payment in cash." I folded the envelope into my pocket, rose, and shook his hand. His grip was firm, with calluses like lunar rocks."I'll call you," I said and made my way out into the afternoon sun.

It wasn't hard to see that Jud Pankow was dying slow. He'd lost the only person he cared about, and I knew he was filling the hours listing every regret, everything he should have said and didn't, and everything he did say and shouldn't have. It was a familiar song and I knew every note of it. I had one asset Jud didn't, though: a clear head.

I figured Stacy's ending would be the best place to start. I'd have to go where I knew the cops wouldn't. Underground.

2.

Home, when I was there, was a second-floor walk-up just off Bermuda Road. It was a tourist-trap motel before it got converted to apartments sometime in the sixties. A painted concrete cactus and a dusty parking lot welcomed me back under the shade of a dying palm tree. A pale lizard on the railing watched with lazy eyes as I jogged up the stairs and jiggled my key in the door for room 208.

My furniture was mostly vintage, straight from the old motel days, spruced up with the occasional estate sale treasure. The combination lock built into the closet door, though, that was new. I clicked on the desk lamp, leaving my curtains closed, and dialed up the numbers by touch. Half the closet was for dress shirts, ties, and my one nice suit. The other half was for business.

Books with faded covers jostled for space on a pair of built-in shelves, from Eichmann's *Treatise on Renaissance Alchemy* to a first edition of Balfour's *Cultes des Goules*. The next three shelves hosted a clutter of pouches, vials, and sticks of chalk—everything for the working sorcerer on the go. Up top, a pair of shoeboxes kept my tools neatly stowed.

I stocked up on a few odds and ends and checked my rummage drawer for a working flashlight. I was in the middle of tugging on a pair of old black jeans, something I wouldn't mind getting dirty, when my cell phone rang. I held it to my ear with one hand, fumbling at my belt with the other.

"Danny boy!" boomed the voice on the other end, a woman with a Creole accent thick enough to cut with a knife. "Where you been hidin'? Everybody's asking about you."

"Mama Margaux, hey. I'm okay, just been a long week. Dealing with some stuff."

"Goin' on two weeks, more like."

I looked over at my rumpled bed and the three empty bottles of Jack Daniels gathering dust in the wastebin.

"Huh, guess it has. Look, I'll come out and see everybody soon. Just haven't been feeling real social lately."

"Tonight," she said. "You come down to the Garden tonight. Don't you say no to me, boy. I'll come and drag you by the ear. Don't think I won't."

I couldn't help laughing. "All right, all right, I believe you. I'll be down later. I have a job to take care of."

"Mm-hmm?" I could hear her disbelief dripping from the receiver. "A job? That what you call fleecing tourists at three-card monte?"

"A real job, though I don't think it's going to amount to much. Mostly just trying to keep my client from going postal on a guy who might be innocent. You know anything about the storm-drain tunnels?"

"I know not to go down there, ever. Full of crazy junkies and worse."

"I know about the junkies," I said. "It's the 'and worse' part I'm concerned about."

She sounded cagey all of a sudden. "Nothin' too particular, but I threw the shells last night, just to see which way the wind was blowing. The Loa say a storm's coming. A bad one."

"Don't suppose your spirits could be a little more specific?"

"You just watch yourself," she said. "There's a whole mess of trouble fixin' to land on somebody's head."

#

When Mama's spirits said trouble was on the way, I knew better than to second-guess her. Still, a job was a job, so I'd just have to hope any dark clouds looming on the horizon weren't headed my way. I pulled up a map of storm-tunnel entrances on my laptop and cross-referenced it with the article on Stacy's death, trying to pinpoint the most likely spot where she would have gone underground. Or where her body was dumped.

I put my hopes on a ditch a few blocks north of Fremont Street. It was four in the afternoon by the time I parked my battered old Ford on the side of the road and walked up to a barbed wire fence. I wanted to be away from here by nightfall, not that it would matter once I went underground. I hadn't counted on the fence, but it wasn't a problem; some adventurous soul had already taken wire cutters and peeled back a hole big enough to slip through, right under a stark No Trespassing sign.

The ditch ran about fifteen feet deep with steep, sloping walls. Garbage littered the water-stained concrete below, a wasteland of crumpled beer cans, scraps of plastic, and glittering shards of broken glass. I climbed down an access ladder, and checked my flashlight for the twentieth time. It was an old clip-on model. It had never failed me before, but this would be a bad place to start.

One of the storm-drain tunnels opened up here, nearly ten feet wide and just as high. Graffiti in a riot of faded colors adorned the walls of the tunnel mouth. Layer upon layer of tags and scrawls and symbols, like a dig site waiting for some archaeologist to peel the paint back a millimeter at a time, discovering ancient wisdom. The freshest tags were harsh, angular, and angry red. They didn't look like modern art. They looked tribal.

The sunlight died a few steps into the tunnel. Gravel and glass crunched under my shoes. I clicked on the flashlight and attached it to my pocket, cursing the feeble beam as I made my way deeper. The tunnel was awash in the odor of mildew and stale water. I kept glancing back at the entrance, at the reassuring blob of daylight, as it faded farther and farther away. After a couple minutes of walking, the tunnel made a sharp bend, and that last comfort vanished.

It felt like being sealed in a tomb. The concrete walls amplified my footsteps to the sound of a gunshot. The echoes of dripping water surrounded me. Something scurried, sending a rock tumbling, and I angled my beam around trying to catch a glimpse of anything but the squirming, thumb-sized cockroaches that fled from the light.

It was dark. Not midnight dark, not even midnight on a new moon. Pitch dark. The kind your eyes can't adjust to, no matter how you strain. Maybe a hundred feet past the bend, the tunnel split into a three-way junction. A faint, distant glow beckoned me down the left-hand turn.

The glow turned out to be a lamp nestled behind a patchwork wall, tiny fingers of light escaping to reach toward me. My flashlight drifted across ramshackle boards and an overturned grocery cart. I almost choked with the stench of mold and rancid trash. The lamp was behind a crude lean-to built with scavenged scrap. As I approached, I thought I heard whispers and the clink of glass on metal.

I froze in mid-step. No telling who I'd run into down here, but nobody lived in a storm tunnel because they were a social butterfly who loved making new friends.

"Anybody up there?" I called out, wincing at how the tunnel threw my voice back at me. "I'm just passing through, not looking for trouble."

A pair of bloodshot eyes peered through a break in the scrap wall. "You Metro?" asked a cracked voice.

"No. Just doing a favor for a friend. Mind if I come closer? Want to ask you a couple of questions."

The eyes narrowed, and I held up my open hands.

"Yeah, all right," the voice grumbled. I approached slowly, taking my time, no sudden moves, like visiting a possibly deranged vagrant in a hut twenty feet below the city streets was the most natural thing in the world. To be fair, I'd been in weirder places.

The lean-to only had two walls, I realized as I came around the side. The back lay open between one wall and the tunnel concrete, and the resident had carved out a little home for himself inside. He had an army-surplus cot, a table with a hot plate and the lamp, and some transparent garbage bags stuffed with clothes. It seemed oddly bright, brighter than the tiny lamp should have been able to muster, until I noticed he'd spattered the inner walls and tunnel ceiling with a coat of paint the color of a dusty eggshell.

"'S for the widows, so I can see 'em when they creep up on me," the man grumbled. He might have been in his late thirties, a little older than me, but his eyes were sunken and his pale skin was pockmarked with acne scars and wrinkles that had come a decade too soon.

"Sorry?"

"Saw ya lookin'," he said, gesturing around him. I realized he meant the paint. "Black widows. Tunnels are full of the bastards. I seen webs with forty, fifty of 'em, just nestled there, waiting. One bite, you swell up like a water balloon. The roaches are bad, but those widows, man, they're mean."

I fought the urge to slap at my arms and legs, already imagining them crawling with shiny spiders. Instead, I took a step forward and offered him my hand.

"I'm Daniel. You been down here long?"

He took it with a firm grip and a nod. "Eric. Been here...man, six years? Seven? Better than the streets, once you get used to it. Nobody hassles me down here."

"Good to meet you, Eric. I was wondering about somebody else who might have been crashing down here. You ever see this girl?"

I fished the ragged newspaper article from my pocket and showed it to him. They'd run it with a high school prom picture of Stacy smiling like a girl with a future made of diamonds. Eric frowned.

"Shit, man, that was the cops that did that." He shook his head.

"That did what? Came and fished her body out?"

"No," he said, "the cops brought her *down* here."

I suddenly remembered the bad feeling I got sitting across the table from Jud. The roller coaster ratcheted up another notch toward the inevitable plunge.

"It was a couple nights before the last rain," he said. "A couple of 'em came down with that poor kid in a body bag. Dumped her about a hundred yards up Tunnel C, near the water intake."

"How do you know they were cops?" I asked.

"Me and a few of the other guys down here, we pressed 'em, wanting to know what they thought they were doing. One of the cops, he flashes a badge in our face. The guy was a detective, no joke. Told us to get the fuck back, and then he shows us the gun in his waistband. We got back."

"You sure it was real?" I desperately wanted him to be wrong. "You can buy badges—"

Eric shook his head, giving me a sad smile. "I used to be on the job, before I got a bad habit and ended up down here. I know badges. They were real cops. Skinny guy with a face like a hatchet, and a bodybuilder with a blond perm. Hatchet-face was the one who liked waving his gun around."

"Did you tell anybody?"

"Man, who am I gonna tell?" He scuffed his gym shoe on the dank concrete. "You think anyone wants to hear anything we have to say? They'd just say I killed her, or maybe those cops'd shut me up for good. I felt bad, but I'd rather feel bad than feel dead."

I nodded. "They didn't leave anything behind, did they? I mean, besides the girl."

"Nah, and if they had, it woulda been picked clean five seconds after they left. Hell, me and my buddy Amos took turns standing guard over the kid's body until the rain came, just to make sure nobody messed with her. It ain't right, you know? It just ain't right. You can have a look down Tunnel C if you feel like it, but I wouldn't if I were you."

"Why's that? Black widows?"

A nervous look crossed Eric's face, his gaze darting toward the darkness at my back. He shook his head and lowered his voice.

"Nah, man. That kid? She's still down here. And she ain't happy about it."

3.

I couldn't guess which habit had sent Eric's life into a tailspin. In Vegas, you can pick your poison: booze, gambling, sex, meth. It's all here and waiting for you, twenty-four hours a day. He didn't come across like a junkie, though, and the sinking feeling in the pit of my stomach told me he wasn't sharing some alcoholic fever dream.

"No such thing as ghosts," I said, keeping my voice light.

He curled his chapped lips into a grin. "You know. You know what's up. Don't pretend you don't. You got that look."

"Maybe I do. Anybody else see this maybe-ghost?"

"My buddy Amos," he said. "He don't live down there no more. He went topside, said getting beaten up on the streets was better than one more night in Tunnel C. Couple of other guys took off a couple of days later, haven't seen 'em since."

"But not you? Aren't you scared?"

Eric waved his hand. "She stays over there, I stay out here. We don't bother each other none. Besides, when she gets close, you know it. There's a smell. Gives you time to run."

"What kind of smell?"

"You'll know it when it hits you. Seriously, man, you don't want to go down there."

I dipped into my pocket, palming a five-dollar bill while pretending to adjust my flashlight with my other hand. I unfolded the cash with a spread of my fingers and offered it to him.

"It's okay," I said. "I'm a magician."

Eric snickered and took the bill with a nod. "You could do a card trick for her, but I don't think it'll help."

"You'd be surprised. I have some really good card tricks."

Eric watched me go. As I continued down the tunnel, the glow from his lamp fading at my back, a sense of cool confidence washed over me. Black widows were one thing, but ghosts? Ghosts I could deal with.

Your typical ghost is just a psychic imprint. They're the aftermath of trauma, despair, an emotion so strong that it doesn't die with the person experiencing it. Scary, but about as dangerous as a filmstrip. If Stacy's murder created an after-impression, I might be able to learn something from it. If nothing else, I could at least banish it and do Eric and his buddies a favor. They had enough ghosts of their own to wrestle with.

Scraps of detritus cluttered the tunnel floor. My flashlight beam flickered across a broken hockey stick, a few plastic bags, a grocery cart lying on its side with one wheel slowly turning in a half-felt draft. I looked back to the middle of the tunnel and froze.

A black plastic sphere sat in the center of the floor, looking less abandoned than carefully placed there, like a prop in a canceled play. I crouched down to pick it up, finally recognizing it as one of those old Magic 8 Ball toys. Taken by a whim, I gave it a shake.

"Is anyone down here?" I asked and then flipped it over. Through a scratched plastic window, I was greeted with the words "Answer hazy, ask again later." I chuckled and moved to put it back down.

Then the ball jerked in my hand, and the answer flipped to "Yes."

The sphere tumbled from my fingers, cracked against the concrete, and bounced into the dark. I slipped a deck of cards from my pocket and gave them a slow, overhand shuffle as I walked deeper into the tunnel. The sinuous riffling of the pasteboard in my hands helped me concentrate.

"All right," I said to the shadows, "we can do it that way."

The underground air had felt damp and cool, like a day in late autumn. Now winter gusted in. A chilling breeze rubbed up against my spine and turned my breath to frost just before the smell hit me. The stench of raw sewage swelled up like someone had opened a cesspool right under my feet. My stomach lurched, and I struggled to breathe as I flipped over the top card of my deck. Queen of spades. I shuffled it back in.

The flashlight beam flickered across a recessed alcove in the tunnel wall. Stringy blond hair, a naked shoulder, bloodless lips. With a whispering rasp, Stacy came out to greet me.

Not all of her, though.

Jud Pankow's murdered granddaughter hovered in the beam of my flashlight, a shambling twitch in her step, staring at me with mad eyes the color of silver dollars. One of her arms was missing. And half a leg. And an oval chunk of her stomach that looked like it had been scooped out with a precision saw. There was no blood, no gore, not even the hint of a wound. Her body just *stopped* here and there, like pieces of her had been edited out of existence.

I knew she couldn't really hurt me, that this was nothing but the memory of Stacy's pain given form and life, but my mouth still went dry. I tried to remember the words of an old Louisiana folk-charm, one I'd used before to put an apparition to rest.

Stacy wrenched her mouth open, her jaw quaking, and rivulets of water poured down her chin, spattering on the concrete floor. Then she screamed and taught me how little I really knew about ghosts.

Her shriek felt like a pair of razorblades slashing across my eardrums, borne on a wind of raw anguish. I staggered back, reeling under a blast of horror given focus and form. Fingers of despair and betrayal clawed at my mind, trying to infect me with her pain, to consume me with it.

I answered on instinct. I passed my free hand over the deck, the jack of diamonds leaping to my fingertips, and I flung it at her. The card caught the Stacy-thing in the shoulder and flew through her, pulsing with a flash of violent purple light. The apparition flailed, its cry cut short, and I reached out to catch the jack as it whirled its way back to my hand.

Like I told Eric, I knew some good card tricks. Not good enough for this, though. I felt like a boxer who expected to go a few rounds with a welterweight only to find himself staring down Mike Tyson. I needed to figure out what the hell this thing was and come up with a plan to take it down before it hurt someone, none of which I could do while it was trying to kill me.

I drew another card, tracing the seal of Saturn across its face with my thumb and flipping it into the air. It hung there as if dangling from an invisible thread, a tiny cardboard barrier between me and the Stacy-thing. The apparition reared back, unleashing another scream, but it didn't touch me. All I saw was the card vibrating in the air, absorbing the lethal torrent.

The card ignited.

Running, I had almost made it to the mouth of the tunnel when a third scream hit me from behind. My hands seized up and sent cards scattering around my feet, useless and inert. My stomach constricted. I dropped to one knee, doubling over, vomiting up a torrent of brackish water as fuzzy black spots flooded my vision. I was drowning in reverse, my air cut off by the flood, my hands scrabbling at the tunnel floor in desperation. Half blind with blood roaring in my ears, I closed my fingers around a fallen card and filled it with the last spark of my power, flinging it into the air.

The torrent stopped. Hacking up spurts of water, I forced myself to my feet. The new shield-card was already vibrating, its power fragmenting by the second. Stumbling to the tunnel wall, I tugged a leather pouch from my hip pocket and tore it open, nearly dropping it from my trembling fingers. I poured out a thin trail of powder, jagged but unbroken, from one side of the tunnel to the other and finished just as the card burst into flames.

The apparition loomed from the darkness and froze. It wavered in the air, radiating confusion, then slipped back into the shadows.

I hunched over, bracing my hands against my knees until I could breathe again. The flashlight beam traced the powder line, letting me touch it up with the remainder of the pouch's contents, just to be safe. The powder was Mama Margaux's personal recipe. I knew it was mostly red brick dust and purified salt, but she guarded the rest of the mixture's contents like it was Colonel Sanders' eleven herbs and spices. All I knew was that anything not made of flesh and bone was instinctively repulsed by the stuff; as long as the line stayed unbroken, the Stacy-thing would keep her distance from the tunnel mouth.

I staggered back up the tunnel, soaked and aching, my throat sore and my stomach in knots. Eric's laughter greeted me as I reached his lean-to.

"You didn't wanna go back there, man. Told you so."

"That tunnel," I gasped, "what's on the other side? Where does it lead?"

"Nowhere fast. Junction goes off to a culvert about two blocks east, but it's sealed with a grate and padlocked. Nobody goes in or out from there."

I nodded. "Good. I'll be back. Until then, stay the hell out of there. Don't let anybody else go back there either."

"Don't gotta tell me twice. Told you, I've been down here seven years. Learned that the best thing to do when you see weird shit is to stay far away from it."

I could still hear him snickering as I walked away. Tourists.

I emerged from the tunnel into a warm Vegas night, the starless black sky lit with an electric glow. A blazing shaft of light from the Strip fired upward in the distance, slicing the air like a neon stiletto. I drove home, stripped off my sodden clothes, and jumped into the shower, cranking the water just a hair shy of scalding as I scrubbed my skin raw.

Stacy was murdered, no doubt in my mind, and her body dumped just ahead of a thunderstorm the weatherman predicted a week ago. It would have been a perfect cover-up, if the storm hadn't been a little late or the coroner hadn't been thorough. Who would want to kill a porn star, and why were a couple of cops involved? Corruption was one thing, maybe a little graft or looking the other way on a petty rap, but dumping corpses was an entirely different level of bad news.

The more pressing problem on my mind was trying to figure out what the hell Stacy had become. The thing in the sewers was no harmless spook show, and I'd never encountered anything like it. I needed a little help to work this out. Fortunately, I knew just where to get it.

4.

Every big city has its own refuge for the occult underground, a place for our crowd to mingle and swap vices
away from prying eyes. There's Dashwood Abbey in New
York, the Salon Rouge in New Orleans, and the Bast Club
in Chicago. In Las Vegas, we had the Tiger's Garden. There
were no dues or secret handshake, and membership was
based on one simple test: the Garden had to *want* to let you
in.

Scrubbed and changed, a fresh deck of cards in my pocket, I made my way to Fremont Street. The pedestrian mall
shone under a canopy of dazzling lights. Cameras flashed
and drunken tourists milled between open-air bars advertising dollar margaritas, while street musicians and blaring
speakers clashed to create a whirling cacophony. Snatches
of song faded into one another, drowned out by the din of
conversation and distant engine sounds. A street performer
with his face painted silver caught my eye as he juggled
pins strapped with LED strips, smearing the air with swirls

of color. Just off to my side, a skinny street rat doing the meth-head bop moved in on me with his eyes locked on my hip pocket. I gave him a look that could cut glass, and he found someone else to be interested in.

The air smelled like cheap cigars and spilled beer. I took a deep breath, letting the music and the commotion move me, falling into step with the churning crowd. I became one with the traffic, one with the street itself, giving in to the chaos.

A heartbeat later I stood in a narrow vestibule on a worn rubber welcome mat, the crowds and the flashing lights ripping away like tearing a bandage from a wound. Door chimes jingled softly behind me. I couldn't remember how I got there.

That's the Tiger's Garden for you. If you look for it, you'll never find it. You could map out every inch of the street, every nook, cranny, and doorway, and it simply wouldn't be there. Clear your mind and go with the flow, though, and if you belong here—and if the Garden wants you—you'll find your way inside.

I walked across the shabby, cigarette-burned, orange carpet, past the coat-rack and the decor that went out of style in the seventies. A few windows lined the sea-foam green walls, covered over with heavy wooden lattices. Nobody had ever seen those windows open, and nobody wanted to tempt fate by having a peek. I inhaled, savoring the smell of fresh Indian cooking, the air teeming with spices and secrets.

"Look," a grizzled voice explained from around the corner, "I'm not saying the Loa aren't objectively real—"

"That is exactly what you said," a disgruntled Mama Margaux snapped. "Own your words, boy."

I knew exactly what I'd see before I rounded the bend. Margaux, holding court in a florid tent dress and nursing a rum punch, squaring off with Corman at their usual corner table. Corman was in his late sixties and built like a retired prizefighter. He wore a rumpled tux with the bow tie undone and draped around his neck. Bentley sat next to him, silver haired and dressed in a funeral suit, reed thin to Corman's stocky. Between the three of them, there were enough empty glasses on the table for a couple nights of heavy drinking.

Corman snorted and waved his whiskey glass at Margaux. "'Boy?' My hair was turning white back when your father was still swinging a machete for Papa Doc."

"You take that back! You take that back *right now.*"

Bentley looked at me helplessly, having unwisely chosen to sit between them. I cleared my throat and walked over, pulling up a chair from a nearby table. The four of us had the Garden all to ourselves for the moment, not that it was ever the kind of place with a waiting list.

"Mama Margaux." I dropped into my chair. "You know Corman's a ceremonialist, you have to make allowances for professional language. Corman, you know we don't alk-tay about apa-Pay ock-Day at the table. Bentley, I see you got a haircut. It looks very nice."

My distraction managed to stop their bickering. Unfortunately, it also turned their guns on me. Three voices with varying degrees of irritation simultaneously demanded to know where I'd been and why I wasn't answering phone calls. I held up my open palms, trying to get a word in edgewise.

"That floozy walked out on 'im," Mama Margaux explained on my behalf, though I wouldn't have used quite those words.

"Oh, dear. Roxy? She was a sweet girl," Bentley said, shaking his head.

"Yeah, she was." I looked over my shoulder and stared right into the buttons of a white chef's jacket. Amar, the Garden's one and only employee, had slipped up behind me without making a sound. He balanced a brass-rimmed tray on one palm, deftly serving another round of drinks, including the rum and coke I was just about to ask for.

"Thanks Amar." I blinked at the glass. "Could we get an—"

"An order of naan," he said with a nod of his turbaned brow. "Of course." He flitted off to the kitchen.

We're not sure whether Amar just works for the Garden or if he's the owner, and he's notoriously tight-lipped on any subject other than the menu. Still, you can't beat the service.

"Sweet's overrated," Corman said, and Bentley shot him a look. Gruffness aside, he must have been doing something right. Bentley and Corman had been together for forty years, and they still acted like newlyweds when they thought nobody was looking.

I tossed back a swig from my glass and savored the spreading warmth in my chest. Perfectly mixed, as always."I don't want to talk about Roxy," I said. It wasn't the truth, but two weeks of heartache and a phone that didn't ring had drilled one hard truth into my thick head: she wasn't coming back. "I got a job. Let's talk about that instead."

"Daniel?" Bentley arched a wispy eyebrow and cradled his glass of gin. I didn't need an interpreter to read the concern in his tone. Bentley and Corman were the closest things I had to real fathers. I didn't talk about the people who raised me; the cigarette burns on my back said enough.

"A legit job. Mostly legit."

I sketched out the broad strokes, then went into detail once I got to the part about meeting the thing that used to be Stacy Pankow down in the storm drains.

"The ancestors can whip up a fuss," Mama Margaux mused, "but I've never seen anything like that. You sure it was the girl, not somethin' else pretending to be her? Anything could be festering down there in the dark."

I shrugged. "I thought of that, but what's the point? Why would anything capable of doing that kind of damage decide to pose as a random ghost and lurk around in a totally abandoned tunnel?"

"The missing body parts." Bentley leaned forward. "That detail demands consideration. Apparitions mirror their creators at the time of death, but the papers didn't say that her actual body was mutilated."

"No, and neither did the guy living down there, who saw her body get dumped. I think he would have mentioned that."

"I heard a story once," Corman said, his expression grave. "Back when I was a professional seer, in the sixties. Supposedly happened to a friend of a friend." Corman looked spooked, and that wasn't something I saw often. Bentley lightly touched his wrist, nodding for him to speak.

"Story goes, this guy crossed the wrong people, so they set up a little surprise for him. Like me, astral projection was his specialty. Going into a trance and sending his soul out to snoop around. Well, one night, a couple of disembodied sorcerers were waiting, and they laid some Tibetan whammy on him. Ripped his soul to pieces. Guy died on the spot, cardiac arrest.

"That was that, until a month later. His wife found the ghost of his arm in their bed. Just his arm, and it damn near choked the life out of her. His head showed up in my pal's closet. Watching him in the night, through a tiny crack, with this insane hatred in his eyes. Then it just vanished into thin air. Next morning, he finds the family dog gutted on the floor, and all the food in the house had rotted overnight."

Amar emerged from the kitchen just long enough to bring two baskets of fresh-baked flatbread, a plate of creamy chicken curry, and another round of drinks. We all tore away chunks of the puffy bread and dug in.

"What they figured," Corman said, "was that he didn't really die. His soul was in pieces, but something kept him from moving on. His mind was dislocated. Fragmented across space and time. The pain would be...inconceivable."

"Explaining why he attacked people he cared about," I said, thinking of Stacy's mad fury. "Like a fox with its leg caught in a bear trap. It doesn't understand you're trying to set it free; it's still going to take a chunk out of any hand that gets close. So how did they fix him?"

"They didn't." Corman tossed back a swig of whiskey. "He just stopped showing up one day, and that's the end of the story. Either the tangled tatters of his spirit unraveled enough to let him move on, or the poor bastard's still out there somewhere. Drifting endlessly through the astral. In screaming pieces."

The table fell silent. We were all well aware of the risks of our profession. Bentley and Corman taught me that the first magician was Prometheus, who stole the secret of fire for humanity and was repaid by having his liver eternally eaten by vultures. It's a cautionary tale that every modern-day sorcerer knows. Still, it was sobering to be handed a concrete example of what can happen when you screw with the machinery of the universe.

"I'm not letting that happen," I said, tearing off another chunk of bread. "Whatever Stacy went through, she's suffered enough. I'm fixing this."

"We're with you," Bentley said with a firm nod. "Where shall we start?"

"Whether it was the cops or her boyfriend or somebody else, Stacy's drowning was no accident, and it's got the stink of magic all over it. I'm going after the boyfriend first. Even if his hands are clean, he'll know better than anyone what she was into before she died. Do me a favor. Put out some feelers, see if anybody is new in town and making waves. Mama Margaux, are you still dating that guy in the coroner's office?"

"Antoine?" she said, arching her eyebrow. "Antoine needs to grow up and figure out what he wants. When he does that, we'll talk."

"Well, if it wouldn't put you out to ask, I'd love to know if the visitor logs show anybody viewing Stacy's body except for her grandfather."

"Done and done," Margaux said.

We drank another couple of rounds. The hours got blurry and the breadbasket wore down to a few scattered crumbs, and eventually the conversation stalled. I pushed my chair back and stretched.

"That's it for me," I said. "I want to get an early jump on this thing tomorrow. I'll keep you all in the loop."

Bentley followed me to the vestibule, resting his frail hand on my shoulder.

"Are you all right?" He looked me in the eye. "Really all right?"

I thought about Roxy, and it took me a second to get the words out.

"I thought she was the one. I mean, you always think that, but...I really believed it. Wedding bells, white picket fences, the real deal. Then one night the dream just died on me." I paused, shaking my head. "I'm sad right now, and that's okay. If I'm not sad I start getting angry, and I don't want to be angry at her. I don't want to twist it around in my head, change what we had into something ugly, you know? I owe her that much."

He stared at me for a moment, then pulled me into a wordless hug.

Suddenly, I stood in the middle of Fremont Street, with only the haziest memory of saying goodbye and walking out the door. You leave the Tiger's Garden the same way you arrive: vaguely, a passenger through an odd and liquid space.

It was four in the morning. Most of the taxpayers and solid citizens had gone back to their hotels to sleep off the cheap beer, and the canopy's neon light show was dead and cold. Fremont was back to its natural state, a litter-strewn wasteland inhabited only by those who had nowhere else to go. A brisk wind ruffled my hair. Fingers of the cold desert night.

I had only walked half a block when I realized I was be-ing followed. Someone clopped along behind me, maybe ten feet back, making a crude attempt to hide in the echo of my footsteps. I casually glanced into the darkened window of a tourist bar, but all the glass showed was a hazy, heavyset blob lurking at my back. Decision time.

A panhandler would have come right up and started talking. This had to be the less pleasant kind of street rat, one dumb or stoned enough to take me for a mark. Probably hoping I'd lead him to my car so he could jack my wallet and my wheels at the same time. I deflated his hopes by stopping in my tracks and whirling around to face him.

With long, stringy hair and cast-off tourist clothes caked with dirt and food stains, my stalker looked like he'd clawed his way out of a shallow grave. His bloodshot eyes widened as he pointed one yellowed, broken fingernail at me.

"I saw you," he said, sounding like he was having trouble finding his words. "You weren't there, then you were. Came out of a door, but you didn't. Poof. Magic."

I sighed. Like any big city, we have our share of people who end up on the streets because they can't get a doctor's help or the drugs they need to function. Schizophrenics occasionally have a knack for spotting wrinkles in the fabric of reality—for example, me, walking out of an Indian restaurant through a door that doesn't actually exist. Of course, nobody listens to them. I was looking for something soothing to say, thinking I'd slip him a couple of bucks and shoo him off, when he gave me a snaggletoothed smile.

"I hear magicians taste like candy," he said, his voice dropping into a growl.

He shambled closer, and now I could see that his teeth weren't just rotten. He had more teeth in his mouth than any human should, crowding each other out and bending jaggedly from diseased roots. Somewhere in the space of a heartbeat, his eyes melted to the color of runny egg yolks.

This was not my night.

5.

As the derelict staggered toward me, I caught a whiff of sulfur on the wind. He giggled like he was laughing at some inside joke he couldn't explain.

"No rules," he rambled. "Hound's gone. Hound's gone, no rules."

I dipped my fingers into my pocket, scooping out my deck of cards.

He paused and broke into a singsong voice. "With the dog away, the cats will playyyy."

I didn't want to be doing magic on Fremont Street. Dead of night or not, all it would take would be one asshole with a cell phone and a YouTube account and I'd be in for a world of pain. We didn't have some austere high council regulating the world's sorcerers and keeping the secrets of magic under their wise guardianship. What we did have was street justice and a collective burning desire to keep anyone from fucking up our action.

Lesson one for any well-taught magician is the story of Prometheus. Lesson two is if you go around showing the world magic is real, if you're *lucky* the worst thing that'll happen is a corrective curb-stomping.

I only saw two real options, since whatever this thing was, I didn't want those teeth anywhere near me. I could run, hoping he wasn't faster than he looked, or I could bluff my way out, hoping he didn't know how badly I wanted to avoid a magical throwdown. I'd already run once tonight and my pride still stung, so the choice was obvious.

I sighed with real exasperation and said, "Seriously, ass-hole?"

He blinked. That apparently wasn't the reaction he was expecting.

"The door," he said, waving his hand, "we all know the door, but we're not allowed to eat. Never allowed to eat. It's not fair. But now—"

"Yeah, yeah, the hound's gone, you said that already. So, what, you were just going to hang out here all night and jump the first magician who walked out the door? The door moves, dipshit."

I tried to be nonchalant, but my heart was pounding. This was bad news. The Tiger's Garden was Switzerland for the occult underground: no matter what your beef was with anybody in the community, and we weren't a big communi-ty, you left it at the door and you made nice. The unspoken rule was that the peace extended the length of Fremont; the idea of waiting outside the Garden and jumping a patron as they left wouldn't even occur to one of us.

I needed to know what we were dealing with, and if this thing—whatever it was—was a lone nut or if we needed to get ready for a real fight. I reached out with my psychic senses, probing at him with a feather touch, trying to glean anything I could.

"Nobody can stop us." His cracked lips spread into a grotesquely oversized grin. "No rules, we can take what we want. Eat what we want. Eat your *toes*. Toes are the tastiest."

"Who's 'we'?"

"The misbegotten children of the abyss." His chin jerked and nose wrinkled. "The inheritors of Lillith. The progeny of filth and regret."

His little rant lined up with what I felt in my gut. I sensed echoes of psychic distress and a wind of madness, halves of two different souls squeezed together with barbed wire and crammed into a malformed human body.

"You're a cambion," I said.

Cambion are what you get when a demon mates with a human. It generally isn't consensual on the human's part, and the relationship doesn't end pretty. Cambion have one foot on earth and one foot in hell, born with the instinctive knowledge that they'll never fit into either world. Not surprisingly, they aren't known for being well-adjusted or sane. I knew there was a small clutch of cambion living on the outskirts of the city, but they'd always kept to themselves and stayed in the shadows.

That is, with one major exception. I used to work for a cambion who was quite the charmer when he wanted to be. He was also the most dangerous man in Las Vegas. We weren't exactly friends anymore.

"I'm going to eat you now." The cambion took another lurching step toward me.

"What's Nicky Agnelli going to say about that?"

His foot froze in mid-step.

"I don't work for him," the cambion said, but I could hear the uncertainty in his voice.

"But you know his name. And I do work for him," I lied. "As do my friends. Mr. Agnelli's going to be very, very unhappy if he finds out you've been harassing us. Since I'm in a charitable mood, I'll make you a deal. You walk away, right now, and I'll forget this ever happened."

The cambion wavered. I stared him down, silent.

"Fine," he snapped, looking like a kid who had just been denied a lollipop. "But I'll find you. One night, one night, you'll wake up in the dark and I'll be crouching at the foot of your bed. I'm going to eat your toes first."

"Turn around," I said calmly. "Walk away."

He spat on the pavement and turned, grumbling under his breath as he shuffled up the quiet street. I waited until he disappeared into an alley, to pull out my phone and rattle off a quick text message to Bentley, Corman, and Margaux. You can't get a connection in the Garden—it doesn't seem to be anywhere a cell tower can reach—but they'd see it as soon as they stepped out the door.

"Leave as a group and make sure you're not followed. Psycho cambion on the street and he knows about the Garden. Put out the word, we need a meeting tomorrow night. Trouble brewing."

I hoped that the cambion's "we" existed only in his head, that he was acting alone and I'd scared him into taking a permanent hike. Still, I wasn't going to risk my friends' lives without making damn sure of it. Now I had to deal with an unsolved murder, a soul-shattered ghost, and at least one rogue half-demon who wanted to eat me for dinner because apparently magicians' toes taste like candy. At least I couldn't complain about being bored.

I watched my back all the way home and took a lot of unnecessary turns. Even still, in bed with the door locked and deadbolt latched, I kept my feet tucked under the covers.

#

The fingers of the desert sun stabbed around the edges of my curtains, shaking hands with my hangover. I pushed myself out of bed around nine. I grabbed a bottle of water and a half-empty pack of convenience store donuts from the mini-fridge, chasing them with three aspirins.

"Breakfast of champions," I muttered, trudging off to the bathroom to shower and make myself look presentable. The steam and spray woke me up, made me feel human again. My first priority was checking out Artie Kaufman. He'd gotten Jud's granddaughter into the porn game, transformed her from Stacy Pankow to "Stacie Velour." Didn't necessarily mean he'd coerced her—plenty of sex workers do what they do out of personal choice—but something about the situation didn't sit right with me.

Fortunately, I had an expert guide in the wilderness. I drove out to the Love Connection, a hot pink storefront squeezed between a dance-aerobics studio and a boarded-up restaurant with a For Lease sign on the door. Foreclosures swallowed the street like a slow-spreading plague, leaving more shuttered shops than open ones.

Still, Paolo was doing all right. You'll never go broke selling sex. I found him with his feet up behind the counter, nursing a two-day growth of stubble and paging through a skin magazine like a law student poring over a textbook. I eased past a standing display of rainbow-colored vibrators and leaned against the counter.

"You forgot the first rule of dealing." I grinned as he jumped and dropped the magazine next to the vintage cash register. "Never get high on your own supply."

"Market research! Gotta know what's trending," he said, running his fingers through his tangled mop of hair. I glanced down at the cover.

"Nuns in leather? Hey, I'm nobody to judge. How are the wards holding up?"

Paolo ran a backroom paper operation peddling fake IDs to the underage spring break crowd. Seventy bucks and one hour could unlock all the pleasures of Vegas, and he would be happy to sell you all the party favors you wanted on the side. We met through a friend of a friend, and he turned into a semi-regular client.

"Like Fort Knox," he said. "Had a couple of cops in here last week, after some punk got caught with one of my licenses and tried to roll on me to stop them from calling his mommy and daddy. They didn't even look at the door to the back room, like they couldn't see it. They just poked around a little, apologized for wasting my time, and took off."

I looked to the back of the store, letting my vision slip slightly out of focus and narrowing my eyes. Honeycombs of ice-blue light glowed against the walls, the "don't notice me" spell still holding strong.

"When did I last reinforce it?" I asked. "Three months? Looks like it's due for some patch-up work. Don't want to risk it failing on you."

It's a tiny grift, as grifts go. Wards like that don't really decay—I've seen enchantments from the eighteenth century that were still chugging along, years after their creators were dust and bones—but Paolo doesn't know that, so he slips me a hundred bucks every few months to wave my arms and chant in doggerel Latin for a couple of minutes.

"We can talk about that later, though," I said. "I'm actually here to shop today. I'm looking for anything directed by Daddy Warbucks, especially anything with this one girl in it. She went by the name Stacie Velour."

Paolo tilted his head. "Whoa. Seriously, man? That's some hardcore sick shit. You always struck me as more of a Playboy kind of guy."

"Research material, not for my personal amusement. I'm trying to find out anything I can about Warbucks for a job I'm working."

Paolo came out from behind the counter and led me down the narrow rows of DVDs, a thousand glossy covers offering me a peek at every kind of sex I could imagine and a few that hadn't occurred to me. I've got nothing against porn, but the sheer amount of it on display, the rote titles and assembly-line feel, was numbing.

"You wanna stay away from that guy," Paolo said, working his way down the stacks as he hunted for a title. "I met him once. He's got a screw loose."

"Yeah? When was that?"

"Last year. I occasionally get some minor-league talent in here. They sign autographs, bring out some fans; I sell a lot of DVDs. It's a win-win for me and the studio. Last summer, he comes out with a couple of his girls and we get to talking. You know, just passing the time. I think the guy's movies are crap, but I don't let it show, because business is business. I guess he started thinking we were some kinda kindred spirits, because he starts asking me about my store inventory, then about my personal collection."

"Like he wanted to see what you were into?"

"Yeah," Paolo said, "so I told him what I thought he wanted to hear. He's asking me about 'special orders', like under-the-counter stuff, and I'm thinking he's a pedo, right? Like he's about to ask if I could hook him up with some kiddie porn. Then he tells me what he's really looking for."

"What'd he want?"

Paolo looked over his shoulder, making sure no customers were in earshot, and leaned close.

"He wanted to know if I could get him a snuff movie."

6.

Paolo sent me away with two DVDs wrapped in brown butcher paper and a fresh chill rippling down my spine. The store's air conditioning gave way to the arid heat of the Vegas sun, but the chill stayed with me.

"Kaufman is one of those guys," Paolo warned me, "where you just know you're gonna be seeing his picture on TV someday, with all his neighbors talking about how nice and quiet he was, and in the background they're pulling bodies out of his basement. Just something wrong with him that you can't put your finger on. Like you look in his eyes and there's nothing really there."

I pulled into the drive-through at Burger King and then headed back to my place for lunch and a movie. The cinematic masterpieces Paolo had picked out for me were volumes seven and eight of *Daddy's Gutter Sluts*. I'd never seen the first six, but something told me I wasn't going to have any trouble following the plot. Loading the first DVD into my laptop, I noticed the company logo: a pair of linked steel rings and the name Second Circle Studios. Cute. The second circle of hell, in Dante's Inferno, was for the sin of lust. Artie Kaufman knew his classics.

Five minutes into the first DVD, I put my half-eaten burger aside. Fifteen minutes in and I felt like I needed to shower with bleach. There was no plot, no characters, just a tired-looking girl and Kaufman acting as his own cinematographer and star. He shot each scene on a handheld camera in one unbroken take, the lens acting as his point of view. He never showed his own face. The video rotated between eight or nine segments and featured four actresses. I immediately recognized Stacy. She wasn't as pretty as her prom picture, not with the swell of a black eye and a fresh cut on her lip.

She showed off her new tattoo in her first scene. It said "Daddy's Girl" in swirling script on the small of her back. She stood in some filthy little hellhole—it looked like a truck-stop bathroom—and looked over her shoulder with a smile as she hiked up her pink tank top for the camera.

"Do you like it?" she asked, the tinny sound echoing over my laptop's speakers.

"Come here," a man's voice answered, almost gentle. Had to have been Artie, holding the camera.

She sauntered close, giving the lens a plastic smile. Then a sudden blur of motion as Artie backhanded her to the floor. The focus wavered when he lowered the camera, showing her on the grimy tiles. A boot slammed into her stomach, leaving her gasping for breath, curled into a fetal ball.

"You're not here to talk, you're here to fuck," Artie said in a monotone, the screen dropping to show his free hand fumbling with his belt buckle. "Don't know how many times I have to tell you that."

Things got worse once his pants came off. This wasn't just rough sex. It was barely sex at all. Each segment was the same: Artie beating down and degrading his actresses while the camera zoomed in for close-ups. "Actress" wasn't even the right word. They weren't acting; they were genuinely terrified. I'd gone to an S&M club once, on a job. I saw some rough stuff going on there, but everybody was into it and nobody was getting any treatment they hadn't willingly signed up for. The whole spectacle had felt more like elaborate play than anything else.

This was the polar opposite. The stream of abuse spilling from Artie's mouth set my teeth on edge. He hated these women. The sex was just a tool to reach his ultimate aim: hurting them. Stacy's scenes were the worst. For some reason, he'd singled her out. I fast-forwarded through a scene where he shoved her head in a toilet, something he'd done with a couple of the other actresses. Then he got creative and did something that sent me running for the bathroom before I lost what little lunch I'd been able to choke down.

Wiping my mouth with a paper napkin, I loaded the second DVD. More of the same. Same actresses, same filthy bathroom "sets", same abuse. I skipped forward five seconds at a time, not sure what I was looking for and feeling sick. My instincts told me there was something here, something to see, but what?

"—go home," Stacy said, cowering on the floor.

I reversed the video.

Her voice was soft and choked with tears. I had to play it four more times before I was sure what I heard her say.

"Don't want to. Want to go home."

Artie's voice wasn't any easier to make out. He lowered the camera, whispering to her in a threatening hiss.

"Anytime, bitch. You think they'll be proud, finding out what you've been doing for a living?"

Stacy finished the scene, her tears leaving mascara trails down her cheeks. Artie's quip hadn't been for the audience. It was a genuine threat. I could only imagine how wholesome Stacy from small-town Minnesota would feel at the prospect of having her grandfather find out about her secret life as a porn star.

"You son of a bitch," I said to the screen. "You were blackmailing her."

Had she finally had enough? Did Artie find out she was leaving and snap? Paolo's words lingered in the back of my mind: he wanted a snuff movie. Maybe he'd decided to make one of his own. Looking back at the last clip, I was starting to get a nasty idea of how Stacy might have really drowned. At the very least, Artie was a blackmailer and a rapist.

Even if he wasn't the one who murdered her, he still took her life.

I put on my sunglasses, drove to the Value Lodge on East Tropicana, and knocked on Jud's door. He squinted into the sunlight, still draped in a tattered bathrobe. Six empty cans of Coors cluttered his bedside table. I stood in the doorway.

"Mr. Faust?"

"You need to go home," I told him. "Back to Minnesota. Tonight."

His face fell. "You're...not going to help me?"

I took off my glasses and looked him in the eye.

"Artie Kaufman is going to have a terrible accident," I said. "I don't want you here when it happens. Go home. Watch the news."

"T-thank you! But I can help, I can—"

"Go home," I repeated calmly. "Watch the news. You'll know when it happens."

He kept thanking me. I didn't want his thanks. I didn't even want his money. I just wanted Artie Kaufman dead.

#

This was going to be tricky. All the circumstances pointed to Artie being responsible for Stacy's murder, but that wasn't the same thing as hard proof. There was still the matter of the two cops dumping her body in the storm drains. Some people might have the juice and the contacts to get that kind of service, but a small-time pornographer isn't one of them. Everybody involved in Stacy's death, one way or another, was going to pay for it.

I still had to find out exactly how she died. Going by Corman's story, it sounded like her soul was literally in pieces, keeping her from moving on. Freeing her was priority one, but I couldn't even start to figure it out without learning all the facts. While I was enticed by the idea of laying a death curse on Artie's head, or just showing up on his doorstep with a baseball bat, I had to keep a cool head and fight smart.

Inspiration struck. I pulled into the nearest parking lot and called Paolo.

"Thank you for calling the Love Connection, where you can make your love connection," he said tiredly.

"Paolo, it's Faust. You still have Kaufman's contact info?"

"I've got a card somewhere, probably. Why?"

"Make a phone call for me, and I'll refresh those protective wards for free next week. Even trade. Deal?"

"What's the angle?"

"I want you to ask Kaufman," I said, "if he's still in the market for a snuff movie. Because you happen to know a guy who might be able to get him one, and you'd just love to introduce him."

Forget booze and drugs: nothing in the world makes a person more prone to stupid, reckless behavior than the pursuit of an unfulfilled fetish. If my hunch was right, I had the key to getting into Artie's inner circle. Of course, I'd have to come up with a nonexistent snuff flick, but I'd cross that bridge when I got there.

I had planned to go home and catch a quick nap before meeting everyone at the Tiger's Garden to discuss our cambion problem, but the two bruisers hanging out in my parking lot—all gristle and fists squeezed into tailored, salmon-pink suits—had other ideas. They walked up to meet my car, waiting patiently while I killed the engine and got out.

"Mr. Agnelli wants to see you," one said, staring down at me from behind sunglasses the color of burnt onyx.

"I don't have any business with Nicky," I said, trying to step around him. He moved to stand in my path, a brick wall of menace.

"Mr. Agnelli," he said pointedly, "has business with you."

They politely escorted me to their waiting Lincoln and put me in the back seat. I figured I was better off not trying to push them into not-so-polite territory. When Nicky Agnelli wanted to see you, you got seen. Besides, I was curious to find out what he wanted. Strange coincidence, being called to a sit-down with the most dangerous man in Las Vegas at the same time as everything else that was going on this week.

Third rule of magic: there is no such thing as a coincidence.

7.

The Lincoln eased its way through the traffic on Las Vegas Boulevard, a white shark in a sea of yellow cabs. The monoliths of the Strip rose up on either side, from skybound twists of crystal and chrome to black art-deco pyramids. Come nightfall they would erupt in a riot of colors and flashing lights, but for now they slept, dusty and quiet, in the afternoon sun.

We pulled into a parking garage halfway down the boulevard. Nicky's boys flanked me as we walked down the ramp and out onto the street, pushing though a swirl of tourists. A woman dressed for tennis and clutching a digital camera did a double take, looking at the suited thugs and then at me as if wondering if she'd seen me on television.

No, no, they're not my bodyguards, I felt like saying. *They're just here to break my kneecaps if I run. Or maybe break them anyway. We'll see how the day goes.*

The Medici was a slice of old-world class in the heart of the city, standing watch over an artificial lake where the waters danced in a syncopated ballet at the top of every hour.

In the lobby, frescoes on scalloped walls depicted the beauty of vintage Italy, and crystal fountains murmured under the electronic clangs of distant slot machines. The thugs marched me across the casino's zebra-striped marble floor. It was early still, just a few locals and older tourists sitting at the cheap slots, but not much real action in sight.

"Let me guess," I said to the suit on my left, "Nicky's one guy short for a game of poker, and he thought of me. He's a sweetheart, he really is."

No reaction. Hell, they didn't even take their shades off indoors. They were the gangster version of the guards at Buckingham Palace. My eyebrows went up when we reached the door to Club Prive, the private salon at the back of the casino. The concierge at the door barely gave us a second glance.

The Club was half casino, half spa—a gallery of private salons in gray velvet and mahogany wood. I smelled some faint, exotic spice in the air, like a warm cologne. It smelled the way old money feels. In Salon Tredici, a cozy little lounge wreathed in a haze of cigar smoke, four men huddled around a table and played mahjong like their souls were hanging in the balance. A small gaggle of onlookers clustered around them, dressed in outfits that probably cost more than I make in a year.

"That's the game, gents," Nicky Agnelli said, flipping over a row of intricate ivory tiles on the aquamarine felt. His long fingers trailed over a string of flowers and Chinese characters, like a piano player warming up for a jazz tune. The other players groaned, handing over fistfuls of colored sticks and dumping over their own tiles.

Agnelli looked like he should be sitting someplace a few hours west, in Hollywood, making movie deals over a three-martini lunch. He looked up and gave us a hungry smile. His ice-blue eyes were wolfish behind rimless, titanium Porsche Design glasses.

"Gentlemen, could I have the room please?"

He kept his tone light, but it wasn't a casual request. The game broke up without a word and the bystanders faded along with my escorts, leaving me alone with Nicky and his girls. They were twins, walking dreams in slinky black cocktail dresses, but I didn't stare for too long. I knew them too well for that. They went by Juliette and Justine, but those weren't their real names. I wasn't sure if dubbing themselves after a pair of novels by the Marquis de Sade was their little joke or Nicky's.

The door slid shut at my back, leaving me caged in the tiger's den.

"Daniel Faust," Nicky said, shaking his head and smiling. "What is this, you don't call, you don't write? I'm starting to think you don't want to be friends anymore."

I put my hands on my hips. "Thought I answered that question pretty definitively, last time we talked."

"Ancient history, it's a brand new day. Sit down, would ya? You're making me nervous."

He looked anything but nervous, but I humored him and took a seat on the opposite side of the mahjong table. Juliette glided over to a minibar, stiletto heels clicking, and opened a decanter of whiskey. Justine circled the table and stood behind me. I tried not to jump when she put her hands on my shoulders. She rubbed them, her slender fingers moving in light circles.

"He's very tense." Justine's voice dripped with amusement.

"Oh dear," Juliette answered, giggling, pouring two glass-es. She smiled at me. Her eyes glowed yellow, like the edge of a candle's flame. In private, Nicky and his crew didn't have to pretend at being human. Their bodies flickered and morphed at the corners of my eye, illusions falling away in bits and pieces only to slide back into place back when I looked directly at them. "Do we make you nervous, Danny?"

Before I could answer, Nicky shook his head and said, "Nah, sweetheart, he's nervous because he's flat fuckin' broke and can't pay rent on his crappy little apartment. My guys saw you on Fremont last week, Dan. You know what they saw you doing?"

"Their mothers?" I replied.

"Funny," he said and turned back to Juliette. "This guy, this fuckin' guy right here, doing a street act on Fremont. Not *real* magic, I mean, he's got a crowd of tourists around and he's pulling scarves out of hats and making coins dis-appear, and they're pissing themselves, he's so good. Daniel Faust. Best sorcerer on the West Coast, and he's busking for spare change."

"That's so sad," Juliette pouted, putting a crystal glass in front of each of us. I left mine untouched. The rich scent of finely aged whiskey mingled with the growing undercurrent of sulfur in the air.

Justine leaned close, her lips inches from my ear, and stage-whispered, "See? Now you made my sister sad. I hope you feel bad about that."

"Mortified." I sighed. "Nicky, what the hell do you want?"

He flashed a mouth of fangs that could scare a great white shark and spread his hands wide. "I want to get the band back together, man!"

"No," I said flatly.

"I want you on my team. I've got some work coming up that needs a light touch, real occult power, and hands I can trust. That's you, buddy. And I'm not talking piecework, temp job garbage. I'm talking you, on my payroll, six figures a year plus perks."

Juliette walked to stand behind Nicky, her fingers draping across his shoulders, mirroring her sister behind me. "You'll love the perks," she said.

I'd be lying if I said I wasn't tempted. I'd been living hand to mouth for so long that a cash envelope like the one Jud gave me felt like Christmas in springtime. It wasn't like I had a moral objection to working for a criminal, either. I *am* a criminal. Then I thought about what Nicky called "ancient history" and my stomach clenched.

"I think you're forgetting something," I told him. "I think you're forgetting that you got two of my friends killed. They were 'on your team' too, remember?"

"Hey," he said, his smile irrepressible, "you can blame me all you want if it helps you sleep at night, but it wasn't me who fucked that job up. I think you know that."

"We're done here," I said and started to rise. Justine held my shoulders with the strength of a bodybuilder and shoved me back into the chair.

"Sleep on it," Nicky said. "It's a limited-time offer, but sleep on it. There was one other thing. You met with an old guy the other day, Jud Pankow I think his name was?"

I never knew for sure how he did it, but Nicky was a walking encyclopedia of Vegas gossip. If anyone worthy of a back-page newspaper article had lunch in this town, Nicky knew what they talked about, what they ordered, and how much they tipped on their way out. I figured he had a world-class seer on the payroll keeping astral tabs on people he considered worth watching. Interesting, though, that he only mentioned our lunch meeting and not my visit to Jud's motel room a couple of hours ago. Even he had his limits.

Even so, I made a mental note to redouble the wards on my bedroom.

"What about him?" I said, knowing it'd be a waste of time to deny meeting with Jud.

"It's sad, what happened to his grandkid. I feel for the guy. I want to make a donation, cover her funeral costs and get him home safe and sound. Maybe put a little something extra in his pocket. Guy that age should be retired and living it up, not working a farm, you know?"

"That's really nice of you," I said, but I knew better. I smelled the hook waiting inside that bait.

"He needs help moving on. And I don't think it's right, you know, that people are holding out false hope, keeping him going like that. That poor girl, she was getting high down in the storm tunnels, a flood came in, end of story. Just a terrible accident."

A low-budget porn director like Artie Kaufman didn't have the juice to get a couple of corrupt cops to do his dirty work.

Nicky Agnelli did.

On the other hand, Artie was a sadist with a motive for murder, and Nicky, for all his faults, didn't go around killing young girls for kicks. He would have been just as sickened by Artie's movies as I was. One man had the motive, one man had the means, and neither one had any reason to be in the other's orbit.

Justine massaged my shoulders, but I wasn't feeling any less tense.

"You want me to drop the job," I said. It wasn't a question.

"I want you to give the old man some peace of mind." Nicky's forehead creased with phony concern. "Tell him that what you found matches the police report, that it was all an accident. Send him home. He'll grieve, but he'll move on. Right now, it's like his granddaughter never died. He can't put her to rest. That's not right."

He apparently didn't know about the Stacy-thing lurking under the city streets. Did he know what I'd discovered about Artie? What I told Jud before sending him packing? I rolled the dice.

"You and I had the same thought," I said. "I just told Pankow to get out of town, that there was nothing I could do for him. You can have your guys check it out. He'll be flying back to Minneapolis tonight."

The second part was true, if Jud did what I told him. Nicky nodded, leaning back in his chair. He couldn't keep the relief from showing in his body language, and that was more troubling than anything. Stacy's murder had him worried. Nicky Agnelli didn't get worried. Ever.

"I looked into it," I said, "didn't find anything but a hinky autopsy report with nothing to back it up. It was a bust, so I sent him home."

"There you go, see?" Nicky said. "You and me, on the same wavelength. Just like old times."

"Now I've got a question for you," I said lightly, thinking back to my encounter with the cambion outside the Tiger's Garden. "What's 'the hound'?"

Justine's nails dug into my shoulders like ten tiny knives.

8.

Nicky took off his glasses and plucked a gray silk handkerchief from his jacket, polishing the lenses. Not looking at me.

"Where'd you—what do you mean? What hound?"

"Ran into a cambion last night. He told me 'the hound is gone' and there aren't any rules anymore. Apparently that meant it was open season on my crowd."

"And you think I should know?" Nicky scrubbed his glasses like he was trying to blot out a bloodstain. "What else did he say?"

"Nothing," I said. "I figured you'd know because, well..." I nodded at him and Juliette as if that said it all.

Nicky blurted out a sudden peal of laughter. Justine's fingernails relaxed, leaving my shoulders stinging.

"Christ, Dan," he said, grinning at me and putting his glasses back on, "that's not racist or anything, is it?"

"I figured you'd have your finger on the local community—"

"And if a black guy steals your wallet, do you grab the closest brother and demand to know where it is, because they all must know each other? And all Asians hang out in dojos practicing kung fu, right, just like Bruce Lee?"

He had a point. I would have had the grace to feel ashamed of myself if their reactions hadn't already given the game away.

"Look," he said, "me and the ladies, we're what you might call exemplary specimens of our kind. Do I know of other halfbloods living in the city? Yes. Do we get together for a regular knitting circle and black mass on Tuesday nights? No. Between you and me, buddy, most of those guys are batshit crazy. Not dependable, and not our kind of crowd."

"Sorry." I faked an apologetic smile. "You're right, that was pretty dumb of me. No offense intended."

"None taken," Juliette said. She flicked a forked tongue across her pearly white teeth.

Nicky shook his head. "My advice to you is to not worry about it. You probably met some lone crazy out there, flapping his gums about nothing. Now, if you'll excuse me, my mahjong partners are waiting outside, and I haven't finished taking all their money. Think about my offer and get back to me."

"Do come back soon," Justine whispered in my ear.

#

The evening light show heralded my return to Fremont Street. The canopy over the pedestrian mall blazed with neon synchronized to a medley of Beatles songs. I hummed along, letting the music move my feet, feeling the street's energy pulling me—

—and then I was inside the Tiger's Garden, still moving, brass bells jingling behind me. Bentley and Corman waved from their table.

"We knew you were about to arrive," Bentley said, holding out a glass of whiskey. Two fingers, poured over a single ice cube. "Amar just brought it over for you, said you were going to order it."

"Right as usual." I took the glass and tossed back a swallow to ease my nerves. It wasn't the quality of the drink I refused in Nicky's backroom mahjong game, but it did the job. "Does anyone else think that's weird, by the way? Anyone at all?"

"It all makes sense if you study quantum mechanics," Jennifer Juniper drawled with a thick Kentucky accent, her chair tilted back on two legs and leaning against the wall.

That was her real name. Her parents were heavily into peace, love, and psychedelics. The only hippie thing about Jennifer was her ubiquitous, blue-tinted Lennon glasses. That, and her pot-growing operation, which she kept hidden from the cops with the aid of some high-quality witchcraft. A sleeve of tattoos sheathed her left arm, the centerpiece a spray of rainbow rose petals around an image of Elvis as the Gautama Buddha.

"This is it?" I asked, looking at the three of them. "Where is everybody?"

"Margaux's coming," Bentley said, ticking off names on his fingers. "Spengler's coming. The Hernandez brothers are on a job in New Orleans. Jorgensen's living off the grid in a cardboard box somewhere. David has a prior engagement—"

"Not that he'd come anyway," I muttered.

"What is it with you two?" Corman asked.

"He knows what he did."

"Brother K is in a cell in the county jail for drunk and disorderly conduct," Bentley continued, ignoring us both. "And Sophia is hiding from what she claims is the vengeful ghost of Merle Haggard and she won't leave her house until the new moon."

"Merle Haggard isn't dead."

He shrugged. "It's Sophia."

Magic is not, as a general rule, the healthiest of passions or the gentlest of muses.

The jingling of bells heralded Mama Margaux's arrival, and Amar appeared just long enough to pull out her chair and offer her a tall hurricane in a smoky glass. The last guest to the party showed up a few minutes later. Dressed to the nines in a Brooks Brothers suit, Spengler was big. Big shoulders, big gestures, a big voice, and big ambitions.

Everybody in the scene knew Spengler. Not for his reputation as a magician, seeing as he was so inept none of us could figure out how he even got into the Garden, but for a web of connections that stretched from Chicago to Calcutta. If you needed a powdered fossil or a bone from a saint's finger, he could have it for you in a week. More importantly for some of us, he was always happy to take questionable merchandise off your hands in exchange for clean cash.

"I'm back from the big sandbox," he said with a wave, "so everybody line up and tell me how much you missed me. I will accept presents in lieu of praise if you're feeling tongue-tied."

"You were gone? Didn't notice," Jennifer said, though she couldn't keep the affection from her voice.

"Two weeks in Saudi, baby, and don't pretend you didn't count the hours 'til my return. I did it this time. Really did it. I hit the score of a lifetime."

"You always say that." She rolled her eyes.

"This time I mean it. This thing I found? People are gonna be breaking down my door trying to throw money at me. You just wait, ye of little faith. Hey, Faust, where is everybody? I thought this was a party."

"Hey, Spengler," I said. "It's just us. Apparently everybody else is drunk, in jail, or temporarily insane."

"So, it's a day ending in the letter *y* then," he said, pulling up a chair.

"That's about right," I said and gave everyone a quick recap of my encounter with the cambion.

"Hound?" Jennifer peered at me over her glasses. "Like a dog?"

"That's what it sounded like. I didn't ask him to spell it for me."

Corman shook his head, leaning back in his chair and contemplating his glass of gin like a philosopher. "This has happened before."

"That's right," Bentley said. "Back in the eighties, when Cormie and I first moved here from California. It was a different crowd in those days, you have to understand. Wilder souls. When the nature of the city changed, most of them either drifted away or met their unhappy ends."

Corman snorted. "What he means is a bunch of coked-up, pentacle-waving cowboys butted heads with the casinos' new management and ended up dead in a gutter. The corporations make the old Vegas mob look like pussycats."

"It was one August," Bentley mused, "a bad one. The kind of summer where the sidewalks blistered and the air smelled like gasoline. That's when the attacks started. Cambion—well, creatures we eventually figured out were cambion—hunting down magicians. A friend of ours was...devoured in his bed. Literally devoured. Not just our crowd, either. They started attacking random citizens. An entire string of missing persons and mangled bodies."

"What did you do about it?" I asked, leaning forward.

"Nothing." Corman shook his head, picking up the story. "We planned to, all right. Had a beauty of a plan, but the attacks just suddenly stopped. And I mean stopped over-night, like turning off a faucet. Couldn't even go looking for payback, because you couldn't find a cambion in this town for a good five years. It was like something scared them all into going underground."

"Scared them," I said. "Or gave them rules. Rules about who they could hunt."

"That'd be your hound dog," Jennifer said. "Gotta be one of us, right? Somebody in our little community. Who else would be able to regulate those critters? Anybody go miss-ing lately who's been around since the old days?"

Corman waved his glass in a circle toward himself and Bentley. "Kid, we *are* the old days."

I took a deep breath. "I talked to Nicky Agnelli today."

The looks from Bentley and Corman could have stripped paint from the wall.

"Wasn't by choice, believe me," I said quickly, holding up one hand.

"What did *he* want?" Bentley asked, a winter chill at the edges of his reedy voice.

"Not important. What matters is I asked him about his community, for obvious reasons. He says they don't have a community and even if they do, he's not in charge and doesn't want to be. Thing is, I dropped the word 'hound' and everyone in the room went stiff. He played it off with a laugh, but Nicky's spooked about something."

"Nicky don't get spooked," Jennifer drawled.

"You know that's right," I told her, "but it was written all over his lying face."

"We need to hit the books," Bentley said. "Cormie and I will start researching anything remotely related to hounds and the underworld. If any of you have a chance to drop by the store, your help would be appreciated and rewarded with essential nourishment."

"Pizza and beer," Corman said. "And if you want something with weird toppings, you're paying for it yourself. No goddamn pineapple this time."

"I'm in," Spengler said. Jennifer just nodded.

Mama Margaux looked at me. "You should come, Daniel. Get your mind off that girl."

Jennifer adjusted her glasses. "Holy shit. Roxy? You two broke up?"

"I don't want to talk about it." *Thanks, Mama.*

Jennifer looked at Spengler. "You know, Daniel and I dated for a couple of months, once. Now I mostly date women."

I leaned back and pantomimed pulling a dagger out of my heart. "Ow. Twist the knife, why don't you? Truth is, I gave you the most thrilling fifteen seconds of your life. Ruined you for all other men."

She buried her face in her hands. "It's true!" she cried, breaking into hysterical giggles. "It's all true!"

I said my goodbyes after the next round of drinks, and Jennifer followed me to the vestibule.

"Seriously," she said softly. "I'm sorry about Roxy. You were cute together. You okay?"

I started to make something up, but instead I just slumped against the wall by the door.

"Ah, shit, Jenny. I will be, all right? Not today, but maybe tomorrow. This helps. Being with friends. Gets me out of my own head for a while."

She leaned in and kissed me on the cheek, leaving behind the faint scent of strawberries.

"Come by my place some night this week. We'll get high, eat popcorn, and watch some bad movies together. Cures all ills."

I saw Bentley lurking a few feet behind her and knew we were about to have "a talk." Sighing, I gave Jennifer a quick hug. "Deal."

Bentley waited until she went back to the tables, and I held up a hand to forestall him.

"No," I said, "I am not working for Nicky again. That's not in the cards."

"But he asked you."

"Of course he asked me. And I said no. On that note, he's connected to the Stacy Pankow murder. I just don't know how yet. He wanted me to drop it, pretending he was just worried about poor old Jud."

Bentley frowned. "What did you say?"

"I said it was already dropped. Which is a big, fat lie. Problem is, he's doing his creepy 'I know everything about everyone' act, and I need to watch my ass if I keep digging into this case."

"You could walk away."

I arched an eyebrow at him. "You know I'm not going to do that."

"Daniel, it's one thing to work around a creature like Nicky Agnelli. It's another thing entirely to work against him. If he's connected to that poor girl's death—"

"Then I deal with him. I gave my word, Bentley. You taught me how important that is. Don't worry, I'll be careful, but I need a helping hand. Can I borrow the Eye?"

He gave me a long look, concern etched in his faded blue eyes, and nodded. "I'll bring it over first thing in the morning."

Back out on Fremont, the night young enough for the crowds to keep churning, the party in full swing, I stepped into a doorway and checked my phone. I had a message from Paolo.

Call me asap, Kaufman wants 2 meet u.

"Showtime," I whispered, my spreading smile cast in the glow of a neon light.

9.

The next morning Bentley brought me a present: a tiny, lacquered casket, like something from a Chinese fairy tale. I opened it and took out the package inside, wrapped in rumpled black silk. A spike of cold shot through my palm and up my arm, fading as fast as it came.

The Black Eye was one of Bentley and Corman's collected curiosities, a small pewter pendant depicting a half-lidded eye with its iris scratched and pitted, dangling from a thin silver chain. Egyptian hieroglyphs adorned the back, but half of them were chiseled away. According to Bentley, the Eye was originally dedicated to a god of forgetfulness, who was in turn forgotten by history.

"What we can read of the back," he told me, "says 'He dwells in spaces between spaces. Name him not, for he craves no name. He is silence.'"

I don't know if I believe in gods, but I do believe in power, and the Black Eye has a kick like a mule. I took a deep breath and draped it around my neck, letting the pendant rest against my bare skin.

One moment, the universe around me was alive and humming with information, with magical potential and the flow of energy, all the invisible conduits and symbols I'd trained for years to recognize and master. The next, my mind's eye was wrapped in cotton gauze, deaf, voiceless, and blind.

That was the blessing of the Eye and its curse. It made you invisible to the world of magic: as far as the unseen world was concerned, you simply didn't exist. Seers couldn't find you, and divining spells washed over you like dewdrops. On the other hand, you were about as mystically powerful as a newborn baby. You were cut off from the tap, pure and simple, like a drunk at last call.

I took deep breaths, struggling not to panic. I lasted almost thirty seconds before I yanked the Eye back over my head, twitching uncontrollably, trying to keep myself from hurling it across the room. I dropped it on the bedspread and sat there, trembling, feeling the hum of the universe wrap its loving arms around me once more.

Magicians are not, as a rule, healthy people. We've all got our hang-ups, be it booze, sex, drugs, you name it. A sorcerer with no obvious vices is inevitably hiding something *really* nasty in her closet. The fact is, they're all just substitutions for our one true addiction. Learning magic, real magic, changes you forever. We play games with the machinery of the universe, witness unimaginable beauty and terror, brush against power undreamed of by most humans. Once that door's been opened and we see the world as it really is, the idea of losing it is the most terrifying thing imaginable.

Wearing the Black Eye feels like gouging out your own eyeballs and stabbing your eardrums with a spike. You know, intellectually, that your senses will flood back the second you take it off, but your animal brain still flails like you're a fish out of water, drowning on the dock. When Bentley and Corman found the Eye, its previous owner wasn't using it to escape detection. He was using it as a torture device.

I didn't see any other options if I wanted to stay under Nicky's radar. Even still, I left the Eye wrapped, shoving the wadded ball of silk into the pocket of my slacks as I hunted for a clean shirt. I could endure it, I told myself, as long as I kept wearing it to a minimum. It helped to think about Stacy's wraith, suffering in the dark beneath the city streets. I could take it. I could take it for her sake, and when I found out who was responsible for our mutual pain, I would exact payment in full.

Paolo had told me to meet him at the Love Connection at ten. That gave me enough time to swing by Budget and rent a car. It would feed my cover story, in case Kaufman was paranoid enough to check, and at the very least he wouldn't see my real license plates. I lightened Jud's envelope a little and paid extra to get the keys for a cherry-red Mustang convertible. I had a story to sell.

Paolo was waiting for me out front and hopped into the passenger seat when I pulled up. He let out a long, low whistle.

"Somebody's moving up in the world," he said, tossing me an envelope. I thumbed through it. Driver's license, social security card, a couple of grocery store discount cards, even an expired video rental membership. The cherry on top was a spread of rumpled business cards, artificially aged to look like they'd been carried around in somebody's wallet for a year or two, and some bogus receipts Paolo had crafted to my specifications.

"I'm not," I said, tapping the envelope, "but Peter Greyson is. You set it up how I wanted?"

"You got the platinum package. That ID is bulletproof. You know you owe me big time, man. Prices on quality paper are going up all the time. Feds closed all the old, easy loopholes after 9/11. Well, almost all of 'em."

I'd bought a nice leather wallet on my way over, and I quickly stocked it with the goodies from Paolo's envelope.

"You're an artist."

"I know," he said with a grin. "So what's the plan?"

"Just get me in, and I'll do the rest. I'm about to become Artie Kaufman's new best friend."

#

Artie lived in Henderson, a half hour's drive southeast of Vegas. His house was nestled on a quiet suburban cul-de-sac, the looping road lined with perfect lawns and scallop-roofed houses with a vaguely Spanish style. He had money, that was for sure. A white windowless van sat parked in his driveway, probably for toting his camera equipment. Not surprisingly, there was no company logo on the sides.

"I wonder if his neighbors know what he does for a living," I said, pulling up behind the van.

"Probably not something that comes up at the Sunday potluck dinners," Paolo said. "Hey, remember what I said. This guy's dangerous."

"That makes two of us," I told him, taking the Black Eye from my pocket and putting it on. I squeezed my eyes shut, leaned back, and gripped the wheel with both hands, riding a sudden wave of panic and vertigo.

"Hey. Hey, you okay?" Paolo frowned.

"Fine," I lied, taking deep breaths and counting to ten in my head. "Just peachy. Stomach's a little upset, that's all."

I felt anything but dangerous getting out of the car and walking up the paved path to Artie Kaufman's front door. I was powerless and about to stroll into the den of a rapist, blackmailer, and possible murderer with no weapons but my wits. For that matter, I had doubts about my wits.

I didn't know what to expect when the front door swung open. Artie's movies were shot with a handheld camera, so I'd never seen him above the waist, and I'd seen far too much below it for my liking. Finding a California-tanned bodybuilder in a muscle shirt and a bleach-blond perm didn't surprise me, though. He carried a mixture of un-earned arrogance and frat-boy wealth like a badge of honor. I realized, as he pumped Paolo's hand and gave him a wolf-ish smile, that I'd want to punch him in the face even if I didn't know what he did for a living.

"Paolo! How the hell are ya, bro? Been too long, way too fuckin' long."

"Hey Artie," Paolo said, looking pained, "this is my bud-dy..."

He paused, looking at me, and my stomach dropped as Artie quirked an eyebrow. *He forgot my cover name.* I stepped up and beamed, projecting a confidence I wasn't remotely feeling.

"Greyson! Peter Greyson, and I gotta say, sir, this is one hell of an honor. I'm a huge fan, huge, huge fan, and when Paolo told me he knew you, well I just had to meet the art-ist himself."

Artie grinned, nearly crushing my hand in his. I made a mental note to steer Paolo away from discussing his and "Peter's" friendship. Great forger, lousy at improv.

"C'mon in, both of you!" Artie said, ushering us inside. "I've always got time for a fan. I was just finishing up a conference call with...well, let's just say they're the biggest distributor in L.A. and they want to buy me out. I'm like, 'Guys, please, my movies top all the sales charts, what do I need you for?' They just don't get it."

Behind Artie's back, Paolo gave me a tiny *no fuckin' way* eye roll and a shake of his head.

"Hey," I said, reciting the ad copy from his website, "you're the most dangerous man in porn. They ought to respect that."

"Damn right!" Artie grinned at me. "Let me show you around."

Artie's house screamed new money. It was styled in art deco and as pristine as an art museum. We followed him down a curving hallway, the ivory walls lit by cubic skylights, even the sun harnessed to show off his wealth. The hall opened up into a living room bigger than my apartment, where black leather sofas squatted on a sea of snow shag carpet, angled artfully around a mammoth flatscreen set into the wall and flanked by five-foot speaker stacks.

Paolo's shaking head stuck with me, and it jibed with my research. Second Circle Studios was a tiny player in the porn game, a one-man operation catering to a very specific kind of fetishist. Whatever Artie earned on his videos, it couldn't be netting the kind of cash needed to buy a place like this. What else was he involved in?

I looked behind him, to the woman strolling toward us on black stiletto heels, and all my thoughts fell away like the losing tickets from a gambler's hand.

She was beautiful, any fool could see that. A pale angel with a body built for daydreams, her scarlet hair worn in a twist over one shoulder. She wore a French maid's outfit barely a step removed from lingerie, her long legs sheathed in black fishnet, garter fastenings on display a quarter inch below the flare of her ruffled skirt. Any fool could see that.

Not just any fool could see the molten glow she gave off when my eyes slipped out of focus, or feel her presence in the room like someone pressing a diamond against my sinuses. Whoever she was, she was so ripe with occult energy that even the Black Eye couldn't entirely keep her from my muffled senses.

She looked at me. Her gaze slid down to where the talisman lay hidden under my shirt, cold pewter pressed against my skin. A reptilian smile played on her painted lips.

"Do you require service?" she asked Artie, her voice tinged with a Scottish burr.

"Yeah, yeah, beers for me and my new friends here."

She turned to leave. Paolo rubbed his eyes, making sure they were working right. "Goddamn," he said, "did she come with the house?"

"She's all right," Artie said, turning on the flatscreen and filling the room with the sounds of ESPN. "Trust me, man, in my line of work, especially when you're as pro as I am? Chicks are falling all over themselves just to get near me."

Somehow I doubted that. We sat down, watching last week's basketball highlights, while I tried to center myself and figure out what had just happened. My magic was worthless with my soul still trapped in the Eye's straitjacket. Just trying to stretch out my senses pushed me to the edge of panic. I counted my breaths and pretended to care about the show, making small talk I could barely hear over the roaring of blood in my ears.

Keep it on, I told myself over and over again. *Just until we leave. Just in case Nicky and Kaufman are connected. Count your breaths and don't blow this.*

The woman returned with a tray and three long-necked bottles of beer, so cold that little volcanoes of frost vapor spilled from their open mouths. I don't drink beer, but I supposed Peter Greyson would, so I took it with a nod of thanks and pretended my heart wasn't pounding against my rib cage. Her fingertips brushed mine as she stepped away, a tiny spark jumping between us and stinging my skin. I wanted more.

"So, Peter," Artie said, "Paolo tells me you're a bit of a collector."

I smiled. He couldn't wait to get right down to business. Even knowing the risks involved, talking to a perfect stranger on a casual acquaintance's say-so, he could barely hold himself back. I figured some natural suspicion would set in sooner or later, but I'd come prepared to deal with that.

"I am," I said. "I like to think of myself as a connoisseur of rare erotica. *Real* erotica."

10.

"Real?" Artie asked. "Like none of that airbrushed Play-boy shit, right?"

I'd rehearsed my lines all night, having conversations with my mirror. Learning how to sell myself as Artie's kind of scum. The words curdled on my tongue, but I smiled when I said them.

"Real," I said, "as in the reality of men, and the reality of women, and their places in the world. Like your films. And...others."

Artie moved closer to the edge of the sofa.

"That's a bold statement."

"I'm not some beta male who's going to tuck his tail between his legs because he has to be politically correct to get laid," I said with an indifferent shrug. Artie laughed, walking over to sit next to me, clinking his bottle against mine. Paolo just tried to make himself invisible, keeping his eyes on the TV.

"I hear that, bro. This is why I love my fans, you know? You really get how the world works. No pretense, no bull-shit."

"How it should work," I said, lifting my bottle in salute.

"Right, right. So, uh, you mentioned 'other' films."

I grinned. "So I did. Mind if I use your bathroom?"

"Yeah, sure, just up that hall on the left, far end."

As I stood up I dipped my fingers into my pocket, quietly sliding out my wallet and letting it tumble to the sofa as I rose. It would look like it fell out by accident. I was count-ing on Artie's curiosity to do the rest.

I had two aims, and giving him a chance to rifle through "Peter's" business cards was the first. The second was recon. If Artie drowned Stacy, he would have kept the recording. Evidence of a capital crime or not, he wouldn't be able to part with a treasure like that.

The idea of killing Artie sounded good to me. The idea of sending him to prison for the rest of his life and getting some public justice for Stacy sounded even better.

Out of sight of the living room, I poked my head into every doorway. He had a spacious home gym, a couple of guest bedrooms that looked like they'd never been used, and then I hit pay dirt. Artie's bedroom was just down the hall from the bath, his king-sized bed buried under a swamp of garish red satin sheets and a pair of samurai swords mounted to the wall. Classy. I searched his drawers as fast as I could, sliding my hand under his clothes and feeling for anything out of place, like maybe an unmarked DVD case.

I came up empty, but a more thorough search would have taken too long and I didn't want to leave anything out of place. The last thing I wanted was for him to come looking for me and blow the entire scam on the spot. I pulled open the door to his walk-in closet, resolving to go back empty-handed if I didn't find any evidence.

It wasn't a closet. It was a magician's shrine.

Books and candles weighed down the wraparound shelves, along with a smattering of wooden beads, tiny brass idols, and eclectic trinkets from half a dozen ancient cultures. The entire unfocused mess screamed "talented amateur," the kind of sorcerer who knows just enough to be a danger to himself and others.

Artie's actresses had their own shelf. A publicity photo of each one lay pinned under magnetic stones, their glossy eyes and mouths stitched over with mortician's thread. I smelled the residue of an anointing oil, something like ginger root and gunpowder. A binding spell, crude but effective.

No wonder they don't run away or press charges against you. They can't.

I didn't see a portrait for Stacy, but an indentation in the dust showed where it used to sit. He cleaned up fast. Another missing picture was more worrisome: Artie's maid. She wasn't on his shelf of enslaved starlets, so who was she?

Looking over his books, the answer came to me, dragging a razor blade of ice across the back of my neck. The collection included the *Grimoirum Verum*, Crowley's private translation of the *Goetia*, even a rare first-edition printing of *The Five Insights* with the censored ninth chapter intact. Artie's books of black magic shared a singular, insane purpose. I knew what the woman was now, why she was powerful enough to glow through the Black Eye's muffling shroud, and the revelation scared the hell out of me.

"You stupid, stupid son of a bitch," I breathed. "You conjured a demon."

Rule number four of magic, the one that any responsible teacher drums into their students' heads until it's as second nature as breathing, is *you do not fuck with demons*. Yes, I'm aware of the irony of a man named Faust arguing against trafficking with the powers of hell, but I've learned from hard experience.

Summoning a demon is easy. Getting them to do what you want, on the other hand, requires a contract and a binding ritual. Imagine facing a trial lawyer so ferocious he makes Clarence Darrow look like a first-year law student. Imagine that this lawyer has had literally centuries of courtroom experience and is incredibly pissed at you for yanking him across dimensions without permission. That's what you're up against when you bargain with a demon. And if you leave the slightest loophole in your contract, the tiniest escape clause, you'll probably be torn to pieces and dragged down to hell, where things will get *really* unpleasant.

So, of course, Kaufman summoned one up, dressed her in a skimpy outfit, and made her serve beer. The stupid bastard was juggling with nitroglycerin and didn't even know it. I would have laughed, except that if he gave the word, his pet demon would rip my spine out and use my skull for a bowling ball. On top of that, he probably had a "defend me at all costs" clause in his contract. Getting physical with Kaufman would make my life nasty, painful, and short. Before I took him down, no matter how I did it, I needed to get his demon out of the way.

I turned around and found myself standing face to face with her.

She stood in the closet doorway, watching. She stared at me like an entomologist studying a rare and exotic insect, or a rare and exotic insect studying its next meal. I had one chance to talk my way out of this, one chance to explain my invasion of her master's shrine. One sentence between life and death.

"So, uh," I said, "you come here often?"

It was not my shining moment.

"You shouldn't be here," she said.

"Are you going to tell on me?"

"If he asks me a direct question," she said slowly, as if considering her words, "I am bound to answer truthfully."

"And if he doesn't?"

She didn't answer. The hint of amusement crinkled at the corners of her eyes. I got the picture.

"He assumes you'll just tell him what he needs to know, doesn't he? Because he thinks he owns you."

"I am...forbidden to speak ill of my master," she said, the line sounding like she read it from a cue card. The look on her face told me what she really thought. I knew I was pushing my luck, but it was time to roll the dice.

"Too bad," I said, "because I think he's a dumbass of mythical proportions. In fact, I believe generations from now, bards and poets will compose epic verse to commemorate his staggering idiocy. Are you sure you can neither confirm nor deny these allegations?"

She smiled, flashing pearly teeth a little too sharp to be human.

"I am forbidden to speak ill of my master. And you need to go back before he thinks to ask me where you went."

I could take a hint. I eased sideways past her, almost close enough to touch, and paused. "Will you tell me your use-name?"

A use-name is an alias of sorts in occult circles. True names have the power to conjure and bind, but we have to call each other *something* or else the entire supernatural world would be reduced to "hey, you" and "that guy over there."

"*Caitlleanabruaudi*," she said, or something similar to it, but my mind suddenly felt fuzzy and some of the syllables sounded like they could only be pronounced by a mouth with two tongues. There are some sounds, and some languages, that are so alien to our nature that the human brain naturally rebels at them. You'd think we'd take that as a hint.

"Caitlin?" I managed to stammer, the rest slipping away from me.

"Caitlin," she echoed. A sliver of tongue flicked across her pomegranate lips, as if tasting the name and coming away satisfied. "Yes. You may call me that. Now go."

I ducked into the bathroom on my way back, flushed the toilet, and washed my hands, making sure to leave them a tiny bit damp. Every con artist knows it's easy to get away with lies the size of Mount Rushmore, but missing the tiny details will kill you every time.

"—barely have to pay them," Artie was bragging to Paolo when I walked back into the living room. "You promise them points based on net profit. It's called Hollywood accounting. Hey, look who's back! I thought you fell in."

"Sorry," I said, patting my stomach and wincing as I sat down on the sofa. "Turns out drinking vodka all night and starting the day with a greasy breakfast burrito is not a winning combination."

My wallet wasn't where I had left it, and my host had a new bulge in his hip pocket. Perfect.

"I've been there," he laughed. "So we were talking about your, uh, collection."

The front door rattled on its hinges, and heavy footsteps slapped against the marble tile. I looked over as our new guest arrived, a hard-eyed piece of bad news in a gray wool blazer. He peeled off the jacket as he walked, giving us a good look at the nickel-plated .38 in his shoulder holster. Clunky cop shoes, cop jacket, cop gun. I tried to make myself very, very small.

"What is this?" he said, looking at the three of us. "A sausage party?"

Artie forced a smile, giving a nervous laugh that didn't fit his bodybuilder's frame. "Hey Carl, just entertaining some fans. Sit down, grab a beer with us."

"Yeah, that's okay, you guys can go back to suckin' each others' dicks. Is she here?" He jerked his thumb toward the back of the house.

"Well yeah, but—"

A thunderstorm brewed behind the cop's eyes. "But?"

If Artie had squeezed his beer bottle any tighter, it would have shattered in his hand. "Just...maybe don't mark her up this time, okay? I've got some friends coming over tomorrow."

Carl sauntered over, resting his hand on his shoulder holster.

"We got a problem here, Artie?" he asked quietly.

"No, no, of course not! Hey, go on back, she'll be happy to see you."

Carl stomped off. A picture formed in my mind, as shiny as the shield on his belt. Now I realized why something about Artie had put me on edge the moment he opened his front door. Down in the tunnel, Eric had described the men who dumped Stacy's corpse.

Skinny guy with a face like a hatchet, and a bodybuilder with a blond perm. Hatchet-face was the one who liked waving his gun around.

It fit Artie and his pal Carl perfectly. Eric had only seen one badge. He just assumed they were both cops. A nasty little suspicion occurred to me.

"Wow," I laughed, shaking my head. "Your friend's pretty intense, huh?"

"He's not my—I mean, he's, yeah. Intense." Kaufman sank into the sofa, pouting like a six-year-old.

"What'd you say his name was? Carl? I was watching something on the news last night about a detective, what was his name?" I pretended to concentrate, then snapped my fingers. "Carl White. That's not Carl White, is it?"

"Nah, his name's Holt. Listen, guys, I'd better let you go, he's in a mood and this could get...I just don't want to deal with it." He handed me one of his business cards, crisp block lettering on soft cream. "Call me tonight, all right? I really want to talk to you about your collection."

I promised I would, and Paolo followed me out into the sunlight. As I revved up the Mustang's engine, he looked at me incredulously.

"That guy totally stole your wallet. It was on the sofa, and I watched him scoop it up."

"I know." I leaned back and smiled. "He was supposed to."

11.

I tugged off the Black Eye, the steering wheel jerking in my other hand. A world of sensations flooded my senses with the force of a brick to the face. I dropped the talisman into my lap and gripped the wheel, taking shallow breaths until I felt human again.

"You," Paolo said, staring at me from the passenger seat with one elbow cocked out the window, "are one weird dude."

"Tell me about it."

"What do you mean he was supposed to steal your wallet? You had me working all night on those IDs!"

"That's right. He should be online right about now, digging up anything he can about Peter Greyson. Look at it from his perspective: he thinks I've got what he wants, a genuine snuff movie, which is also illegal as hell. I might be legit, I might be a crackpot, or I might be a cop trying to snare him in a sting. If he thinks he's got a handle on who Peter Greyson is, he'll feel safer, more likely to stick his neck out. Also, now I have a reason to go see him again, once I discover my wallet is missing."

"So the business cards you had me do up—"

"Are for a real outfit in Los Angeles. EpiCalc was an accounting-software company that went belly-up last year. Kaufman will see the company's legit, but he won't have any way to verify whether Peter really was a sales manager there. Then there's the receipts. If you see an ATM receipt showing a person's account is fifty-eight bucks overdrawn, and then a liquor store cash receipt from that same afternoon for a twenty-dollar handle of vodka plus he's splurging on a rented Mustang, what's the first thing that comes to mind?"

"The guy's in a downward spiral," Paolo said.

"Right. Probably needs cash, too, and fast. Put the story together, and Peter Greyson is a desperate man in a bad situation. He's the kind of person, in other words, who Kaufman can wave some money at and bend over a barrel."

I pulled up outside the Love Connection. Before he got out, Paolo gave me a long look.

"Careful. He's got an ego, but he ain't dumb. That cop buddy of his looks like real trouble, too. You sure you aren't in over your head?"

The real trouble, I thought, *is the woman who could have shredded us both into bloody confetti without breaking a sweat, but Paolo doesn't need to know that.*

"If I'm not in over my head, I'm not trying hard enough. Thanks for the assist, Paolo. I've got it from here."

I took the side streets on my way across town. I wasn't afraid of being followed; I just needed time to think. I kept the Mustang's top down. The breeze felt good on my skin, an antidote to the desert heat.

Detective Carl Holt. Same Holt, I'd bet cash money, as the one who gave Jud Pankow the runaround. He and Artie had dumped Stacy's body and now he was in charge of investigating the case. Nice arrangement. Carl and Artie weren't friends, that much was obvious. I had Artie pegged as a typical bully, happy to slap around women half his size but easily cowed by a more dominant personality. Carl fit the bill. Hell, he had a key to Artie's house and walked in like he owned the place.

To see "her," I reminded myself, *and unless there was somebody else in the house, that means Caitlin.* I remembered Artie's protest about "marking her up" and bristled, squeezing the steering wheel.

What kind of demon would Artie summon? Obvious answer, the number one go-to choice for every wannabe sorcerer out there: a succubus. Thing is, according to all the lore I'd read, a succubus's kiss could be just as potent as mainlining heroin. Just as addictive, too. I ran the numbers in my head and built a theory.

Artie binds Caitlin to his service. Artie murders Stacy. Artie introduces Caitlin to friendly Detective Holt and gets him hooked on her supernatural charms. The offer couldn't be simpler: "You can romp in the sack with my pet demoness any time you want; just help me cover up this pesky little murder first."

Both men had something to hold over the other. Carl could expose Artie as a killer, and Artie could take Caitlin away and introduce Carl to the joys of occult drug withdrawal. Mutually assured destruction. No wonder they hated each other.

I could work with that.

#

"So what are my options?" I asked Bentley, leaning against the front counter at the Scrivener's Nook. He looked up at me from behind an antique cash register, arching an incredulous eyebrow.

"Well," he said, "he can order his demon to tear you to pieces, or he can have his police officer friend shoot you and cover up the murder. Or maybe he can just beat you to death with his bare hands. It sounds like he might be abusing steroids, and that sort is prone to uncontrollable rages, I understand."

I looked around at the clutter of books, stacks upon stacks covering vintage tables and overflowing mahogany shelves. Bentley and Corman's store existed in a constant state of controlled chaos. They prided themselves on a filing system dictated by whimsy and decor that was trendy two hundred years ago. Every time I came in, I felt like I'd walked into a Charles Dickens novel.

"I was kind of hoping for some more concrete guidance in the research department? Maybe from the backroom collection?"

"Just exorcise her. You know how to do that," Corman said, easing his way up a ladder on the other side of the store with a box of hardcovers precariously balanced against his hip. I jogged over to hold the box while he finished his climb.

"She's not possessing a human. She's an incarnate, I'm sure of it."

"Incarnate demons are rare for a reason," Bentley fretted. "The sheer power required to create a physical body out of nothing but raw spiritual energy...most of them just can't do it. They have to climb inside a human or an animal to survive in our world. You're absolutely certain?"

"Kid knows how possessions work," Corman grunted, saving me the effort. "If he says she's an incarnate, she's an incarnate."

Bentley held up a finger. "Point of order? Can we use 'it' rather than 'she'? It's an important distinction. Daniel, I know that these men are...abusing her, and I understand how you feel about that, but you must remember that you aren't seeing what you think you're seeing. That isn't a woman, or even a person. It's a creature born of sin and corruption in its purest form."

"What he's saying is..." Corman reached down to take another book from the box. "She'd gut you as soon as give you the time of day, no matter how nice she smiles."

"I get that," I said, pretending I hadn't had Caitlin on my mind since the second we met. "If I'm going to take these guys down, though, I need to get around her somehow. Look, Kaufman must have a binding contract somewhere in his house. If I burn the contract, doesn't that—"

"Set the demon free on the spot?" Bentley said. "Oh, yes, most assuredly, at which point it will thank you with a wet and messy death. Oh, and you'll have succeeded in unleashing a free-willed menace upon the world to spread havoc and misery however it pleases."

Corman shook his head. "Bad play, kiddo."

"Don't suppose I'd have any chance in a straight-up fight?" I asked.

Bentley tapped his bony finger against his chin. "You're talking about an incarnate demon with at least a few centuries of power and experience. How do I draw a comparison for you? Let's see. Cormie, what was that delightful science fiction movie we watched last weekend?"

"*The Terminator*," Corman grunted.

"*The Terminator*." Bentley nodded. "Have you seen it, Daniel? You might find it instructional."

#

I had hoped to come home with answers. Instead I brought back a fifth of Bacardi, a two-liter bottle of Coke, and a microwave pizza from the convenience store down the block. I knew I'd been having too many nights like this in a row since Roxy left, but it was a comfortable rut.

I booted up my laptop and got things ready. Time to call Artie. I kept a box of burners in my closet, cheap Nokia flip-phones with a few hours of prepaid time for jobs like this one.

"Mr. Kaufman?" I said when he picked up, trying to sound harried and breathless. "I'm so sorry to bother you this late, I'm sure you're busy. This is Peter, Peter Greyson from this morning? Paolo's friend?"

"Hey, Pete!" he boomed. "How the hell are ya? Sorry we had to cut things short, bro."

"Totally understand, you're a busy man. I didn't leave my wallet over there, did I? I dropped it somewhere, and I've been going nuts trying to find it all afternoon."

"As a matter of fact, you did. I found it in the sofa cushions just like, five minutes ago. I was about to call you and let you know."

I exhaled with mock relief. "Oh, man, thank you, you're a lifesaver."

"So, Pete," he said slowly, building himself up to it, "you said you're a collector. Paolo said you might be able to get, you know, some really rare videos?"

"I have one that you might like. Listen, normally I'd share it for free since you're my favorite director, but I'm in a little jam here—"

"Say no more, bro. We're both men of the world. It's all ups and downs, am I right? So how do you feel about a nice fat stack of cash in your hand? I can make that happen, if you've really got what I'm looking for."

"Oh, I've got what you're looking for."

"Yeah?" he breathed. I felt like a phone-sex operator, getting him all hot and bothered. Grimacing, I tapped my keyboard.

"I'm not saying anything on a phone line, you know, but, well, listen to this."

Before calling Artie, I had logged on to Netflix and took a quick spin through the horror section. I'd queued up a one-star-rated film described as "raw, brutal torture porn" and paused it on a scene where a masked killer with a drill was terrorizing a naked co-ed.

I held my phone up to the cheap computer speakers and hit play, treating Artie to six seconds of flesh-tearing shrieks. The special effects were terrible, but I bet the screams sounded pretty believable on his end of the line.

"Just saying," I murmured into the phone, hitting pause.

"Holy shit, bro."

"It's three hours long. Her throat gives out about two hours in, though."

"Yeah," he breathed, "yeah, I think we can do business. Hey, my usual poker night is tomorrow. Why don't you come on by, sit in for a few hands, chill with us, and then we can have a private viewing?"

"Wow, I haven't played poker in years," I said, "but I guess I can give it a shot. You guys play for real money?"

"Five-hundred-dollar buy-in. You could make some real money, you play your cards right."

"I don't know. I really need every dollar I can scrape together right now. Five hundred's just about everything I have left."

"Come on," Artie said, "trust me, these guys I play with are chumps. You'll probably steamroller them. Every dollar counts, right? And even if you lose, I'm gonna pay you a lot more than that for the video. You walk out with cash in your pocket, no matter how it goes down."

I counted silently to five, letting the tension simmer. "Oh, all right, I'm in. What the hell, right? Could be fun."

I promised to be there at seven sharp and hung up the phone. The poker invitation stank like a rotten fish. He wanted the video that badly, practically drooling into the phone, but we couldn't meet to trade it before the game started? Or tonight, even? My gut said Artie didn't intend to pay me a dime. He believed I was a desperate man in dire straits. Desperate and reckless enough, maybe, to be pushed into putting the video on the table when I'd lost everything else.

The lion's den awaited. Artie Kaufman, a sadistic killer expecting a prize that I didn't have. Carl Holt, a corrupt cop with everything to lose. Caitlin, who had literally clawed her way out of the pits of hell. Then there was Nicky Agnelli's connection to the whole mess, a big fat question mark dangling from the barrel of a gun.

I only had one chance to yank the rug out from under Artie. If we made it to the end of the night and he figured out my "movie" was nothing but a blank DVD, no way was I getting out of his house alive. I didn't like my odds. Still, I had two good reasons not to drop the job and walk away: Jud and Stacy Pankow. They both needed my help to move on, in their own ways. I'd live, if I walked away, but I wouldn't be able to live with myself.

12.

I woke with the dawn and guzzled a bottle of water to
chase away my hangover. Then I stumbled into the shower,
letting the warm spray blanket me while I rested my forehead against the cool tile wall. Hazy dreams slipped between my fingers, dancing at the edges of my mind. I
thought I had dreamed about Caitlin. Imagined her standing there, in the darkness of my bedroom, watching me
sleep.

I toweled off but didn't get dressed yet. Instead I went to
my closet and pulled out a couple of dog-eared books, flopping down on the bedspread to page through them. I needed an edge for tonight, a card up my sleeve in case things
went sideways.

"The Harlot's Curtains," I read aloud, my finger sliding
across the page. "Oh, Aleister, your magic was dodgy, but
you sure knew how to sell it."

The enchantment called for a lodestone, some powdered
amethyst, and a dram of pigeon blood, among other ingredients. While it's true that you can get anything you want in

Las Vegas, that's a privilege generally reserved for high rollers. The rest of us have to improvise.

Once you know how magic works, once you've tasted its waters, you realize how few concrete rules there are. Most sorcerers come up with a deeply personal catalog of symbols and patterns expressing their unique approach to the art. I knew a guy who collected those advertisements for escorts you find scattered all over the sidewalk on the Strip. He read them like tarot cards.

If you can figure out another magician's mindset, you can take their spells and translate them into your own metaphor. Half an hour of legwork gave me a list of equivalent ingredients, my own version of the Harlot's Curtains. All that remained was to put the enchantment together. I pushed the bed aside, uncovering the patch of floor where I'd carefully cut away the carpet and exposed the bare wood underneath. Chalk dust from a hundred rituals scuffed and streaked the faded boards.

Four hours later I sat cross-legged, my naked body glistening with cold sweat, and blood roaring in my ears. The room danced with light from a triad of black candles. The last words of my invocation fell from my lips with the last of my energy, gutter-Latin escaping my body on a gasp. I had lost track of time along the way, carried aloft by a spell that wove itself from the desert air. A white poker chip from the Sands Hotel, a long-gone legend of the Strip, glistened in my open palm like a beacon in the shadows.

It seemed like such a tiny thing, but it would have to do. I took another shower and got ready to fight.

#

I rang Artie's doorbell at five minutes to seven, and he opened it so fast he must have been standing just on the other side.

"Hey, hey!" He beamed, pulling me into an awkward hug. "Look who's here, the man of the hour!"

I'd been patted down by professionals. Artie's clumsy slapping at my hips and back, disguised as a friendly greeting, was anything but. *No, I'm not carrying a gun,* I thought. *Why are you worried that I would be?*

I did have a sealed puffy mailing envelope tucked under one arm, with a blank DVD inside. Artie eyed it greedily as he stepped back.

"Is that it? The real deal?"

"Real as a heart attack," I said, patting it. "I'll show you thirty seconds of the footage, from anywhere in the video, to prove it's legit. If you like what you see, we talk price."

"Sounds like a plan," he said, leading me into the living room, "but first I hope you're ready to play some serious poker."

A professional-grade poker table took a place of honor in the heart of the room, the sofas and chairs pushed back against the wall. My psychic senses strained in vain, but the Black Eye was back in place around my neck to protect me from Nicky's seer. The Eye's power weighed against my lungs, a constant suffocating pressure, the kind of frustrating ache that keeps you from getting a moment's rest. If I needed to use the chip in my pocket, the Eye would have to come off first. On the other hand, if things went that far sideways, crossing Nicky Agnelli would be the least of my problems.

Kaufman's buddies were the kind of low-rent hoods you'd expect to see brewing meth in a trailer park. One wore a pair of amber shades and a visored cap, like he thought he was competing in the World Series of Poker. The other one couldn't keep still for five seconds at a time, his head and hands constantly twitching. Whatever he was on, it wasn't the expensive stuff. Shades and Twitch gave me lethargic waves from the sofas, then looked at Kaufman as if waiting for a cue.

Caitlin emerged from the kitchen, saloon-style doors swinging behind her, and the breath caught in my throat. She wore a green satin gown that clung to her body like a raindrop to a leaf, scooped dangerously low in the back. It matched her eyes. She handed me an open bottle of beer. Her touch lingered just a moment longer than it needed to.

You're not seeing what you think you're seeing, I told myself, remembering Bentley's warning. It didn't help.

Artie came up behind her and grabbed her ass. I almost recoiled from the sudden look in her eyes, a glare of pure burning hatred. I saw how fast it melted into a charming smile as she turned to face him. I fought my overwhelming desire to take my bottle and smash Artie's face in. Woman, demon, I didn't care. This was wrong.

"Do you require service, Master?" she asked him.

"No, but I sure as fuck do," called out Detective Holt as he stomped his way up the hallway. "C'mon, we got time for a quickie."

"No, we don't," Artie said. "Game's starting, everybody to the table."

Carl's brow furrowed. He tugged off his jacket and tossed it onto the back of a chair, openly wearing his shoulder holster, before closing in on Artie. "Sorry? Didn't hear that."

"Later. You can have her after the game."

Carl hissed through gritted teeth, "We have a *deal*, Artie."

"We talked about this last night," Artie said, pitching his voice almost too softly for me to hear. "We agreed—"

"Fine," Carl snapped, throwing up his arms and dropping into his chair at the poker table. "Fine, be that way, fuck it. Everybody, get your asses over here. Let's get this over with."

I concealed a smile and sat down opposite Artie. My theory was right: Carl acted like a heroin addict jonesing for a fix, which made Artie his dealer. Whatever Caitlin did for the detective behind closed doors, it had long since warped from a desire to a desperate need.

That wasn't good news for me. The only thing more dangerous and unpredictable than a junkie is a junkie with a loaded gun.

The five of us paid cash into the pot, and Artie dealt out stacks of plastic chips. There were a few too many back-and-forth glances between him and his two friends for my liking. I saw a setup coming from a mile away, but with the Eye weighing down my neck like a millstone I couldn't do anything but watch close and try to stay sharp.

Half an hour later, I was down by three hundred dollars and looking for the number of the truck that hit me. Lady Luck was colder than a woman scorned, but I'd figured out why. As expected, the bastards were hustling me. They'd worked out a system and kept it tight. A tug of the ear here, an anxious finger tapping on the emerald felt there, little signals to help them work with a singular purpose: burning me down. I figured they'd split the take after they sent me home empty-handed. That was their plan, anyway.

Carl didn't seem to be in on it. He was too impatient and distracted to be any good, burrowing down to his last stack of chips even before I did. He'd take himself out of the game soon enough. I deliberately threw the next few hands, watching every discard, working out the nuances of their system. It didn't hurt that Twitch barely knew what game he was playing, and Shades couldn't keep himself from grinning like an idiot every time he caught a decent hand. If not for the hustle, this would strictly be amateur night.

I sank down in my chair like a whipped dog, digging into my pocket and tossing a handful of crumpled bills onto the felt. "I shouldn't do this," I said. "I really shouldn't do this, but count me in for another three hundred."

"The table turns fast," Artie said with a wolfish smile. "You can still go home a winner."

"I'd better, this is my rent money."

"Gonna have to blow your landlord again," Carl muttered, then slapped his cards on the table. "Fold. And I'm out."

Now it was the four of us, and Artie and his buddies were happy and complacent. Just where I wanted them. Twitch was the weakest link. I decided to take him out first. I waited until he signaled to the others that he'd been dealt a great hand, and then I waved Caitlin over.

"Another beer?" I said.

When she came back, I took the bottle with an outstretched hand and "accidentally" dropped it into Twitch's lap. He jumped up, spattering beer onto the felt as he dropped his cards, yelling louder than I'd dared to hope despite my oh-so-sincere apologies. Artie got up to find a towel. Caitlin bent over to pick up the bottle from the floor, stealing everybody's attention, and I had two seconds to switch my useless seven of hearts for Twitch's ace.

When things finally settled down, Artie and Shades folded their hands like clockwork, confident that Twitch had this round locked up. The look on their faces when I beat him with a lousy two pair was priceless. A tiny victory for a tiny hand, but the real reward was making Twitch look like an idiot incapable of managing a grade-school hustle. He blew the next hand all on his own, too flustered to pay attention. Artie and Shades froze him out by silent consent after that, leaving him to dangle even as he kept signaling his hands, telling me exactly what he was holding.

Off balance and out of the loop, Twitch went into a nosedive. We whittled him down, dividing up his stake until he barely had any chips to his name. I kept my victories small, occasionally tossing a hand to Artie or Shades on purpose, wanting them to stay confident.

The shoe came around the table and it was my turn to deal. "I don't know about you guys," I said, "but I'm starting to feel lucky."

13.

Luck comes naturally when you make it yourself. I palmed a couple of cards from the shoe as I dealt out the next hand, slipping them up my sleeve and wedging them against the band of my wristwatch for safekeeping. Then I took the kid gloves off and started winning.

Twitch dropped first. Cleaned out and withering under his buddies' glares, he mumbled something about needing to get back home and skulked out the door. Shades was next on the chopping block. I cut into him again and again, my stack of chips growing. He winced at each loss like I'd leaned across the table and gut-punched him. He suddenly remembered it was getting late and he had to be at work in the morning, offering limp apologies as he chugged down the last of his beer.

"There you go," Artie said from across the table, forcing an enthusiasm into his words that his eyes didn't match. "Like I said, you could make some money tonight."

"Night's still young."

He slapped a roll of bills onto the table. "Any objections?"

"None."

He paid into the bank and gave himself a fresh stack of chips, mirroring mine. Meanwhile, Carl watched Caitlin like a cat eyeing a mouse in a cage. He suddenly slapped his palm against the table, making the chips jump, and stood up.

"Have to make a phone call," he snarled and stomped out of the room. Artie and I shrugged at each other and got down to business.

With the signals from his partners gone, so was my biggest advantage. We went back and forth for a few hands while I looked for a way into his head.

"Sorry about your loss, by the way," I said as I laid down a winning hand.

His cheek twitched. "What loss?"

"That girl, what was her name, Stacie Velour? Heard she drowned. Damn shame. You must have been broken up over it."

"Barely knew the bitch," he said, staring hard at his hand. "We just worked together once or twice."

I tossed some chips into the pot, raising the stakes, keeping my tone conversational. "Weird rumor on the Internet. Somebody said there's a version of her autopsy report floating around, claiming she drowned two days *before* the rainstorm. Strange, huh?"

He nearly bent his cards in half.

"Internet's bullshit," he said, a faint stammer in his voice. "Bunch of pencil-neck geeks sitting in their mommas' basements, making shit up."

"Yeah." I nodded slowly. "That's what I said too. Still, I heard they're going to assign more cops to the case, give it another review. Just to be safe."

That was all it took. Flustered and nervous with his thoughts a mile away from the table, Artie made mistake after mistake, and I punished him for each and every one. I cut into his stacks of chips like a surgeon with a scalpel fetish, the clock ticking just shy of midnight by the time I finished cleaning house. I didn't know exactly how much was in my pile, but it was a hell of a lot more than Artie had planned on losing.

"Sure you can still afford the video?" I asked, taunting him a little. It wasn't bravado; I needed him angry and reckless for what I had in mind.

"I'm good for the money," he growled.

"I'm sure you're good for it, but do you *have* it? In cash? I don't take checks."

Carl came back to the table, thrusting his phone at Artie. "It's your brother."

He took the phone. I couldn't make out the words on the other end, but I could hear shouting.

"No, look." He could barely get a word in edgewise. "No, I understand how important he is to...no, that's not...yes, I know how serious this...all right, all right, fine. Goodbye."

Carl beamed with triumph as Artie handed the phone back.

"You're an *asshole*," Artie snapped.

Carl pointed at Caitlin. "I get her how I want, when I want, where I want. That is the deal. You don't like it, I can stop holding up my end of the deal and we can have this conversation someplace a lot less friendly. I want her *now*."

"Fine," Artie said, throwing up his arms, "fine, take her in back. Just don't cut her again, Christ. Or at least clean up after yourself this time. I'm not your goddamn maid."

I should have been jubilant. Artie was out of his mind, easy to wrap around my finger, and Carl and Caitlin were about to step out of the picture. I had every advantage, every card in my favor. Everything was going according to plan.

I looked at Caitlin. She stared at Carl, dead eyed, resigned.

Fuck the plan.

I picked up my padded envelope and dropped it on the table, pushing it to the middle along with my pile of chips. "I've got a better idea," I said. "One more hand. If you win, you get all my winnings, and the video, and I walk out of here with empty pockets."

"And if you win?" Artie asked.

I pointed to Caitlin. "I get her."

The room fell quiet. Artie looked at me for a moment, squinting. "You know what she is?"

I reached around my neck, unclasped the Black Eye, and put it on the table. The sudden rush of power, the whirl of sensations and currents, rode in on the pounding of my heart. I'd have to answer to Nicky if his seer was watching, but that was the least of my problems right now.

"I'm sure you recognize this symbol," I said, knowing he probably had no idea what he was looking at. "I'm an adept of the Golden Dawn. We've been watching you for a long time, Mr. Kaufman. You're obviously a magus of great power, but we didn't know until now just how much respect you deserved."

"Yeah," he said, nodding slowly, "I—I do. I do deserve respect."

"This is bullshit," Carl said. "You can't be taking this seriously."

Freed of the Eye, I stroked the envelope with my fingertips, tracing the sigil of Pluto across its face and flooding it with a stream of energy. *You want this. You NEED this.* A simple trick, but with Artie confused and pulled in four directions at once, the crude enchantment drew his eyes like a mound of diamonds.

"Unless, of course, you're not allowed to wager her," I said with a pointed glance at Carl.

"She's mine, and I can do what I want with her," Artie said, getting up from the table and walking into his bedroom. Carl followed him, arguing at his back, utterly ignored. Artie came back with a sheaf of papers in his fist. He dropped it onto the center of the table.

The contract could have come from any courtroom in the country, though this one appealed to a very different set of laws. I flipped through it, nodding. *Bound for eternity in the name of the thirteen forgotten martyrs, witnessed by the emissary of the Lucifuge, oath of dire perdition for any who might sunder these chains, etcetera, etcetera.*

"Signed in blood," I said, leaning back in my chair. "Nice touch."

"You can't do this." Carl glowered. "You can't let him take her!"

Artie slid the shoe over to him. "I'm not losing. Now deal for us."

I stood in the middle of a three-way crossfire. If I lost this hand, it was all over. Artie would figure out my "snuff movie" was a scam, and either he'd kill me or he'd order Caitlin to do it. Meanwhile, Carl looked like he wanted to put a bullet in both of our heads. This ride was out of control with no happy ending in sight.

My heart sank at the smile on Artie's face. Our last round was a straight-up showdown, no room for tricks or bluffs, best hand wins. I had a literal ace up my sleeve, but with all three of them watching me like hungry hawks I had no way to get at it. I was going to die from a simple twist of bad luck. That, and sticking my neck out.

Caitlin sauntered over to the table, stroking Carl's shoulder like a lover as she leaned down to whisper in Artie's ear.

"Break him, Master," she purred, punctuating her words with a flick of her tongue against his earlobe, "or let me do it for you."

He turned his head, startled, while Carl stared at them like a jealous lover. It was all I needed. I slipped the ace from my watchband, palming a worthless card in its place. I pretended to rub my neck and dropped the spare card down the back of my shirt.

"I think we're done here," Artie said with a smile, laying down a gleaming span of cherry-red diamonds. A queen-high flush. Good hand.

"Agreed," I said, showing him three sevens and two beautiful little aces. Full house.

That's when everything went wrong.

Carl's pistol cleared his holster in a heartbeat, the barrel aimed right between my eyes. His grip was as shaky as his sanity, but at this range he'd blow my brains all over the shag carpet without even trying.

"You can't have her!" he shouted, spittle flecking the table felt. I squeezed the arms of my chair, trying to keep my cool with the gun barrel hovering inches from my face.

"Easy pal," I said. "I'm not the one you should be aiming that piece at. Your friend sold you out."

"What are you talking about?" he said, his gaze wavering between me and Artie.

"Stacy Pankow. You think it's a coincidence I'm here to-night?"

"Who the fuck is Stacy Pankow?" Carl said.

"You knew her as Stacie Velour. You know, the girl whose body you dumped in the storm tunnels? The murder you covered up? You're an accessory."

"He can't prove anything," Artie stammered.

"He offered me a trade," I said, "yesterday, before you showed up. My movie for his. I turned him down because I needed the cash, but man, did it sound juicy."

"What movie?" Carl said, looking at his partner in crime. "What's he talking about?"

I rested my hands on the table. "The video of him mur-dering Stacy. What, you didn't know? You didn't know he kept a souvenir?"

"He's lying!" Artie said, but the gun wavered in Carl's grip.

"Am I? Am I lying about the DVD in your safe? The one that pins you with a murder rap? Think about it, detective. He goes down, you go down with him. You know what happens to cops who get sent to Ely Prison? It's not pretty."

That was a lot of hunches, and if I was wrong on a single one of them, I was good as dead. I didn't even know for a fact that Artie had a safe in his office, except I knew he'd be keeping Caitlin's contract somewhere out of harm's way and it was a likely bet.

"Tell him," I said, "tell him to open his safe. *Make* him open it."

Artie glared. "Carl, will you please shoot this son of a bitch? If you don't have the balls, give me the gun and let me do it."

"I think," Carl said after a moment's thought, "I would like to see your safe now."

He marched us into Artie's office, but he kept the gun trained on me, giving me a jab in the back with the barrel. Artie went behind his desk, opening a polished birch cabinet to reveal the gunmetal-black face of a small safe.

"This is stupid," he said, looking back at Carl. "You are about to feel really, truly stupid—"

"Open it."

I held my breath as Artie keyed in the combination. Tumblers clanked and the door swung wide to reveal...nothing. A few loose papers. A thin stack of cash. A passport. I'd gotten it wrong. There was no recording, not here.

"I'm sorry," Artie said with a sneer, "you were expecting something different? Now waste this asshole!"

"Gentlemen," I said, brandishing the white casino chip I'd enchanted that morning, holding it between my thumb and forefinger. They paused, uncertain.

"The fifth rule of magic, and my personal favorite: always make a dramatic exit."

I flipped the chip in the air. It spun end over end, slowing as it reached the top of its arc, and exploded.

14.

The chip erupted with a blinding flash, smearing a green haze across my retinas as every light in the house died at once. I dove for the door. Carl's pistol barked twice, streaking the room with white lightning. I scrambled around the corner as another pair of shots blasted into the wall and blew away chunks of stucco.

The house swam in darkness, only the blinking of a digital clock painting the shadows a baleful crimson. I ran to the living room to grab what I needed from the poker table and ducked underneath just in time, watching Carl charge past me on his way to the front door. I kept my footsteps light on the shag carpet, moving as fast as I could, ducking into the bathroom as Artie's bedroom door flew open. He didn't have a gun, but he'd grabbed one of the samurai swords. He waved it over his head and raced through the house.

I crouched between the toilet and the sink, engulfed in shadow. I looked to my left and my heart jumped into my throat. Caitlin perched like a bird on the rim of the bathtub.

Her eyes shone in the dark, no longer green. Now they were the color of polished pennies. She put her finger to her lips.

"Shh," she whispered. I nodded.

She held up one finger and pointed left, shaking her head. Then she pointed right and held up her open palm, as if telling me to wait. Finally she dropped her hand. I didn't think; I just ran. She could have been leading me right into Artie and Carl's arms, but my instincts said otherwise.

I made it to the kitchen and dug through the cabinets, hoping I could find what I needed. I was almost done with my makeshift creation when the overhead fluorescents flickered back to life. Artie and Carl barged through the swinging doors, zeroing in on me—and froze.

"I wouldn't," I said calmly, letting them take a good look.

I stood in an arcane circle painted on the linoleum floor with a box of sea salt I'd stolen from Artie's cabinets. It was a sloppy rush job done in the dark, but I held my ground like it was an iron fortress. In my left hand, I held Caitlin's contract.

In my right hand, I held a lighter.

Caitlin stood in the corner, looking between the three of us like a cat who couldn't decide which mouse to eat first.

"*Wait!*" Artie shouted, at Carl as much as at me. Carl kept his gun steady, glaring daggers.

"You know how this works," I told them, sparking the cheap plastic lighter. "Contract goes up in smoke, she goes free. I imagine she'll have a lot to say about how you two have been treating her."

Carl hesitated, looking between me and Artie as if not sure who to believe. I lowered the contract an inch, almost close enough to touch the open flame.

"Call him off," I warned Artie. "If he shoots me, I drop the contract against the lighter, and bad things happen. Really excruciatingly bad things. Caitlin, tell him what you'll do to him if I set you free."

She smiled and said, *"Everything."*

"It's suicide!" Artie cried. "She'll kill you too!"

"Not while I'm standing in a circle of art. She can't cross the salt."

"That's not even a real circle! The glyphs are all screwed up!"

"This," I explained, "is an Astrum Argentum grounding pattern. It works just fine, I can promise you that. Sure, I'll be trapped inside, but I'm hoping she'll get bored and go away eventually. If nothing else, I'll have time to plan my next move. You won't."

A serpentine tongue slithered across Caitlin's lips, leaving a glistening trail in its wake.

"What do you want?" Artie stammered. "Money? Girls? Drugs? You've got to want something!"

"The truth. About Stacy Pankow."

"I don't know anything about—" he started to say, then clutched the hilt of his sword to his chest as I dangled the papers a little closer to the flame. "All right! All right, it was my brother's idea—"

"Don't tell him anything," Carl growled.

Artie shook his head. "I wanted to be on the inside, and to do that you've got to make a kill, all right? It has to be a special kill, and you have to use the special spell after, so we were filming a scene and I just held her head under the water. I held her and wouldn't let her up and she kicked and thrashed around but I just *wouldn't let her up.*"

Tears streamed down Artie's cheeks, his confession spilling out in a babbling cadence. I could only follow every third word or so, but it sounded like bad craziness. "You were filming," I said. "Focus, Artie. Where is the recording? I want it."

"I've had it with this bullshit!" Carl shouted, raising his gun. Artie spun, bringing the sword down hard and fast. Carl's right hand, fingers still clutching his pistol, fell to the kitchen floor.

Carl gripped the stump of his wrist, staring at his spurting blood with wide, incredulous eyes. "You—" he stammered, slumping to the floor.

"I—I told you," Artie said. "I told you not to."

Carl's face went stony gray, shock taking over as his blood spattered across the floor. His mouth opened and closed like a fish on a hook, but no sound came out.

"I told him," Artie said.

"Focus. The recording. Where is it?"

"No way! I tell you that, you've got no reason to give me the contract back!"

"All right," I said, nodding, "we do it the proper way, then. We invoke an Unbreakable Oath. You're an expert magician, you know how those work, right?"

"O—of course I do!"

"I pledge," I intoned gravely, "by the Unbreakable Oath of the Great Brotherhood, in the knowledge that I will burn in eternal hellfire should I break my word, that I shall trade you this contract, unharmed in any way, in exchange for the recording of Stacy Pankow's murder. I further vow that no harm will come to you from me or mine, and that there will be peace between us for the rest of our days. Do you accept this pledge?"

"I...I do," he said, his head bobbing like a metronome.

"And so the Oath is sealed, by our magic and our word, forever and unbreakable. Now then, as you know, since I made the pledge, it's tradition for you to fulfill your part of the bargain first. Where's the video?"

"Under my mattress, in my bedroom! But it's yours now! It's yours, okay? Take it, I don't need it! Just...give me the contract? Please?"

"Before I do," I said, "there's one thing you need to know. Something you absolutely must understand."

"What? Say it!"

"I lied," I said and held the contract to the flame. It went up like flash paper, blazing with a crumpling implosion of sound and the stench of brimstone. The last remnants of blackened ash tumbled from my fingertips like cherry blossoms on a gentle wind.

Caitlin smiled as she sauntered across the kitchen floor, taking her time. She paused to stand over Carl. He blinked, staring blankly from glassy eyes, bleeding out and barely conscious.

"You, I'll see in hell," she murmured, taking hold of his head with one hand and wrenching it with a sickening crack. She dropped his corpse to the floor and looked at Artie. "He was in shock. Torturing *him* wouldn't have been any fun at all. I'll fix that when I get home."

Artie pressed himself against the refrigerator, cornered, blubbering.

"But as for you...oh, you. Artie, Artie, Artie. Your ambition was admirable. I don't fault you for it." Caitlin's Scottish brogue grew harder as she took hold of his trembling arms, pulling him into an embrace. "But you *humiliated* me. Did you think the bill for that would never come due? Did you think you could leave the restaurant without paying the check?"

He struggled against her, helpless, weeping. "I'm sorry! I'm sorry!"

I closed my eyes. Part of me wanted to make a run for it, a mad dash to the door just to escape being any part of this, but Caitlin was too quick, too strong. I knew I'd never make it. I stayed in my little circle of salt, hoping it would be over fast.

"Do you know," she told him, "that with every slap, every insult, every indignity, I was taking solace in thinking about what I was going to do to you for all of eternity? No tears now, Artie, this is just a taste of what's to come. Just my little way of saying 'goodbye for now, see you again soon.'"

I held my breath.

"Little magus," she said, and I realized she was talking to me. I opened my eyes. She held Artie in her arms, coiled in a parody of a seductive embrace.

"You should watch this," she said, flashing a smile lined with shark teeth.

Then she bit into his cheek. Slowly.

I don't know how long it lasted. Two hours? Three? I had my eyes shut for most of it, standing on wavering legs, listening to Artie scream in pitches no human throat should be able to reach as Caitlin painted the walls with his blood. In the end it was just choked gurgling and chewing noises.

At some point I realized I didn't hear anything but the distant hum of air conditioning. I opened my eyes. Caitlin stood there, watching me, her pale skin and emerald gown drenched in gore. She wore a thoughtful smile. I glanced toward the corner of the kitchen and immediately wished I hadn't, struggling to keep my stomach under control.

"Now then," she said, "what are we going to do with you?" She strolled around the edge of the circle of salt, eyeing it, looking for a break in the pattern."It was a good bluff."

"The Unbreakable Oath?" I said. "Yeah, no such thing. Still, you can toss anything to a drowning man. Tell him it's a life preserver and he'll probably take it."

"Not that bluff. This one."

She slid one foot effortlessly across the line of salt and stepped inside the circle with me.

15.

I tried not to tremble as I looked into Caitlin's copper eyes, her teeth a heartbeat from my throat. The scent of her perfume mingled with the stench of gore, becoming some new and unearthly scent that whispered of charnel houses and night-blooming flowers.

"I was trying," I said, swallowing hard, "trying to make a real circle, but it was dark, and I didn't have much time—"

"Shh," she said, putting her finger to my lips. I tasted Artie Kaufman's blood.

So there it was. I should have listened to Bentley and Corman. I should have done a lot of things that I didn't. In the span of a second, a thousand regrets flashed before my eyes.

At least I had something to be proud of. Artie and Carl would never hurt anyone again, and Jud could rest easy knowing he'd gotten some justice for his little girl. Not much of a balance against my life of crime, but I'd done a little good in the end. Caitlin rested her hand against my chest, feeling my heart pound, drinking in my fear. I raised my chin and looked her in the eyes. If nothing else, I could go out with a little dignity.

"I'm not going to beg," I said softly.

"Beg?" A smile glinted in her eyes. "Oh, I'm sure I could make you beg. Another time, perhaps."

She curled her other hand in my hair, letting me feel the scrape of her fingernails, razor-sharp and hungry. My eyes closed as she leaned close. Her lips brushed against my cheek, a gentle kiss that left an electric tingle in its wake.

When I opened my eyes, she was gone.

I stood alone in the carnage. Just me, two corpses, and a houseful of evidence. Sunrise would bring visitors. Witnesses. Emotions were an indulgence I couldn't afford right now. I took all the horror and shock and bottled it in the back of my mind, safely out of the way while my professional instincts took over.

First stop, Kaufman's bedroom. I was nowhere near his size, but my clothes and shoes were sticky with his blood and they had to go. I found some clunky sneakers and a T-shirt and gym pants that fit like a tent, but at least they'd get me home. I slid my hand under his mattress, closing my fingers around a tiny wedge of plastic. The black Sony memory card must have come straight from Kaufman's camera. The stick went into a shopping bag along with the Black Eye, the cash take from the poker game, and the money left in the office safe. Not a bad little payday. I walked through the house with a hand towel from the bathroom, wiping down every doorknob and surface I might have touched.

I didn't want to go back into the kitchen, but I had no other option. Holding my breath and reeling at the stench, trying not to look at the corner of the room, I rummaged through the cabinet under the sink for a plastic bucket and an assortment of cleaners. A pour of this and a dollop of that resulted in a witch's brew straight out of *The Anarchist Cookbook*.

I splashed the concoction across baseboards and dribbled it in a trail along carpets, spreading the nostril-searing slop in every room I'd visited except for the kitchen. I wanted those bodies found and identified. I used the last of the bucket's contents to soak my old clothes, piled close to the door, and watched the blue flames rise at a touch of my lighter. The arson would be obvious, but that was the point. It's a lot easier to leave a crime scene in hopeless confusion than it is to make it pristine.

Flames licked the windows, mirroring the glow from the rising sun, as I hopped into the Mustang and rolled out of the driveway. Once I got two blocks away, I paused at a stop sign and used my burner phone to call 911 and report the fire, hanging up when they asked my name. My next call was to Jud.

"Is this—" he started to say, and I cut him off fast.

"Don't talk. Just listen. The job's done. Watch the news tonight. Now lose this number and never contact me again."

I opened the back of the phone, pulled out its SIM card, and dropped it on the asphalt. I jumped out of the car and ground it to broken fragments under my heel. The rest of the phone wound up in a Dumpster half a mile away. I dropped off the Mustang at the rental place, signing off on it as Peter Greyson, and took a cab to a convenience store a few blocks from my apartment. All direct connections between me and the two dead men, and most of the indirect ones, were sliced away clean.

Under normal circumstances, I'd have congratulated my-self on a job well done. Jud Pankow had hired me for pay-back, and he'd gotten it in spades. Carl and Artie's deaths were no great loss to the world, and nobody got hurt in the crossfire. Still, I didn't feel like celebrating. I'd lied to Jud. The job wasn't done, not by a long shot.

Stacy's half-formed wraith still wailed under the city streets. I'd have liked to think that taking down her killer would set her free to move on, but she wasn't that kind of ghost. Artie had done something beyond mere murder: in the kitchen he'd babbled about a "special kill" and a "special spell."

It was my brother's idea, he'd whined. The same brother, I assumed, as the one who read him the riot act over the phone about letting Carl have as much time with Caitlin as he wanted. His brother needed seeing-to.

Then there was Nicky Agnelli. He had a hand in this grim mess, and I still didn't know why. If my paranoia held true and he'd been keeping magical tabs on me, he'd know what I had done by now. Taking off the Black Eye in the middle of Artie's house, exposing me to Nicky's pet seer, made sure of that. Nothing I could do about it now. I'd just have to hope I was wrong, that Jud was the one he was watching, or that I'd lucked out and nobody was looking my way. If not, things were about to get a lot more complicated.

And then there was Caitlin. Maybe she'd gone back to hell. Maybe she hadn't. I wasn't sure what to think about Caitlin, only that I couldn't stop seeing her every time I closed my eyes.

I went home, put Kaufman's clothes in a trash bag, and fell back on my bedspread. I'd long since burned through the last of my adrenaline, moving on nothing but momentum and survival instinct. I didn't have the strength left to do anything but sleep.

#

Orange light washed against my curtains as the hammering of a woodpecker dragged me from a fitful sleep. No, not a woodpecker, it was my main cell phone vibrating against my end table. I pushed myself up, groaning, and reached for it. Four missed calls. Wonderful.

"I'm here," I said, rubbing my eyes.

"Daniel." Bentley's voice was a mixture of reproach and fear. "What did you do?"

News had spread fast. Naked, I ambled over to the desk and turned on my laptop, stifling a yawn.

"I, ah...things got complicated."

"Did you kill those men?"

The *Las Vegas Sun*'s website showed a picture of Artie's house, the front window smashed out and his doorframe licked by fire. The headline screamed, "Double Murder, Arson in Henderson."

"No," I said, clicking the article, "but I was there when they died."

"...home of porn director Arthur James Kaufman, who successfully won out against obscenity charges in Georgia in 2011. One victim has been confirmed as Detective Carl Holt, a thirteen-year veteran of the Las Vegas Metropolitan Police Department's homicide division. Holt was decorated last year for valorous..."

Memories of last night hit me like a fist. It had been easy not to think during the cleanup. Making sure I didn't leave a trail for the cops was a more pressing concern than thinking about how Kaufman screamed until his throat gave out, or remembering the smell when Caitlin peeled open his—

I dropped the phone and ran to the bathroom, falling on my knees in front of the toilet, heaving until nothing came up but a trickle of bile.

Bentley was still on the line when I stumbled back to my desk. "It's complicated," I told him.

"...robbery may be a motive, but first responders reported seeing what they described as a 'satanic shrine' hidden in Kaufman's bedroom..."

"What happened to it, Daniel?" Bentley demanded.

"It?"

Her.

"Kaufman's demon," he said. "It got loose, didn't it?"

I dug in my mini-fridge, looking for something to get the taste out of my mouth. I took out a small bottle of ginger ale, cracked it open, and chugged half of it.

"I think she left."

"Left?"

"Went back to hell," I said. "Sounded like she had some serious fun and games planned for those two. Listen, can we discuss this later? I'm not up for it now."

"We'll need to discuss it. I'm not sure if you understand how serious—"

"Serious as a heart attack," I told him. "Believe me. But right now I'm trying to keep my stomach from climbing up my throat, so I'd be grateful for a change of subject."

"Fine. I'll bring you up to date. We had our little research party last night, trying to learn anything we could about this 'hound' that the cambion ranted about."

"And?"

"Nothing," Bentley said. "Found plenty of material on hellhounds, gloomhounds and the Hounds of Gnar'peth, none of which you'd want to encounter in a dark alley, but nothing that could ride herd over an entire community of half-demons. Spengler even brought over some of the rarer volumes from his personal collection, but we came up empty. Either it was merely a quirk of this cambion's insane mind, or someone is using 'hound' as a title or a pseudonym."

"It was worth checking."

"We had an unfortunate confirmation that this wasn't a one-time affair. Jennifer was attacked outside her home. Don't worry, she's fine. It turns out cambion aren't immune to military-strength pepper spray. It was your friend from the other night—"

"The toe-eater?" I said, remembering his odd fixation.

"—the very one, along with a woman in rags. He's made allies."

"Just what we need, more problems. Hey, you and Corman don't own a camcorder or anything like that, do you?" I picked up the lozenge of black plastic, turning it in my fingertips. "I've got a 'duo pro' memory card here and I need to see what's on it."

"We still have our Handycam from our anniversary vacation last year, but I'm not sure what it uses. You're welcome to take a look at it."

"Perfect, I have to bring back the Black Eye anyway. Hopefully I'll never have to wear the damn thing again."

The answer to the secret of Stacy's death, and her tormented half-life, lay on that card. I didn't want to watch it. God, I didn't want to watch it. If I was going to put things right, though, the only way forward was down.

16.

Three hours later I came back home with a Sony camcorder in one hand and a grocery bag in the other. Bentley
and Corman had laid down nearly a thousand bucks for the
thing and used it exactly once, on a trip to Niagara Falls.
The bag held a Chinese takeout dinner and a bottle of Jack
Daniels. I'd been drinking too much lately, but no fucking
way was I watching this thing sober.

I poured three fingers of Jack into a plastic cup and
broke out the chopsticks, digging into my sweet-and-sour
pork while reading the camera manual. It looked like I could
just load the memory card into the camera, then use a cable
to transfer its contents onto my laptop. Simple enough.

I rigged the cables and moved the file, a movie clip with
a string of random numbers for a title, onto my laptop. The
icon sat there, anonymous and innocent, waiting for me to
click it. Two more drinks and I was almost ready. Seemed
funny how I'd just seen a man torn to pieces right next to
me but this seemed so much worse. Maybe because one of

them deserved it, and one was a dumb, innocent kid from Minnesota who never asked to go out like this.

I launched the movie.

Instead of his usual handheld style, Artie had put the camera on a tripod for Stacy's final performance. She stood in the same grimy bathroom where he'd shot their other movies, staring into the lens, sniffling.

"I want to go home," she said in a halting whisper.

"We talked about this," his voice echoed from behind the camera. He sounded distracted, an edge of tension in his voice I hadn't heard before.

"I don't care. I just want to go home. Please let me go home."

"One more," he said. "Do one more for me, and you can go home. I'll buy you a plane ticket."

Her eyes, red from crying, widened. "You mean it?"

"I promise. We can go to the airport as soon as we're done here, if you do a good job for me. You can be with your granddad for dinner tonight. Wouldn't you like that?"

She caught a tear as it rolled down her cheek, brushing it away with the back of her hand. "Yes. Thank you. Thank you."

"Do you love me, Stacy?"

"I love you," she said, her voice breaking.

"Good. Now take off your clothes."

She undressed, her hands shaking, and he stepped out from behind the camera. My stomach muscles tightened, bracing for a punch that never came. Instead he held her, almost gently, and whispered in her ear as he stroked her hair. She nodded, sinking to her knees before him on the dirty tile floor, and he used her one last time.

Then he drowned her in the toilet.

My fingers flinched against the keyboard, wanting to skip this, to fast forward through her death spasms as she kicked and thrashed, but I held back. My teeth clenched. I hoped she'd somehow fight him off, escape, even though I already knew how this movie ended. He held her head down until her body finally went limp, standing motionless over her like a clockwork executioner.

Then Artie hauled her up by her hair, dropping Stacy to the floor and rolling her onto her back with his shoe. Open eyes stared towards the camera, stared at me, a plea for help that never came.

He walked out of the camera's sight and came back with a leather pouch in his fist. He straddled Stacy's corpse and crouched down, chanting in a sibilant whisper. I cranked the laptop's speakers until my room filled with a static hum. The words were foreign, Eastern-sounding. Chinese? I couldn't be sure. His burly shoulder blocked part of the view, but he waved the bag slowly over Stacy's face before putting the opening to her lips.

A faint glimmer of light, like a silver mist, drifted from her bloodless lips to the pouch. He tugged the drawstring taut, still chanting, rising and walking off camera as a few final driblets of light leaked from her mouth and boiled away like water vapor.

"A soul-trap," I said to the screen, "but you screwed it up, you impatient amateur bastard. You stole half of what she is, and the rest is stumbling around in the dark like a wounded animal. Where did you put the pouch? Show me where you put it."

He wandered in and out of frame, ignoring the dead girl at his feet, his phone to his ear.

"Hey, bro, it's done," he said. "What? I don't know. It doesn't...it doesn't feel like anything. I don't know, I just expected it'd be...cooler. Just feel kinda numb, I guess. Maybe I need to do it again."

You'll never get that chance, I thought. *The one thing I did right.*

"Yeah, I did it just like you told me. I'll bring you the bag. So am I in?" He stopped, grinned, and did a little fist-pump. "All right, awesome! Totally worth it, bro. We're gonna be kings. Yeah, all right, tell Mom I said hi."

Hanging up the phone, he looked toward the camera, as if realizing it was still recording. Something flickered across his face. A moment of doubt? Guilt? He reached out and turned the camera off.

In the darkness of my apartment, I stared at my reflection in the black void of my laptop screen. I drank my whiskey in silence.

I'd heard of soul-traps, knew the theory, but I'd never seen one in action before tonight. This was the realm of truly hardcore black magic, the kind that takes decades to master. Unlike Artie, his brother knew what he was doing. But why was he doing it at all? Stacy's murder wasn't some random thrill killing; it was part of a plan, and any plan that would make a slug like Artie into a "king" had bad news written all over it.

One thing was clear: Stacy's half-souled wraith wasn't going anywhere until I got my hands on that pouch and used it to put her back together again. I decided to pay a visit to Artie's mysterious brother and see if he wanted to do this the easy way or the hard way.

I hoped he'd choose the hard way.

#

A tenor saxophone purred under the clink of glasses and low, seductive laughter. I sat in a leather-backed chair, cigar smoke swirling through the hazy air, and tried to remember how I got there.

The nightclub was a swath of mahogany and scarlet, elegant and baroque, the kind of place you see in photographs of prewar Berlin. All around me lovers talked, drank, shared cigarettes in the dark. Everyone but me, sitting alone in front of an empty stage.

"A drink for you, sir."

A prim man with a white jacket and a towel draped over his arm, his lip adorned with a pencil-thin mustache, set a tall glass of something amber and smoky on the small table beside me.

"I didn't order this," I said. I didn't think I'd ordered it. I couldn't remember.

"Compliments of the lady, sir."

"The lady?"

"The lady on stage," he said with a flourish and stepped to the side. I looked up to the stage. Caitlin smiled back at me, draped in a scarlet dress that matched her flowing curls. She cradled her fingers around a standing microphone like a 1940s radio starlet in the footlights.

I'm dreaming, I realized. Normally that would be enough to jolt me awake, but instead I sank deeper into my chair as she began to sing, an invisible band striking up a slow, torch-song melody.

"You flew to the clouds but your ghost's in my bed
The scent of you bringing back words we both said
In the dark, in the dark o' my love..."

I leaned forward in my chair, watching her sing, drinking her in. The lilt of a violin caressed the air, notes flowing on a breeze of hopeful melancholy.

"Every life that collides, every scar left behind
Of long memories and longer goodbyes
You're gone but you linger, my love..."

I thought about Roxy and the night she left, throwing her things into a suitcase like she was trying to stone it to death while I paced the room and railed against the inevitable.

"Roxy, will you—stop. Will you at least *talk* to me?"

The nightclub suddenly gone, I stood in the memory of my own apartment and watched myself on the other side of the bed, torn between misery and rage.

"We did talk," Roxy said, not looking at me, rummaging through the drawers and throwing clothes in the suitcase as fast as she could pull them out. "We've been doing nothing but talking. You don't *listen.*"

"So that's it. After all we've been through together, just like that, we're through?"

She paused, frozen over the suitcase, then nodded as she slammed it shut and reached for the zipper. "Yeah. We're through."

"She broke your heart," Caitlin said, standing beside me.

I shook my head as the voices of the memories faded, silently acting out their desperate pantomime.

"I broke hers," I said, "or we both did. It gets hazier the more I think about it. It's easy to tell stories about the people we leave behind, turn them into monsters in our heads, you know, so the loss doesn't hurt so much. Truth is, we both said some things we shouldn't have, we dug the knives in deep, and she packed a bag and got on the next bus for Reno."

"Something to be said for a clean break," Caitlin mused, watching the silent argument.

"Nothing clean about it. People go, but they stay," I said, tapping my forehead, "up here. The hard part's learning to move on, to let it all go instead of wallowing in regrets. I've imagined a thousand different ways this night could have played out, a thousand ways I could have kept her from walking out that door, but you know what? It doesn't matter. This is what happened. This is what's real. The more I accept it, the less it hurts."

"You can't live in your dreams," Caitlin said, "though it is a fascinating way to learn about people."

Dream-Roxy stomped out the door, lugging her suitcase behind her. Dream-Me sat on the edge of his bed, face buried in his hands. I looked at Caitlin with dawning horror.

"You're really here," I said. "I'm not making this up. You're here. In my dream. In my *head*."

"Problem?" she asked with a smile.

The world caved in. A brutal weight squeezed the breath from my lungs, raw panic overtaking me like a knife in my heart, like an arachnophobe dropped into a vat of spiders.

"No," I gasped, shaking my head, "you can't be here—"

"Daniel," she said, taking hold of my shoulders. "Daniel, I did not come here to hurt you. You don't need to be afraid. Daniel!"

A swirling vortex engulfed us, the dream dissolving in raw chaos. I couldn't hear, couldn't think, couldn't do anything but shake my head and struggle in her arms.

"Show me," she said sharply in my ear, "show me what you're afraid of."

So I did.

17.

I knew the room in a heartbeat. The cheap clapboard walls, the dingy garage-sale furniture, and the teenager tied to a chair with a burlap sack over his head. A sea of upturned and unwashed faces watched with reverent awe, sitting cross-legged on the floor or sprawled out on beanbag chairs. Someone in the back strummed a Peter, Paul and Mary song on an acoustic guitar.

A strange calmness washed over me. Standing in the echo of my past, I could almost pretend it was a show or a movie I was watching, instead of something that happened to me.

A tall man stood beside the chair. His hand rested on the boy's shoulder. He dressed like a seventies folk musician, with a string vest, a fuzzy goatee and a lazy, bloodshot smile that never left his lips.

"The angels are with us, children," he said. "The angels will guide us and ease our path to spiritual ascension. Come now, angel. Come and speak unto us, that we may hear your wisdom."

The sound that erupted from under the burlap hood was anything but human. The bound figure twisted and squirmed, joints popping and body contorting as he struggled to escape the ropes.

"*Chilkat gamun!*" the boy howled, his words distorted and leaping in pitch. "*Chilkat gamun rabadai!*"

Onlookers gasped as the chair lifted from the ground, slowly spinning, hovering an inch over the pea-green rug as the torrent of arcane words grew louder, more furious.

"Be at peace!" the man said, holding up his hands to calm them. "The angel greets us, but he bears a message of warning. Some of you have not been doing all you can for the family. Some of you have not been sharing freely of your hearts, your minds, and your labor. He says to look inside yourselves, to question if your devotion is true!"

Caitlin leaned against the wall and folded her arms, one eyebrow raised.

"That 'angel'," she said pointedly, "is a fledgling demon of the Choir of Wrath. It's speaking in gutter flensetongue, and it's promising that man a number of sexual mutilations involving battery acid."

I felt tired. Old hurts and old angers helped to smother my panic, leaving me numb in the balance.

"We called him the Shepherd," I said.

"The Up With People reject?" she asked.

"I was seventeen and on the run. Hungry and desperate. When he found me, I was using some crude misdirection charms to hustle a tourist. People like me, people with a spark of raw magical ability and no real training, were like catnip to him."

"A cult." Caitlin's nose twitched with disdain. "So he'd get one of you possessed, claim he was translating angel-speak, and give your marching orders. What'd he do if he got a demon who spoke English?"

"Square it ahead of time. I don't know what he offered them, but they'd say whatever he wanted them to. Usually that his spiritual powers would be a lot stronger if his bed wasn't empty that night."

She peered around the room. "Which one is you?"

I pointed."I'm the one tied to the chair."

The chair fell to the carpet with a thud and Dream-Me slumped against the ropes, unconscious under the hood. The onlookers applauded, hugging one another, some with tears of wonder in their eyes.

"I had the bare essentials for learning sorcery," I said, "talent and insatiable curiosity. He only wanted the talent. He tried to starve the curiosity out of me, tried to torture it out of me with 'ritual penance,' tried...other things, but it just made me fight harder. I knew I needed to escape.

"That's when he decided that being a host for the 'angels' wasn't to be shared among all of us any longer, that instead I'd been specially chosen to be their one and only vessel. And instead of once a week, they had so much to tell us that they needed to come every single night."

Caitlin stared at me, horrified.

"Humans can't endure..." she started to say, then shook her head. "How many times were you possessed? By how many demons?"

"I lost count after thirty. Usually a different one every night. Night after night I was a puppet, a prisoner in my own body. The physical pain was excruciating, but that was nothing compared to what it felt like inside my head. The torrents of psychic filth, like someone pissing inside your brain and carving their initials on the back of your eyelids just to show they were there—"

We stood in a grassy meadow under a warm summer sun. Caitlin pressed her finger to my lips.

"Shh," she said. "I know. You don't have to talk about it."

"Where are we?" I squinted at a French manor at the top of a hill. "This isn't one of my memories."

"No. It's one of mine. A peaceful place. I thought you might like it. How did you get away?"

I shook my head. "I don't remember. I remember running. I got out somehow, and they chased me, but...there's a place in the city, an occultists' hangout with an invisible door. It pulled me inside, and I passed out cold on the carpet. A couple of friendly magicians found me and took me in, taught me, made me strong."

Caitlin tilted her head, taking me in with a curious stare.

"You were already strong. Your survival is proof. I'm curious—I would like you to explain something."

"Ask."

"After what you endured at the hands of my kind, and knowing full well what I am, you still saved me. You not only saved me, you risked your life to do it. Why?"

I shrugged. The answer seemed obvious.

"Because what they were doing to you was wrong," I said, "and it needed to be stopped. Doesn't matter who you are. Doesn't matter what you are. Wrong is wrong."

She blinked.

"Curious," she said again, and I found myself staring at my bedroom ceiling. Alone in the darkness, I put my palm on my chest and felt the beating of my heart.

#

Nothing felt entirely real as I turned on the shower, scrubbing my hair under the spray and turning over the events of the dream. I'd heard of shared dreams before, but I'd never expected to experience one firsthand. Or did I? For all I knew, the entire thing was just my imagination on overdrive. It wasn't like I hadn't been thinking about Caitlin.

Finding Artie Kaufman's brother was priority one, but for that I needed a name. I'd been thinking about Artie's house, how it was so much nicer than he should have been able to afford on a low-end porn director's budget. If his brother had helped him pay for it, his name might be on the deed. I got out of the shower and toweled off.

"I love living in the future," I muttered to myself as I sat down and called up the Clark County property information website. Property records are public information, and thanks to modern technology I just had to type in Artie's address and let the computer do all the work. When the results came back, I shook my head at the screen.

"Owner: Carmichael-Sterling Nevada"

I'd heard of them. The Carmichael-Sterling Group was an out-of-state concern looking to make a play for some Vegas action. In the last year they'd bought up the old Silverlode Casino and a couple of off-Strip hotels, looking to rehab and reopen them under new management. Their big claim to fame, though, was the Enclave: a sixty-five-story luxury hotel and casino whose unfinished steel skeleton now loomed at the south end of Las Vegas Boulevard. When it finally opened its doors, word had it, the Enclave was going to make Dubai look like a beggar's slum.

So why the hell were they paying for a porn merchant's house out in Henderson? Public relations departments have nightmares about this sort of thing. I dialed their contact number and hit buttons until a live person got on the phone.

"Carmichael-Sterling Nevada, how may I direct your call?" chirped a perky voice on the other end of the line.

"Mr. Kaufman, please," I said, hoping there was only one of them at the company. The receptionist asked me to hold, and after another couple of rings it went to voice mail.

"This is the desk of Sheldon Kaufman, director of finance," said a deep, sonorous voice. "I'm away from my desk right now, but if you leave your information at the tone I'll call you back as soon as I return. If this is an emergency, please call Arthur Shaw at extension—"

I hung up. *Sheldon Kaufman. Pleased to meet you.* Looked like the group's finance guy was spending company funds on a dream house for his brother. I put on a button-down shirt and a pressed pair of slacks, digging out a pair of wire-rimmed glasses from my dresser drawer. They were fakes, nothing but plain glass in the frames, but they made a nice accessory when I was trying to project a certain image.

I wanted a closer look at Sheldon Kaufman's office, and I knew exactly how I was going to get it.

18.

I made a second call before my drive over, putting on a thick Southern accent just to be safe and asking for the public relations department. They sent me to the voice mail for a woman named Meadow Brand, and again, I hung up without leaving a message. All I needed was a name.

Carmichael-Sterling had bought up a three-story wedge of granite and glass on the outskirts of the city, perfectly modern and perfectly forgettable. With a leather valise in hand, I jogged up a short flight of steps and through a softly whirring automatic door, adjusting my fake glasses as I cased the room.

A row of overstuffed powder-blue chairs curved along the inside of the lobby wall under the watchful eye of a rounded receptionist's desk. Not many people around, a few coming and going from the elevator banks or wandering down the hallway behind the front desk, but my gaze immediately shot toward the security camera looking down from its steel perch in the corner of the room.

I put on a smile and strolled up to greet the receptionist. I could see the tilt of her computer monitor from where I stood, but not well enough to read her screen without being obvious. Between that and the lack of any kind of building directory on display, this wasn't going to be the cakewalk I'd hoped for.

"Hi!" I said, "Peter Greyson, *Las Vegas Sun*. I'd like to speak with Meadow Brand, please."

"Certainly, sir," she said, her voice trailing off as she rattled her keyboard. "I'm sorry, I'm not seeing you on the schedule. Did you have an appointment?"

"No, this is regarding an urgent piece of breaking news. We're running with it in this evening's edition, and we'd really like to have an official comment from Carmichael-Sterling on the matter."

She looked at me like she'd just bitten into a lemon. Dealing with this was above her pay grade. "Well, I'm sorry, sir, but she's booked in meetings all day. I could possibly set up something for you tomorrow?"

I made a show of looking over my shoulder, then leaned toward the desk, pitching my voice low.

"You might want to tell Ms. Brand," I said, "that our readers are going to be very curious about why the Carmichael-Sterling Group was bankrolling a Satan-worshipping porn director. Said director having been brutally murdered in a home your company paid for."

Like I said, the real-estate connection was a PR person's worst nightmare. No sense letting a good catastrophe go to waste. The receptionist paled and reached for her telephone.

"I'll see what I can do, sir, if you could have a seat please?"

I wandered over by the chairs, watching in my peripheral vision as she cupped a hand over her mouth and whispered into the telephone. The back and forth went on for a couple of minutes before she finally hung up and called me over.

"Sir? Ms. Brand has an opening in her schedule. If you'd like to go up to her office, she's in room 371 on the third floor. She'll be free in about ten minutes."

Probably frantically calling people, trying to figure out what I was about to confront her with and get her ducks in a row. "Great, thanks! Oh, before I go up, do you have a washroom?"

She pointed me to the men's room down the hall, a short walk past the elevator banks. I ducked in just long enough to unzip my valise and pull out a sheaf of papers, random tax forms I'd picked up at the local library and scribbled numbers on. At a distance, they looked just boring enough to be important. I returned to the hall, walking fast and trying to look harried, and made a beeline to a couple of middle-manager types hanging out by hallway water cooler.

"Hi, sorry, this is my first day," I said, trying to look helpless as I held up the papers. "I'm supposed to bring these to Mr. Kaufman's office right away, but I have no idea where the finance department is. Can you point me in the right direction?"

"One floor up," one of them told me. "Take the elevators up, go to the end of the hall, and turn left. Shel's office is right there. I don't think he's in today, though."

I thanked them profusely and strode back toward the lobby, hitting the stairwell and jogging up the steps two at a time. I'd only have a few minutes before Meadow started to wonder where I was. Sheldon Kaufman's office was dark, his Ikea-grade furniture shadowed behind a small glass window. The doorknob barely jiggled when I turned it, locked up tight, but I'd come prepared for that possibility. After a moment listening for any oncoming foot traffic, I fished my lockpick kit out of the valise and selected a tension wrench and a slender metal rake.

I gritted my teeth as I slid the tools into the lock and felt along the pins for pressure. If anyone happened to stroll around the corner right now, I'd be sunk. Fortunately, most office buildings have laughably cheap interior locks, installed under the assumption that all they need to keep out guys like me is a sturdy front door and an alarm system. That's a lousy assumption.

The tumblers clicked. I slid my picks back into the valise and let myself in. I'd barely lifted my foot over the threshold when I froze, a sudden sharp pressure flaring behind my sinuses. Like any sorcerer worth his salt, Sheldon had warded the place. If I let my eyes go slightly out of focus, a webwork of delicate saffron-yellow threads glowed against the navy-blue carpeting.

I used the same kind of wards to guard my apartment. If I tripped the spell, nothing would happen to me, but he'd instantly know someone had set foot on his territory. If he was really good, he might even get a mental image of me or worse, echoes of my thoughts. I could slice through the threads like a knife through butter, attacking the wards at their root and cutting them off before they could sound an alarm, but then he'd know he'd been invaded the next time he came back to the office.

I didn't have time to do this the right way, taking hours to gently unravel and replace each strand of magic, covering my tracks. It was brute force or walk away, no other options. I didn't want to put him on guard...or did I?

By now Sheldon had to know his brother was dead. He'd had some hand in Stacy's murder, giving Artie the soul-trap, so he'd be worried and wondering if any evidence at the house pointed his way. He'd also know Caitlin was on the loose. I realized I was playing this the wrong way. I didn't want Sheldon relaxed. I wanted him terrified. Scared people make stupid decisions.

I gathered my focus, gaze fixed at the middle of the floor, slowly raising the knife edge of my hand high above my head. A knot of tension rose, burbling up, filling my hand with trembling energy until I let out a sudden exhale of breath and dropped hard to one knee. My hand slammed down on the carpet. The threads of his warding spell unspooled like the parting of the Red Sea, whipping away and dissolving into thin air. When Sheldon came back, he'd know he had an uninvited visitor.

I rummaged through his desk, not entirely sure what I was looking for but hoping to find some kind of lead. All of his folders and binders were distressingly mundane. Apart from the wards, you'd never guess Sheldon Kaufman was anything but an ordinary accountant.

I pulled out his bottom drawer and found a .40-caliber pistol, a Sig Sauer P226 with matte black grips. Definitely not standard accounting gear. I left it untouched and checked out the rest of the office, feeling every passing minute weigh heavier on my shoulders.

His desk blotter drew my eye. He had a calendar-style pad, most of the boxes filled with scribbled notes on meeting this person or that or his various lunch reservations, except for Tuesdays. Every Tuesday was carefully circled, the lettering clear as he listed his golf arrangements.

"Red Rock Country Club," I murmured. "Tomorrow morning. Sounds great, Sheldon, I'll see you there."

That was all I was going to get. Not the windfall of information I had hoped for, but at least I knew where he'd be tomorrow, assuming he didn't break his routine. It was the closest thing I had to a lead, so it would have to do. I locked the door behind me and jogged up the stairs to the third floor.

I heard a brusque voice as I approached Meadow Brand's open office door, and slowed down to listen to the one-sided conversation.

"—no, I just want to know what you were thinking. *Were* you thinking?" she snapped. "You'd better be there tomorrow. Lauren's flying in from Seattle tonight, and we *will* get this sorted."

I poked my head around the corner, giving a little wave. Meadow Brand sat behind her desk, a larger woman who knew how to dress for her curves. She held her desk phone in one hand and an iPhone in the other, tapping out a text message as she spoke.

"I have a reporter here, I have to go," she said, hanging up. She flashed me a million-dollar smile and rose to shake my hand, her grip reassuring and firm. "Sorry about that, please, have a seat. I was starting to think you got lost."

"The receptionist said you needed a few minutes. I didn't want to rush you." I nodded to the telephone. "Problems?"

"Nothing newsworthy," she said with a practiced chuckle. "When it's finished, the Enclave Resort and Casino will be the new heart of Las Vegas. You don't build a piece of history without the occasional miscommunication."

Something had nagged at the back of my mind, like an itch I couldn't scratch, ever since I walked in the door.

Glancing around the office, past a motivational poster of a balloon soaring over the Grand Canyon, I spotted the source. A foot-high kachina doll, a masked Hopi warrior in turquoise and black, perched on the shelf behind Meadow. I'd seen them before, mostly as tourist kitsch brought back from Arizona, but none of those blazed so strongly with magic that they left an imprint on my psychic retina. I was too slow to conceal my surprise. Meadow followed my gaze, looked back to me, and grinned.

19.

"Do you like it?" Meadow gestured at the kachina doll. "It's not authentic, I'm afraid, I made it myself last summer. Arts and crafts are kind of my thing. Not as good as the real ones, but still, not bad for a first try, huh?"

"It's great!" I told her, feeling my gut clench. I couldn't tell what the doll was capable of, not without a closer inspection, but it told me one vital fact: Meadow Brand was some kind of magician, just like her coworker Sheldon. The two of them would have to know about each other. The question was, how close were they?

"So," she said, folding her hands on the desk. "I know what you're here about, and I'm glad you're giving us a chance to set the record straight instead of just running off and printing wild innuendo. The truth is, the house in Henderson was purchased for Sheldon Kaufman, our director of finance. Like most of the group's employees, he was relocated from our home office in Seattle once we launched the Enclave project and established Carmichael-Sterling

Nevada as a subsidiary of our parent company. The house was a perk, you could say."

"Sheldon Kaufman," I said, nodding slowly and putting on my imaginary reporter hat. "So Artie Kaufman is...?"

"His brother. His estranged brother. The black sheep of the family, for what I hope are obvious reasons. A few months ago, they made an attempt at reconciliation, and since his brother was on the verge of homelessness Sheldon agreed to let him use the house. Sheldon, meanwhile, bought a condo closer to the office and started living there.

"Artie swore to Sheldon that he'd gotten an office job and cleaned up his life. If Sheldon had any idea, any idea at all that anything untoward was happening in that house, he'd have evicted his brother immediately. As it stands, he's very, very embarrassed by the whole affair, not to mention heartbroken over his brother's death. I do hope you can respect his privacy, if you decide to go forward with this story."

I made a show of thinking about it, adjusting my glasses and pretending to make a few notes.

"When you explain it that way," I said, "I'm not sure there's even a story worth running. It all sounds pretty cut and dried. I'll talk to my editor, but I doubt we'll pursue this any further. Personally, I'd rather be reporting on the Enclave's progress. This city needs some positive news."

"I agree wholeheartedly." Meadow beamed. "Now, I'm not promising anything, but play your cards right and a certain someone might get invited to the preview-night press gala."

"I'll be there with bells on," I said, shaking her hand as I rose from my chair.

The story was solid enough to be legit. I'd have believed it myself, if I didn't already know the brothers were in dirty business up to their necks together. Of course, the best lies are always wrapped in verifiable truth. It makes the filling easier to swallow.

Out in the parking lot, strolling in the arid sunshine and turning the situation around and around in my mind, I barely noticed the windowless van pulling up alongside me.

Then someone jabbed a stubby plastic wand against the small of my back and hit me with eighty thousand volts of electricity.

Every muscle in my body went rigid, and I flopped like a fish on the pavement, hitting the ground hard. Faces blurred around me, hands lifting me, pushing me forward as the van's side door flung open. The stun gun hit me again, firing against my hip. I couldn't control my own limbs, couldn't fight back as a black canvas bag dropped over my head and rough hands yanked my wrists behind my back, securing them with plastic zip-ties.

Nicky, I thought. Nicky must have found out I lied to him about dropping the investigation. So what happens when you screw over the biggest racket boss in Nevada? A bullet in the head if I was lucky.

Zip-ties clenched my ankles, tight enough to cut off the flow of blood and leave my toes tingling. I felt weak in the wake of the shocks, not in pain so much as exhausted and shaky. I rolled on the corrugated metal floor as the van lurched into gear, only for a pair of hands to hoist me to a sitting position with my back against the wheel well.

"Don't talk," a man's voice growled in my ear, "don't move, don't fucking blink under that hood. If you so much as think about pulling any tricks, you'll find out what a stun gun against your balls feels like. Understand?"

I nodded. It felt like the safest choice.

"This is so wrong," moaned a younger woman's voice. "We shouldn't be doing this."

"Shut up, Melanie, nobody put a gun to your head and forced you to come along."

"And now he knows my name," she said, "idiot."

"It ain't gonna matter," the man said. I didn't like the implications of that.

#

We rode in silence for about half an hour. I kept my mouth shut in part to avoid further shocks, and in part hoping my captors would let something slip. They were pretty good at impersonating statues. After their little exchange, all I heard was breathing and the thump of bad tires against bad road.

I ruled out Nicky. These guys were good but they weren't that good, and none of Nicky's people would have made an outburst like the girl had. Someone connected to the Kaufman brothers, then? It might not even be a current grudge. God knows I'd made enough enemies in my time, but not many of them had the resources or the guts to pull off a daylight kidnapping.

I experimentally flexed my wrists against the zip-ties. No good. If they'd handcuffed me, it would be a different story, but I wasn't getting out of the tight plastic strips without a sharp surface and a really good angle.

There was a certain strange comfort in being utterly helpless. With no avenue of escape and no options, my breathing slowed, burying my panic under quiet contemplation. Obviously I was in serious danger, and the man's last words hinted that they were taking me on a one-way trip with an unhappy ending, but I wasn't dead yet.

I counted turns, getting a feel for the speed of the van, in the hope of figuring out where we were headed. Their wheelman was too good for that. I gradually realized that he was zig-zagging across the city, looping around entire blocks and making random turns, a pattern to throw off anyone following the van and make a mess of my internal compass in the process.

Eventually the van slowed, gravel crunching under the wheels, and came to a stop.

"I'm cutting the ties off your legs," the man said, "so you can walk. You kick me, I fry you. Understand?"

I nodded. He sounded a little too eager to use the stun gun again. The sliding door rattled open. Hands hoisted me to my feet and helped me out of the van, down onto the gravel. I trudged forward, steered by a beefy hand on my shoulder, gripping hard enough to make my bones ache.

The surface underfoot changed from gravel to hard concrete, a metal door clanging shut behind us. A warehouse, maybe?

"We shouldn't be doing this," the girl said.

"Shut up, Melanie. He's gonna get what's coming to him. That's final. We all agreed."

"We didn't all agree," she said. "You and him agreed and bullied the rest of us into it."

"You're still here, though."

"Trying to talk some sense into you, yeah."

We walked down a long, smooth ramp. Dripping water echoed under the faint rattling of chains and the murmur of hushed voices. The man shoved down hard on my shoulder, planting me in what felt like a metal folding chair. Two pairs of hands quickly tied me down, leashing my ankles to the chair legs.

I squinted as the hood yanked away and a dangling light-bulb flared in my eyes. As my vision swam back into focus I made out dirty faces and ragged clothes, maybe a dozen people gathered on the workshop floor of a derelict factory. Machines rusted on broken tracks, the dying afternoon light streaming in through cracked skylights twenty feet above our heads.

They weren't all human. Maybe none of them were. As my gaze swam over them, their features warped as if main-taining a human face took constant effort. I saw flashes of broken fangs in lopsided mouths, patches of ratlike fur, scales, and glimmers of hungry yellow eyes.

Cambion, I thought, slumping in my chair. Because I didn't have enough problems this week.

I spotted the girl who'd spoken in my defense right away. Melanie hovered at the edge of the crowd, looking hesitant and guilty. She was maybe nineteen and unlike the others, who mostly looked homeless and half-starved, she bore the markings of a suburban girl who bought her punk couture from Hot Topic. The emo mop of neon-blue hair was a nice touch.

The halfblood with the stun gun loomed over me, a bruiser whose veins popped and rippled over his muscles like tiny snakes under his skin. "That's right, Dorothy," he said, "you ain't in Kansas anymore."

I looked up at him, dumbstruck.

"Really?" I said. "Of all the badass things you could have said, that's the line you decided to go with? Look, here's a homework assignment for you: go and rent some vintage Schwarzenegger flicks, learn how to—"

This time he pressed the stun gun against my rib cage. He was considerate enough to wait to talk until I stopped twitching and flopping.

"Not so funny now, are ya?" He jabbed the plastic wand toward my face. "Not so funny now!"

"Enough," a voice rasped from the back of the crowd. The cambion parted, looking fearful as a familiar face approached my chair. The toe-eater. Great. "Before the sorcerer dies, does he have any last words?"

"Yeah," I said, pointedly glancing at the girl before looking back to him. "Why are you doing this? I mean, you're a hobo whack job who thinks mages taste like Twinkies, I get that, but some of your buddies here actually seem lucid. What'd I ever do to you?"

The cambion with the stun gun stroked it against my cheek, his finger resting on the trigger. "You put us back in chains, motherfucker," he growled.

"We were free!" the toe-eater cried, baring his cracked and yellowed teeth. "We! Were! Free! No rules, no rules, and you ruined us!"

The cambion around him nodded, murmuring their assent, but they looked more frightened than anything else.

"I don't even know who you people are," I said. "Let me level with you. I've done a lot of bad things to a lot of people, and I remember each and every one of 'em. Whoever you think I am, whatever it is you think I did, you've got the wrong—"

"*You loosed the hound!*" the toe-eater roared, pointing a blackened fingernail at me as he trembled with rage.

The hound, again. I still had no idea who or what the hound was. A few nights ago Toe-Eater was stalking me on Fremont Street, celebrating the hound being gone. Now the hound was back, and it was my fault? What had I done since—

"Caitlin," I said aloud, the pieces clicking together. "Caitlin is the hound."

The skylight exploded. The crowd of cambion jumped back, flailing and scattering, as a thunderstorm of broken glass rained onto the concrete and glimmered like diamonds in the dying light. Caitlin plummeted in its wake like a hawk plunging after its prey, landing on the heels of her high leather boots and rising gracefully from a crouch. A long white coat draped her willowy form, billowing around her, and she brushed a speck of glass from its tailored shoulder. She turned to me and smiled.

"You called?"

20.

"Bitch!" screamed the cambion with the stun gun, charging her like a maddened bull. She didn't hesitate, turning and flicking out her arm. A blur whined through the air, and the cambion crashed to his knees, clutching the ivory handle of a knife protruding from his neck. His eyes bulged, blood guttering down the front of his shirt, his throat convulsing.

"Correction," Caitlin said, "the proper title is 'hound.' You're the bitch. Now then, would anyone else like to do something foolish?"

The cambion fell on his face, his breath rattling as he died. The others wavered on their feet, only a few of them still clustered behind the toe-eater. Not Melanie, though. She stared at Caitlin like a kid who just got caught forging her report card.

Caitlin pulled back one side of her coat. A coiled bull-whip rested on her hip, its brass handle engraved with swirling sigils.

"Most of you know me," she said as she surveyed the room, "but for those who do not, I am Caitlleanabruaudi, the Wingtaker, hound of Prince Sitri's court. You gather here in violation of hell's law, and I stand in judgment. You live, or die, at my pleasure. So who would like to tell me what I want to know, in the hopes of putting me in a good mood before I pass sentence?"

"We spit on your law!" the toe-eater snarled. "We spit on your prince! You have no authority over us!"

The other cambion had looked intimidated by him before, even openly frightened, but now they seemed intent on edging as far away from him as they could. Anybody could see which way the wind was blowing. Anybody but him.

Caitlin held up a slender hand, offering a faint smile that didn't reach her frozen eyes. "I can be gracious, even in the face of rebellion. Tell me who put you up to this and you can walk away."

"No one!" the toe-eater shouted. "We are free and ungoverned! We will not be ruled by your bastard prince or any of his puppets!"

"You know what?" Caitlin said. "I actually believe you. What a shame."

The whip flashed from her belt, slashing across the air and landing with a thunderous crack. Flames surged from the handle and raced along the leather like it was a trail of gasoline. The toe-eater turned to run. He never had a chance. She lunged out her arm, and the whip coiled around his neck and hauled him to the concrete floor. The fires engulfed him in a storm of napalm.

The air stank with an unholy blend of burnt tires and pork. The cambion thrashed and shrieked. Caitlin held the whip fast, yanking him back down every time he tried to get up or roll free. The others backed away as the burning man flailed at them, screaming for help.

It didn't take long. Caitlin waited until there was nothing left but a charred husk, barely recognizable as anything close to human, before flicking her whip free. The fires died as she coiled the lash around her arm and hooked it back onto her belt.

The crowd watched her in horrified silence.

"You will go and tell others," she said calmly, "that the hound has returned, that order has been restored, and the law will be obeyed. Be thankful. You all got a second chance tonight. I don't give thirds. Now go. Except for *you*, Melanie. You come here. *Now*."

The cambion shuffled off, alone or in pairs, out into the night. The punk kid came over, her shoulders slumped and head down. She approached Caitlin like you might approach a lioness in the wild. Caitlin put her fingers under the shorter girl's chin, forcing her head up. She looked Melanie in the eyes.

"She wasn't in on it," I said quickly. "I mean, she was here, but she didn't want to be. She tried to talk them out of it."

"I know," Caitlin murmured. "Melanie, this is getting tiresome. You know this isn't your crowd. You don't belong here."

"I know," she stammered, on the verge of tears, "I know, but...I didn't realize. I mean, I thought it was just talk. I didn't think they were really going to hurt anyone—"

"Shh," Caitlin said. "Now...you know I have to punish you for this. You understand that, right?"

A tear rolled down Melanie's cheek. "I know."

Caitlin pointed at the first corpse, the hilt of her dagger still jutting from his throat. "Go get my blade."

Melanie wrenched it from the bloody corpse, her face pale, looking torn between tears and throwing up. She carried it to Caitlin, holding it loosely between two fingers.

"You will take this home with you," Caitlin said, "and clean it until it is pristine. So clean you could cut your dinner with it, yes? While you do, I want you to think about what happens when people rebel against the law. You'll bring the blade back to me tomorrow, and I'll decide what to do with you then."

"Yes, ma'am," Melanie stammered. Caitlin waited until she'd vanished from sight before letting out a pent-up sigh.

"Melanie is a good kid," she said, her tone suddenly casual. "She really is, but she's going through a phase right now."

"What are you going to do to her?" I asked. I must have sounded horrified. She took a look at me and giggled.

"Tomorrow? Nothing. She'll spend all night torturing herself with guilt and then start agonizing over what I might have in store for her. She won't sleep a wink. Docile as a kitten by tomorrow night. I'll tell her I'm proud of her for learning her lesson and give her a big hug. It's all psychology."

"Pardon me for saying, you don't seem like a hug person."

"What, you mean that?" She gestured toward the two corpses on the floor. "That's my job, Daniel."

"Yeah, you'll have to forgive me, I'm a little confused about that. And didn't you, you know, go back to hell when I freed you?"

She walked behind my chair, sliding another dagger from inside her coat. She sliced through my zip-ties. I rubbed my aching wrists, clenching and unclenching my fingers against the bloodless tingling.

"Number one, you're confused because you're not supposed to know any of this exists. We're irritated enough that you occult-underground types even know what cambion are, but that cat got out of the bag during the Dark Ages. Number two, I don't live in hell; I live in Las Vegas. There really is a difference, though it's sometimes difficult to tell, especially in August."

"How did you know I was in trouble?" I asked. She sliced my ankles free, spinning the ivory-hilted dagger in her hand before slipping it back into her inner coat pocket.

"I've been following you, silly. I hoped that the people who set me up would come after you for revenge. Instead I snared a clot of feral little opportunists. Not the prize I wanted. Don't give me that look; you were never truly in danger."

"The people who set you up? Besides Artie Kaufman?"

"That pig had nothing to do with it. He was just the babysitter. He did what he was told. His brother's the key, and I never saw his brother, just heard him on the phone."

I stood up, shook my legs out, and contemplated Caitlin. She looked like she'd just stepped off a Paris runway, even after murdering two men without thinking twice about it. Corman's words lingered in the back of my mind. *She'd gut you as soon as give you the time of day, no matter how nice she smiles.*

Maybe I was falling for a pretty face. Maybe I was just dumb enough to want to ride this train a little farther, a little closer to the end of the line, to see what I'd find there. I could justify it all day long, talk about how I needed help closing in on Sheldon Kaufman, how it was necessary to free Stacy's soul, but those were just excuses. What I said next, I said because I wanted to.

"We should compare notes," I told her.

"Are you sure that's safe?" she asked with a twinkle in her eye.

"Not remotely."

"Smart boy. All right, but if we're going to talk, we're going to do it over a meal. I'm famished."

I glanced nervously at the corpses, and she put her hands on her hips. "I don't eat *carrion*," she said. "Come on, my car's outside."

A white Audi Quattro with napa-leather seats sat in the abandoned factory's parking lot. It squawked as she unlocked the doors from her keychain.

"Here's all you need to know," she told me as she strode toward the car. "A good-sized chunk of the western United States is under the authority of the Court of Jade Tears and its honored ruler, Prince Sitri. I am his hound, his whip-hand, the keeper of his law on Earth, and his court's appointed persecutor—"

"You mean prosecutor?"

She just rolled her eyes.

"Among other things," she said, "many other things, this means policing the local cambion population to ensure they don't do anything stupid, and protecting them should they need help. Most of them, like Melanie, are fine. The ferals are the problem."

"Wait, that kid's the norm? I thought they were all psychotics except for a few."

I got in the car while she tossed her coat and weapons in the trunk. Underneath she wore a white silk blouse and a black pencil skirt, the hint of a silver pendant gleaming at her neckline. She slid into the driver's seat. The engine purred to life. Her fingertips caressed the wheel.

"Most cambion," Caitlin said, "are perfectly well-adjusted and normal, relatively speaking. You don't know about them because they're very good at hiding."

"How many are there?"

"A generous handful. My prince's court is one of the few that doesn't have an open-season policy on them. Many feel that, being half human, they're abominations and impure by nature."

"Gee, thanks," I said. The Audi rumbled out of the factory lot and onto the street.

"We, however, deem them worthy of existence and protection so long as they obey our laws. As a result, more than a few halfbloods migrate in from the Midwest and East Coast, looking for a place to thrive. The other courts' shortsighted loss is our long-term gain. As usual."

"So you're...the sheriff?"

She grinned. "The sheriff, the diplomat, the occasional guidance counselor. Any business of the prince's on Earth is my responsibility. I do occasionally need to go home for work or pleasure, but by and large, this world is my oyster so long as I'm strong enough to keep the job. Ah! Here we are."

A valet ran over to take her keys as we pulled up to the curb. We walked together through the casino, under a ceiling painted the color of a midsummer sky. When we got to the restaurant, I eyed the marquee over the doors dubiously.

"Uh, Caitlin? Isn't this one of Gordon Ramsay's places? Don't you need reservations at least a week ahead of time to get in?"

She glanced over her shoulder at me.

"I don't, no."

21.

True to her word, Caitlin only had to whisper a few words to the maître d' and we were whisked away to a two-seater table with a view of the kitchen. The prices on the menu were the scariest thing I'd seen all day, but my pockets were stuffed with cash from Artie's poker game and the company was nothing to complain about. Caitlin picked out a ginger liqueur with lemon and bitters from the drink menu, and I ordered a Vesper martini.

"Here's what I don't get," I said. "How did you get snared by the Kaufman brothers in the first place? I've seen remnants of infernal contracts before. They're always give-and-take, 'you do this and I'll do this.' Not the one you signed, though, it gave all the power to Artie and left you…"

I was going to say "virtually a slave," but I fell silent, seeing the storm clouds brewing behind her eyes. Her lips pursed in a tight scarlet line.

"I was sent a message, which I believed authentic, that my prince wished me to meet with one of his agents in a hotel room. It was an ambush. There were several people waiting for me, under hoods and masks, and they...forced me to sign it."

I shrugged. "I don't get it. What'd they do, hold a gun to your head? I doubt that would slow you down much."

"They have something that they shouldn't," she said, seeming to choose her words with great care, "a bit of old magic that has no place in this world, something venomous to my kind. Its very existence is a sensitive topic."

"How sensitive?"

Caitlin sipped her drink, giving me a hard look. "Sensitive enough that if you so much as knew its name, I would be obligated to tear your throat out. Find another question to ask."

"So you were captured. Sheldon and his friends gave you to his brother, who kept you in that house. What did Detective Holt have to do with it?"

"He was the entire reason I was there. I had one purpose: to seduce him, addict him, and keep him pliable. He was vital to their plan. Understand that the Kaufmans had no idea who I was, beyond my basic nature. I heard them talking on the phone once, and Sheldon told Artie, 'If she can't do a job on Holt, get rid of her and I'll tell our benefactor to find us another succubus.'"

I frowned. "So it wasn't personal for them. They asked this 'benefactor' to find them some random succubus, and he or she led them to you."

It didn't hang together, though I wasn't sure how. Some detail nagged at me. The waitress came back.

"We'll have the beef wellies for two," Caitlin told her.

"The cambion," I said as soon as the waitress walked off, "that's the problem. Wait—you just ordered for me."

Caitlin nodded. "I did. You'll love it. Best thing on the menu. What about the cambion? They didn't know anything; they were just acting out."

"That's the problem. They didn't know anything. Just that you were gone, right? You up and vanished one day, and the toe-eater and his buddies figured it was party time."

She narrowed her eyes as she put her cocktail glass to her lips. "Right, and?"

"So how did they know I was the one who set you free? Somebody had to have told them. We sure as hell didn't leave any witnesses behind."

"I haven't spoken to anyone about it. You? Who did you tell?"

I had to think about it. Gossip was like breathing for Bentley and Corman, but they wouldn't have said a word. I frowned, suddenly realizing who could have pointed the ferals my way.

"Nicky Agnelli, that piece of shit."

Caitlin glared. "What *about* Nicky Agnelli?"

"You know him?"

"Of course I know him. He's been a thorn in my side for years. He's always wanted my job. Not to serve, mind you, but to use the office to further his greedy little ambitions."

I gave her a quick recap of my week, from finding Stacy's wraith in the storm drains to my unexpected interview with Nicky at Club Prive.

"I knew Nicky was either keeping tabs on me or on Stacy's grandfather with his pet seer, so I used an artifact to shield myself when I went to Kaufman's house. I took it off, though, on the night of the poker game. If his guys were watching, Nicky knows exactly what went down there. This was payback. He must have leaked the details to the toe-eater and figured the ferals would do his dirty work for him."

"*Khlegota*," Caitlin spat, the flensetongue word slipping into my eardrums and doing cartwheels of spite. "I imagine the Kaufmans paid him to track down a succubus they could capture for their little plan. By sending them at me, he earned his filthy money and got me out of the picture."

I nodded. "That's Nicky's flavor, no doubt about it. As long as I've known him, he's always been a five-moves-ahead kind of guy. So what now? Are you going to go after him?"

The waitress brought over our plates, and Caitlin fell silent, looking pensive. The rich aroma of the beef Wellington opened my eyes wider than a pot of espresso.

"I can't," Caitlin said. "Nicky wasn't abandoned or cast out like most halfbloods. His father is a duke in Prince Sitri's court, and he's very protective of his family's reputation. I don't dare move against him without ironclad evidence."

I sighed. "Which Nicky knows. He's also the kind of guy, in my experience, who has a knack for keeping his hands clean."

"Choir of Pride," she muttered, slicing into her meat, "they're insufferable, every last one of them."

The first bite melted on my tongue, a perfect blend of tender beef and puff pastry, the juices laden with flavor. "This is fantastic," I said. "I forgive you for ordering for me."

"See? Trust me. What's your next move?"

I scooped up a forkful of glazed vegetables and contemplated it.

"Well, now that Nicky wants to kill me, that has to be squared. It'll keep, though. His gambit with the ferals failed, and he's gotta be thinking I suspect him. He won't try again anytime soon."

"What makes you think he won't just shoot you?"

I shook my head. "Because Nicky Agnelli has a very strained relationship with the Vegas occult underground. We leave his rackets alone, and he leaves us alone. If he did anything to change that though, like for instance going all Al Capone and capping one of us, or anything else that could be traced back to his doorstep...well, he's tough, but he's not tough enough to handle every sorcerer in the city coming down on his head at the same time."

"Sounds like we both have scores to settle."

"Not just with him. I'm going after Sheldon Kaufman. The only way to free Stacy is by getting my hands on that soul-trap and trying to put her back together somehow. I can't go all guns blazing, so I aim to shadow him a little and see what I can find out about this 'plan' of his. How about you?"

"Recovering the...old magic I spoke of is my first priority. Second is seeing that Sheldon joins his brother in hell. I have plans of my own, after what they did to me."

But you can't take the direct approach either, I thought as I savored another bite of beef Wellington. *Not as long as Sheldon's packing the kind of power to force you into signing another one-sided contract. You'd end up right back where you started, or worse.*

"Sounds like we're walking the same road," I said.

"I'm not opposed to walking together a bit longer," she said with a smile that suddenly faded. "But Daniel, heed me on this. Should you find what I seek, do not try to claim it for yourself. You will be tempted. But you would regret surrendering to that temptation, just as I would regret what I would have to do to you."

"Would you like my word of honor?"

"You're a sorcerer. Your 'word of honor' is just as worthless as mine. I will settle for your affirmation instead."

"Then I affirm," I said, "whatever you're hunting is yours. All I want is Stacy's soul, so I can put things right."

Caitlin smiled, teasing. "How noble of you. A knight in tarnished armor."

"Nothing noble about it. I took her grandfather's money and said I'd do a job for him. The job's not done yet. Simple as that."

She held up her last forkful of beef, studying its succulent texture in the light.

"You interest me," she mused. "Dessert?"

She insisted on ordering again, but after that meal, I couldn't complain. The waitress brought over plates with a gooey, glistening toffee cake and, to my bewilderment, a stick of butter.

"I know gourmet food can be high-calorie," I said, "but that's overkill."

"Try it." Caitlin wagged her fork at me. "Have I steered you wrong yet?"

The texture felt all wrong, softer than butter. As I put a forkful to my lips and tasted the cold rush of brown sugar and cream I let out a little murmur of pleasure.

"Brown sugar and butter-flavored ice cream," I said. "Perfect."

"Quite. Believe me, I know temptation."

That was what worried me, but I was having too much fun to let my better judgment get in the way.

"So how long have you lived here?" I asked.

"I was appointed as the prince's hound in the mid-eighties. Wonderful time. Still have my leg warmers some-where. I'd been to Earth a few times before, but...much earlier."

"It was an interesting decade. Good music, too."

"The best music," Caitlin said. "Duran Duran, Howard Jones—"

"Howard Jones was great. How about Tears for Fears?"

"Saw them in concert!"

I laughed. "I bet you're fun at concerts. So is it all work and no play for you these days, or do you actually get to relax once in a while?"

"What do you call this?" she said with a grin. "I'm always on duty, but I find little ways to amuse myself. What about you? How do you make ends meet?"

"A little of this, a little of that. Some jobs I'm more proud of than others. If I'm ever really low on cash, I can go down to Fremont and do my busker routine for a few hours. I do a little magic. Not magic-magic, I mean. Sleight of hand."

Caitlin leaned back in her chair, arms crossed, a lopsided smile on her lips. "Show me."

"Seriously? It's not very impressive compared to the real thing."

"Show me anyway."

"If the lady insists," I said, dipping into my pocket and holding up my car keys. I gave them a jingle. "I need to borrow your napkin."

"I'm going to want that back," she said, handing it over to me. Our fingers brushed with an electric tingle. I folded the keys up in the middle of the linen napkin, tying them into a bundle as I explained.

"Like most people, I have trouble with losing my car keys from time to time. They just go missing, like they've got a mind of their own. One day I thought I'd fix that by tying them down, like so." I trapped the keys at the bottom of an elaborate knot and held it up, shaking it so Caitlin could hear them jingle inside their napkin prison. I offered it to her. "Here, hold it just under the knot."

"All right," she said, the bundle dangling from her fingertips, "what now?"

"Well, now I go back to the drawing board, because it didn't work at all. Go ahead, take a look."

She looked dubious, untying the bundle, then laughed as she shook out an empty napkin. The waitress brought me the check in a slim folio.

"All right, so where did the keys go?" she said.

"Your guess is as good as—" I started to say, then opened the folio. The keys tumbled out, clattering on the table. "Oh. I guess they wanted to go home with the waitress."

"Naughty keys."

"I know, terrible date etiquette." I paused. "Er, that is, are we...are we on a date?"

22.

Caitlin smiled brightly, but the expression faded just as fast, like a bouquet of flowers left out in the desert sun.

"It doesn't," she started, hesitant, "it just doesn't work. We can't, I mean...it's just dinner."

I bit my lip, feeling like an ass. "Of course, right. So, uh, I'm going to follow up on Sheldon Kaufman. I want to know what his scheme's all about. With his brother and Carl Holt dead, I figure it's pretty much all over, but desperate people make stupid moves."

"We can only hope," Caitlin said. "Don't underestimate him, Daniel. He's not like his brother."

I thought about the high-end wards in his office, and the gun in his desk, as I padded the check folio with cash and set it on the table. "He hasn't met me yet."

"I'm serious. It's been a while since I've been able to have a decent conversation with someone who wasn't, well...someone who wasn't either afraid of me or scheming against me, or both. Don't go getting yourself killed before we have a chance at another."

"Count on it. Hey, I was wondering something when you crashed the party back at the factory. Where'd you get the name Wingtaker?"

Caitlin dabbed her scarlet lips with her napkin.

"It's a very long story," she said, "and you wouldn't like how it ends. Suffice to say it's how I earned my position."

She was half right, earlier. I wasn't scheming, but was I afraid of her? Standing next to Caitlin was like walking into a lioness' den wearing a suit made of T-bone steaks. No amount of infatuation could make me forget what she was, or drown out the memory of Artie Kaufman's dying screams.

So why did I linger on the steps outside the restaurant, flirting around the edges of a goodnight kiss like a teenager? In the end, she just rested her hand on my shoulder and favored me with a smile. I took a taxi home.

I dug out an old Howard Jones CD and played it on my laptop. I lay back on my bed, hands clasped behind my head, letting the music carry me back in time. A fresh bottle of Jack waited on the end table, but for the first time in weeks I didn't feel the need to pour a nightcap. The music was better.

#

I set the alarm to wake me up a little before dawn. Lots to do, if I wanted to get the drop on Sheldon Kaufman today. I grabbed a breakfast burrito and a paper cup of black coffee from the gas station on the corner, then hit the thrift store as soon as it opened. Fortunately, they had exactly what I was looking for: a white polo shirt, pristine white slacks, and matching Nikes with a pale silver swish. I looked exactly like somebody who should be serving drinks and taking car keys at a fancy country club. Either that or selling you a vacuum cleaner.

Blending in was easy. Getting in was something else entirely. Red Rock Country Club was a gated community in Summerlin, basking in the shadows of the Spring Mountains. Howard Hughes founded Summerlin and it still bore his thumbprint. The locals could afford the best of everything, and that included the kind of guards who had real training and real firepower.

A cab dropped me off in the Carmichael-Sterling parking lot so I could pick up my car. Thankfully, none of the cambion had come back after the kidnapping to slash my tires. I drove into Summerlin with the morning sun at my back. On the passenger seat, a small beige tote bag concealed the extra goodies I'd brought from home. When I reached Red Rock's east gate, where a guardhouse kept watch over the manicured road, I took a left and circled the community with one eye on the outer wall.

The problem with security, real and bulletproof security, is that it's ugly. By way of example, take a look at a supermax prison or better yet, a liquor store in the bad part of town. The rich and beautiful want to feel safe in their homes, but they don't want to look out through barred windows or ruin their view of the canyon with strings of razor wire. There's always a compromise between safety and aesthetics, and that compromise is where guys like me wriggle in.

"Perfect," I murmured as I came back around, now watching the houses on the outlying streets. Mail jutted out from an overstuffed mailbox on one corner, the lawn behind it at least two weeks overgrown and browning in the heat. The neighboring driveways sat empty, their owners probably off at work, nobody keeping a helpful eye on the place. I pulled into the driveway and parked. My car should go unnoticed and unchallenged there until I got back, and it was close enough that I'd have a chance of reaching it should things go wrong. Not a good chance, but better than nothing.

The seven-foot brick wall ringing Red Rock was pretty, but some concertina wire would have made it a lot harder to climb. I took a running jump, grabbing the edge of the hot, rough stone and hauling myself up and over while the toes of my sneakers scrabbled for purchase between the bricks. Landing hard on a manicured lawn, a lance of pain jolting up my shins, I quickly looked around for cameras or bystanders before jogging to the sidewalk and putting on my best impersonation of an innocent taxpayer.

I took it slow on my way to the country club. Heat mirages glistened in the distance over spotless streets. My entire goal was not to be noticed, and being out of breath and soaked with sweat tends to draw attention in polite company. The scenery stole my breath faster than the heat. My gaze lingered over cars I'd only seen on *Top Gear*, polished to glow in the desert sun and parked in front of three-million-dollar houses.

I couldn't imagine having that kind of money. I'd always just gotten by, living hand to mouth, trusting my wits and the winds of fortune to provide when cash got tight. It wasn't the luxury that drew my eye, though, it was the idea of a stable, secure life. Hell, maybe start a family of my own. Grill up burgers in the backyard and play catch with my kids instead of chasing nightmares in the dark.

I felt guilty just for imagining it. *You'd fuck it up just like your old man did. You're poison and you know it, so drop the daydreams and stay focused on the job.*

I walked a little faster. I wanted to get the taste of this place out of my mouth.

The country club was in full swing, members dining on the elevated patio under sun umbrellas or gathering on the rounded drive. Freshly waxed golf carts whirred past me in a tiny parade. I skipped the front doors and walked down a grassy slope to the side of the building, looking for a service entrance. A kid in a short-order cook's hat leaned against the stucco wall beside an unlabeled door, smoking a cigarette and occasionally glancing at his plastic wristwatch. He gave a start when I walked up, and I held up a calming hand.

"Relax," I said, "I'm not here to bust you for the smoke. Want to make an easy fifty bucks?"

"Is it illegal?"

"Not at all. I'm just doing a favor for a buddy, and I need a little help."

I told him what I wanted, and he talked me up to seventy-five. I peeled four twenties from my wallet and told him to keep the change. He let me in through the service entrance, walking me through the back of the Palmer Lounge. A lonely janitor pushed a buffer across the floor in the darkened room.

The kid pointed the way. "Go up the hall, and out on your right. Pull up around back and wait for me to give the signal. If you get caught, I don't know you, all right?"

"Know who? I was never here."

I walked briskly down a service hallway, eyes forward, gait strong. The key to walking around places where you're not supposed to be is to look like you're too important to be interrupted. Most people are non-confrontational by nature, and if you give them a good reason not to challenge you, they won't. I pushed through another pair of doors and found myself on the edge of a secluded, fenced parking lot for the club's golf carts. Numbered keys dangled from a corkboard next to the door. I helped myself.

My stolen cart hummed along the path. I paused within eyesight of the back doors, where small knots of golfers waited for their partners and checked their bags before heading out onto the rolling lawns. The course was gorgeous, a sculpted landscape in vivid green contrasting with the russet mountains in the distance, but I kept my eyes on the people.

Last summer I'd taken on a corporate job, ferreting out an embezzler at a local bank. It was more private-eye work than sorcery, and I'd caught the culprit with the help of a handy little audio bug about the size of my thumbnail. Not quite legal, but I found a company in England happy to sell them so long as you sent a statement on letterhead attesting that you were a police officer. I dipped into my tote bag and pulled out the bug along with a stick of Juicy Fruit. A few seconds later, the tiny marvel was securely affixed to the underside of the cart's dashboard with a glob of freshly chewed gum, out of sight and ready to work.

My new friend, minus his short-order hat, led a foursome to the edge of the path. He squinted, hand over his eyes, spotted me and gave an emphatic wave. I stepped on the gas, then froze.

The portly, curly-haired man standing next to the kid must have been Sheldon. He looked like his brother, minus the dye job and the bodybuilder's physique. With him was a

woman in her late forties, refined like an old-time stage actress, and a gangly man who looked like a hundred and fifty
pounds of nervous energy. Rounding out the foursome was
Meadow Brand, Carmichael-Sterling's other resident magician. She'd recognize me the second she saw me.

I jumped out of the cart and waved emphatically to a
passing caddy. "You! You! Hurry, there's no time!"

He paused, bewildered, gesturing to a side door. "But I
have to—"

"No! No time! Mr. Kaufman needs his cart now! Come
on, come on, get on, here you go, just drive it right up
there." I hustled him into the cart. "There you go, quickly
now, he's a great tipper, *go go go!*"

I watched with relief as the cart puttered up the lane,
right on schedule. Heading back inside, bag on my shoulder, I hunted for an employee restroom.

An empty stall wasn't the most dignified listening post,
but all I needed was a locking door and a quiet space. The
bug's receiver was a squat chunk of plastic about the size of
a television remote, a Cold War relic with a jack for a set of
headphones. A burst of static worried me, but I fiddled with
the knobs until distant, scratchy voices echoed over the line.

"—Holt's dead, my brother fucked up, we all know that,"
said a man's voice. Had to have been Sheldon. "The question is, what are we going to do about it?"

"Absolutely nothing," said a woman's voice, not Meadow's. She was beyond calm. Icy. Ethereal, like nothing could
lay a finger on her. "This saves us the trouble of disposing
of him ourselves, and it will take at least a week to reopen
the investigations on his desk. Our work will be done by
then. It won't matter."

The other man spoke up. "Can you guarantee that? Can you *guarantee* that? The risks we're taking—"

"You haven't risked a goddamn thing, you little pansy," Meadow Brand snapped. "We've all done our parts except for you. When's it going to be, huh? You have a new excuse for us?"

"Tomorrow night. I had to get my wife out of town, okay? She's going to Rio for a week. I've arranged everything. It's Amber. It has to be Amber—she's the only one who qualifies."

"Why don't you just kill your wife?" Sheldon asked. His casual tone chilled my blood.

"I don't love my *wife*," the other man said, and a chorus of laughter spiked the needle on the receiver.

I blinked, one hand cupped over my ear. *What the hell are you people up to?*

23.

"Be strong," the calm woman said, "and remember, if it was easy, it wouldn't be worth doing. I chose the three of you because you have the drive and the courage to accomplish this great work. We do this not because we can, but because we must, for the good of—"

"I don't want to interrupt the pep rally," Meadow said, "but can we talk about the four-hundred-pound gorilla in the room? How the fuck did our succubus get free, and is it going to come after us? I don't like loose ends."

The other woman sighed loud enough to crackle over the receiver. "I assume Sheldon's brother was seduced by foolish promises. 'Release me and I'll grant you power and wealth,' that sort of thing."

"He was a halfwit," Sheldon muttered. "And what am I going to do with the trap he gave me? He totally botched the ritual; there's not even an entire soul in there."

"We don't need it anyway," Meadow said, "unless Tony here wusses out. Again."

The calm woman said, "We'll keep it. Just in case."

The golf cart's engine sputtered. Heavy canvas bags slid against metal.

"Why are you being so mean to me?" Tony's voice grew softer as he got out of the cart, walking away from the bug.

"'Why are you being so meaaaan to me?'" Meadow mock-whined. "When you put on your big boy pants and step up to the plate like the rest of us, I'll start taking you seriously. You get the respect you earn."

"Enough," the other woman said. "Both of you. Tonight is crucial. I called our friend as soon as my plane landed. He's covering his end of this business, but that won't mean a thing if we aren't working in perfect harmony."

Perfect harmony? I thought. *Oh, that's just an invitation for somebody to mess with you. I think I'll accept.*

"Can we talk about the construction permits, please?" Tony said, his voice fading. "If we have to revise these blue-prints, I need to know before next week."

I only heard a few more words as the foursome walked away from the cart, off to play a round of golf on a bright and sunny day. I didn't feel the sunshine. Something was wrong here, seriously wrong, and it made Stacy's murder look like a drop in the bucket. I bagged up my kit and left the bathroom.

I figured I could loiter in the parking lot out front and shadow one of them when they left. With my car parked well outside Red Rock's gates, though, I wouldn't get very far. Another trip to the Carmichael-Sterling office, if I handled it right, might yield a home address or more infor-mation about the other two players. An Internet search wouldn't hurt, either. Options riffled through my mind like poker cards as I walked through the lobby toward the exit, discarding hand after losing hand.

"Oh, caddy," called a voice behind me.

Caitlin rested a golf bag against the hip of her plaid trousers, wearing a snug turquoise blouse accented by a white cap. She beckoned me over with a smile.

"You'll do. Carry my bag?"

I raised an eyebrow, but obligingly shouldered her bag as we walked out onto the green.

"Fancy meeting you here," I said. "I'm guessing it's not a coincidence."

"No coincidences in magic, isn't that something you people say?"

She flagged down a golf cart and we drove out to the first hole. I searched for something pithy to say, but the best I could come up with was, "You look great."

"Thank you! Just a little outfit I threw together. Is the plaid too much?"

"It's golf," I said. "I think the plaid's just right."

"That was my thought. Do things properly or go home."

We got out of the cart, and she studied the curve of the green, a light breeze ruffling her curls.

"What club should I use for this hole?" she asked.

"I...have no idea. I don't know how to play."

She grinned, sliding a six iron from the bag. "You're a terrible caddy. How did you ever get this job?"

"No idea. This strange woman just came up and hired me, and I couldn't bring myself to say no."

"Have to watch out for those strange women," she said, her club slicing through the air with a whistle. She struck the ball square on, sending it flying in a gentle arc toward the hole. "Hmm. Might birdie this one. So tell me what you learned today."

She drove the cart while I gave her a rundown of what I'd heard.

"*Their* succubus?" She glowered. "Oh, they're going to get it. So Sheldon and this Brand woman both work for Carmichael-Sterling?"

"Right, and the other man, Tony, talked about construction permits. I'd bet all four of them are transplants from Carmichael's home office in Seattle."

My phone buzzed against my leg. I took it out and glanced down. Caller unknown. Shrugging, I put it back in my pocket.

"And they're collecting souls," Caitlin said. "A specific number of them. Some sort of sacrifice, perhaps."

"Souls that have to 'qualify,' so there's definite criteria involved. The question is, why would—" I paused as my phone started buzzing again. "Excuse me."

I put the phone to my ear. Before I could even say hello, a thin, frightened voice rasped, "Mr. Faust?"

"Maybe," I said, "who's calling?"

"You have to help me," he said. "Please, you have to help me, there's no time."

I slumped. "Wow, did you catch me on a bad week. Look, I'm a little tied up—"

"It's Mr. Agnelli. He's going to kill me."

"Nicky Agnelli?" I said, sitting bolt upright. Beside me, Caitlin's eyes went hard.

"He had me watching you, Mr. Faust, but I saw too much. I looked places I shouldn't have and now he's going to get rid of me—"

"Okay. Okay, calm down. Where are you, right now?"

"Running. I'm running," he gasped, "but the twins are after me. Please, I've seen what you can do; you're my only hope! There's a parking garage on Lamb Boulevard. Meet me on the fifth floor, in an hour. Please, come quickly!"

"All right," I said, "I'll be there."

I hung up.

"Well?" Caitlin asked.

"I think that was Nicky's pet seer. He says Nicky's trying to kill him, and he needs a rescue. I figure it's a seventy-five percent chance of being a trap. Maybe eighty."

"Let's go," she said, nodding firmly. "If he's really on the run, he could be the evidence I need to bring Nicky down for good."

I shook my head. "I'll go. If it's a trap, it's a trap for you, not for me."

"You can't know that."

"I know the odds. Think about it. You said it yourself, this guy is just what you need. Nicky knows that too. He couldn't come up with a better piece of bait if he tried."

Caitlin folded her arms. "And if it is a trap, and you walk in alone?"

"Then I take my chances. Nicky wants to kill me because I got in his way and I hurt his pride. He's still a business-man, though, and he won't risk his life to wage a vendetta when he can take his time and get me weeks, months, years from now. You, on the other hand, he *needs* to kill or recapture because he knows you're loose and you have a pretty good idea of who set you up. I'm not sending you into a death trap, Caitlin. I won't do it."

"And I don't want—" she paused, clenching her arms across her vest. She shook her head. "Go. But you call me, as soon as it's over. I want to make sure that you're...I want to hear how things went."

"I don't have your number."

She plucked my phone from my hand and thumbed over to the contacts menu, adding herself to the roster. *Cait*, the new listing said.

"Go," she said.

#

I booked it back to downtown Vegas, keeping an eye on the clock. If this guy was for real and Nicky's twin enforcers had his scent, he might already be dead. Wishing he were dead, maybe. Justine and Juliette liked to play with their food. I didn't want to go up against those two without a lot of preparation and maybe a platoon of marines in my back pocket, but I knew I might not have a choice.

I called Bentley as I drove, keeping one hand steady on the wheel, and left a quick message when his voicemail picked up.

"It's Daniel. Look, I don't want to worry you, but you need to know I'm going to meet with somebody, and there's no gentle way to say this. If I vanish or something happens to me, it was Nicky Agnelli. Spread the word and drop the boom on his ass. I don't think it's a problem—I'm sure I'll be fine, but just in case. Just in case."

My one hope was that Nicky's desire to keep the peace with Vegas's occult underground outweighed the sting to his pride when I stole Caitlin out from under him. Tough call. I'd find out when I got there.

The Lamb Boulevard parking garage sat half empty this time of the afternoon, the snaking aisles lined with rental cars and the occasional plate from California or Arizona. Cars grew sparser as the floors climbed higher, leaving the upper deck a decent place for a clandestine meeting. Or an execution.

A short, balding man in an off-the-rack suit paced beside a rusted Camry, rubbing the back of his neck. I pulled up nice and slow, not wanting to spook him, while keeping a sharp eye on the scattering of cars on the roof. The Vegas skyline rose up around us, dusty and sleeping in the sun.

I pulled into a spot about ten feet away, easing out of my car. I showed him my open hands. He pressed his back to his car, jumpy as a cornered rat.

"Mr. Faust?"

"That's right," I said, not moving any closer. "Just me. Let me guess, you're Nicky's seer. That's your shtick? Remote viewing?"

He nodded. "I was born with it. I've worked for Mr. Agnelli for years. It's always been minor things, harmless, like watching local celebrities and political figures. Gathering gossip and insider business news."

"Not anymore, huh? What's Nicky's interest in Stacy Pankow's murder? Why did he warn me away from pursuing it?"

He shook his head. "He doesn't care about her. But you freed that...that creature. You're threatening his plans and worse, theirs. The people he works for."

"Sheldon Kaufman?"

"He's just another pawn!" the man snapped, ruddy faced as his eyes darted from side to side. "A few weeks ago, I started using my talent to watch Mr. Agnelli. I knew I shouldn't, but he's been so different lately. He's changed. Driven, utterly consumed with his work. I wanted to know why."

"Slow down," I said, "and take a deep breath. What's Nicky after? What's his end game?"

The seer waved his hand. "Something in hell. Putting his father on some demon prince's throne, making daddy proud of him. It's all rubbish. It's small time."

I furrowed my brow. I figured Nicky just wanted Caitlin bound and out of the way so he could make a play for Vegas. "That doesn't sound small to me."

"Compared to what they want? He's dancing on strings. And Lauren Carmichael, she's the puppet master. Carmichael-Sterling's CEO. You don't understand, she's been planning this for *decades*. Everything that's happening now, it's just one tiny piece of her grand design."

I thought back to my glimpse of the golf foursome. "Lady in her late forties, stylish, about this tall?"

"That's her," he said, his head bobbing like a metronome. "She has the ring, the damned ring, and it's just a tool to her. She went to India. She went to India, but it wasn't her who came back."

"Breathe," I said. "Just...breathe, okay? What ring?"

The seer paced relentlessly, spittle flying as he raved, his agitation growing. I wasn't sure if he was out of his mind with fear or just plain out of his mind, but I kept my distance.

"What's she's planning, it's monstrous. I wasn't supposed to look. I wasn't supposed to, but I looked. The plans for the Enclave. Not the ones they filed with the city, the *real* plans. I know what she's building, what that place really is. Haven't been able to think straight since I saw, but that's not the...tonight! That's why I ran, why I called you. Tonight is critical, that's, that's—it's critical. You have to stop them. You have to!"

I held up my hands, trying for a soothing tone. "Okay, okay, I will. But you need to calm down, all right? Tell me exactly what I need to stop. Focus for me."

"They're going to kill a man." He took a deep breath and let it out in a heaving wheeze. "He has what they need, the last piece of the puzzle. He's a fence, local, I'm trying to re-member his name—"

"Think hard," I said, my stomach muscles tightening.

"It was Spend, no, Span." He looked me in the eyes, sud-denly lucid, and snapped his fingers. "*Spengler!*"

The seer's head exploded in a spray of red mist.

24.

Sniper!

A flock of pigeons soared from their perch on the roof's railing, startled by the gunshot. I hit the ground, my body pressed to the hot asphalt. I frantically scanned the horizon for some glimmer of light, the reflection of a riflescope, but the shooter was a ghost. The seer's corpse lay sprawled on the ground. Nothing was left of his head but some torn flesh and splintered bone at the end of a shattered spinal column.

Fifty-caliber round. Jesus. They weren't taking any chances.

I trench-crawled the few feet to my car door, looking up at the handle as though it were a million miles away. The low wall encircling the parking deck gave me a little protection, but I'd have to stand up at least a little bit to open the door and get in, exposing me to fire.

And the longer you wait, the more time they have to reload and drop a bead on you. Move!

I held my breath, got up on my knees, and yanked open the car door, clambering inside and lying flat on the front seats. Bracing myself, I swung up into the driver's seat and scrambled to jam my keys into the ignition. I nearly dropped them, my hand shaking, but the engine revved to life and I threw it into reverse. I spun back out of the parking spot, the car door still open and swaying on its hinges, then stamped my foot on the gas.

The car hit the ramp hard enough to bottom out. The chassis jolted and threw up sparks. I hauled the wheel around, bending low with my head just high enough to peek over the dashboard. My phone vibrated in my pocket.

"Not now," I muttered through clenched teeth. The car fishtailed as I swerved around the next lane and down the ramp to the third floor. Every tier of the garage had a railed balcony open to the sky, a shooter's paradise.

I whipped around to the next level, careening straight toward an elderly tourist in the middle of the lane. She clutched a token cup for the penny slots. I slammed on the brakes, tires screaming, and stopped hard enough to throw myself forehead-first against the steering wheel.

I pressed my fingers against my head, checking for blood. The skin was sore to the touch but unbroken. The engine rumbled. The old woman looked at my car, looked at me, and flipped me the bird before hobbling along.

"Yeah," I breathed, adrenaline coursing through my veins. "I deserved that."

My phone rang again. I tugged it out of my pocket and checked the caller ID. Nicky.

"What," I answered flatly.

"This is Justine, and Juliette is with me, and you're on speakerphone. You almost hit that old lady. That was *terrible*."

"You should feel bad," Juliette added.

"Yeah?" I said, sitting up in my seat. "Well at least I didn't just shoot somebody in the fucking *head!*"

"Probably because you can't afford a gun," Justine said.

"What's the point of buying a military-grade sniper rifle," Juliette asked, "if you're not going to use it? I made that shot from almost twelve hundred meters. Can you make a shot from almost twelve hundred meters, Danny?"

"What we're saying," Justine added, "is people should take pride in their work."

"What," I seethed, "do you two psychopaths want?"

"We want to make sure you understand that man was crazy," Justine said.

"Cuckoo for Cocoa Puffs," Juliette added.

"He had to be put down," Justine said, "like a rabid dog. It was for his own good. What did he say to you?"

Why don't you ask your seer? I wanted to say. *Oh wait, you can't.* For once, Nicky and the twins were flying blind. If they didn't know he had spilled the beans about tonight, that put me a step ahead of them. That was a first.

"He told me you were going to kill him."

"A seer and a prophet," Justine said. "What else did he tell you?"

"He was about to tell me something about Nicky, but then something happened. What was it? Oh, yeah, you shot him."

"Oopsie," Juliette said.

"He would have lied to you anyway," Justine said. "Besides, he was so painfully boring. You should come have a chat with my sister and me. We're much more fun."

A horn blared. I jumped in my seat. The headlights of a car flashed in my rearview mirror. I waved a feeble apology, put the car into drive, and rolled down the ramp toward the exit.

"I think I'll pass," I said. "Give my regards to your boss."

I hung up the phone and pulled up Spengler's number in my contact list.

Two weeks in Saudi, he'd said back at the Tiger's Garden. *This thing I found? People are gonna be breaking down my door trying to throw money at me. You just wait, you'll see.*

People were going to be breaking down his door all right.

"Hey, it's the big guy!" his voicemail message said. "I'm out doing important stuff with important people, so leave a message at the beep and if *you're* important, I'll call ya back."

"Spengler, it's Daniel. You're in danger. Call me. Now. As soon as you get this."

Spengler's house was a good forty minutes away. I leaned on the accelerator, clutching the wheel as I speed-dialed Caitlin with my free hand.

"Daniel," she said, picking up on the first ring.

"You were right. The seer fingered Nicky. He's got some kind of crazy scheme to put his dad on your prince's throne."

"Impossible. Flatly impossible. Prince Sitri has held that throne since the dawn of the Byzantine Empire. There's no scheme he hasn't seen coming from decades away. It's been rumored that half of the plots against him were started *by* him, just for his personal amusement."

"Yeah, well, Nicky seems to think he's got a good shot, and selling you to the Kaufman brothers was part of the plan."

"Choir of Pride," Caitlin seethed. "Insufferable. Every last bloody one of them. Where's the seer? Is he with you? Bring him to me."

"The twins got to him first. With a sniper rifle."

"Are you all right?" she said, suddenly alarmed. "Did they hurt you?"

"No. They made sure I knew they could have, though. Nicky doesn't want a war on his hands. He'll find a plausibly deniable way to kill me. They just wanted the seer taken out before he could spill the beans."

"*Khlegota!* No chance of intercepting the seer's soul, either. I guarantee they had someone waiting on the other side for him."

"You can do that?" I asked. Admittedly, the afterlife is something I try to spend very little time thinking about.

"Right now, that man is likely chained to the floor of a very deep, very dark, very unpleasant pit, where he can't tell anyone what he knows. I'm sure they've taken his mouth as well."

Something about the casual way she said that, like it was business as usual, sent shivers down my spine.

"At least we know we're on the right track," she said. "Nicky's guilty. He'll pay in good time. And pay dearly."

I leaned on the gas, shooting through a yellow light and weaving around a gas truck.

"There's more," I said. "The inner circle over at Carmichael-Sterling has their own game. They're going after a friend of mine tonight, a fence named Spengler. I'm on my way to stop them."

"Do you need help?"

Yes, I thought, *but they've still got the magic that made you Kaufman's thrall the first time around, and I'm not putting you through that again.*

"I've got this," I told her, trying to sound more confident than I felt. "This all ends tonight. We send these out-of-towners running back to Seattle with their tails between their legs. Then we can focus on putting the screws to Nicky. Easy as that."

Nothing was ever that easy.

#

Spengler lived in a McMansion at the end of a sleepy suburban street, every house the same shade of forgettable beige. I always figured he'd go for something as big and ostentatious as his personality, but I guess when your job risks landing you on more Interpol watch lists than your average terrorist, you learn the value of camouflage.

I pulled in behind his BMW and jumped out, running to his front door. I leaned on the doorbell, listening to it hammer out a staccato chime inside, wondering if I should chance picking the lock. If I was too late...

The lock clicked. Spengler pulled the door open, the big man draped in a black silk kimono spattered with white flower patterns.

"All right, all right already!" he said. "Oh, hey, Dan. What's up?"

"Do you not check your goddamned voicemail?" I said, shepherding him inside, shutting the door, locking it, and sliding the deadbolt tight. Spengler's home was the kind of pristine you only get from hiring a cleaning service once a week. Art from the Renaissance masters decorated the walls. A few of the pieces were real, long missing from a smattering of museums across Europe. A better investment than gold, he always said.

"My phone's charging, and I'm kinda getting ready for a date here. My sexy little Candi is coming over in about fifteen minutes, and I've got a sweet tooth, if you know what I mean."

"Call her and cancel."

He looked down at me, not sure how seriously to take my tone. "Dude, Candi's two hundred dollars an hour, and if I cancel now I'm going to have to pay her anyway."

"Spengler," I said, "listen to me very carefully. There are people coming here, right now, to kill you. Now pick up your phone. Cancel. Your. Prostitute."

While he called Candi, I tried to call the cavalry. I put out calls to Bentley and Corman, Mama Margaux, Jennifer, getting nothing but messages and busy signals. The idea of the two of us taking on a whole team of adept magicians at the same time didn't fill me with hope. Plan B was taking Spengler and getting the hell out of here, but not without figuring out what Carmichael-Sterling was after. At the very least, I had to deny them their prize.

"You'd better be serious about this," Spengler said, hanging up his phone. "Because I can't be paying women and *not* having sex with them. It's wrong. It's wrong on so many levels."

"Let me make a long story very short." I cornered him, leaning in and talking slow. "A pack of magicians is coming over here to kill you and steal something from your collection. They're determined, ruthless, and they're responsible for several murders already, so don't think for a second you're going to talk them out of it. I need to know what you've acquired in the last month or so. It has to be something recent, or they would have come after you before tonight."

He shook his head, looking worried as reality sank in. "Man, do they not know I'm protected? I'm the supplier to the stars, and I don't just mean the occasional bump of Peruvian marching powder. Everybody knows I can get you your heart's desire, so why would anyone kill the golden goose?"

"Because," I said, holding up a finger, "they only want one egg. These aren't our people, they aren't a part of our community, and they don't give a fuck whose toes they step on. You're a bump in the road to them."

"I've only made one buy in the past couple of months, from my trip to the sandbox."

"Saudi," I said, "the big score you were talking about at the Tiger's Garden?"

He nodded and gestured for me to follow him through the house. Mahogany bookshelves lined one wall of his study from floor to ceiling, looming over an overstuffed leather armchair and an antique standing globe. He gave the upper half of the globe a twist, pulling it back on concealed hinges. A snifter of cognac and a pair of glasses waited inside.

"We do not have time—" I started to say, but he cut me off with a wave of his hand.

"Under normal circumstances," he said, lifting out the bottle, "I wouldn't show this to anybody. I'm gonna have to ask you to keep quiet about it."

He reached into the recess, hooking his fingers around a catch, and gave it a tug. A section of the bookshelves clicked and swung open.

"Welcome to my safe room," Spengler said.

25.

The room behind the bookshelf was about ten feet square and fortified like a bunker. Grainy footage from outside the house, front and back, flickered on a bank of monitors along with a bird's-eye view of the street from what looked like a camera mounted on a tree branch. To the left of the security console, a pump-action shotgun and a pair of stubby handguns hung from a chrome wall rack.

I whistled low, tracing a finger along the shotgun's barrel. "You planning for a siege?"

"Hope for the best, plan for the worst," Spengler said, pulling the door shut behind us and twisting a lock that looked like it belonged on a bank vault. "I've got about two months of surplus military MREs and bottled water in those boxes behind you. The room's fireproof, with a rooftop ventilation system that draws and purifies air from outside. I can shut off the ventilation in an emergency, but only for a couple of hours."

"Better odds than the Alamo, but I still think we should hit the road. Show me what you found in Saudi Arabia."

He pulled back a green tarp, unveiling a wooden crate against the back wall of the safe room. Its weathered slats bore customs stamps and faded brands from half a dozen nations.

"Getting it back here was almost as hard as finding it in the first place," Spengler said, lifting the lid, "but totally worth it."

Nestled in a bed of sawdust and paper clippings, the crate held an ebony casket just big enough for a toddler. My first instinct was to recoil, to yank the crate lid from Spengler's hand and slam it shut, to seal the casket away in darkness.

"I know, right?" he said, reading the look on my face. "You get used to it, but the first reaction is pretty strong."

I shook my head and took a step back. "There's something in there."

I didn't know how I knew it. I just knew it. Something lived in that casket, something much older, much crueler, than any infant. Something with the patience of a trap-door spider and nothing but time. Swirling carvings adorned the casket's face, hard to make out at first. I traced the lines with my eye and they resolved into the figure of a man, impossibly thin and long, clutching a pan flute.

"What is it?" I asked, trying to tear my gaze away.

"It's the Etruscan Box." His eyes blazed with a mixture of pride and raw greed. "*The* Etruscan Box. My holy grail. I've been chasing this thing for a decade, putting out feelers from here to Siberia, and finally I picked up its trail. Poor bastard I bought it from had no idea what he'd inherited from his old man."

"But what is it?"

"Lotta stories about that," Spengler said. "Legends passed down from explorer to explorer, all from people who spent their lives hunting the Box and never caught a glimpse. Remember, we don't know a whole lot about the Etruscans before Rome finally rolled over them, but they were around for a long time, a *really* long time. They had some savage witchcraft up their sleeves."

He reached into the crate. I held my breath as he grabbed hold of the casket's lid, but it refused to budge.

"See? It doesn't open. It doesn't want to open. Doesn't matter. I'm just selling the box as-is. I put it up on the Internet under a coded auction listing, and you wouldn't believe the people I've got bidding on this baby. Some of the biggest players in the occult underground from coast to coast—throwing cash at me like it's Judgment Day and they're trying to get rid of all their money before Jesus comes back. The top bid is already over two million bucks and climbing."

"So these stories," I said, "what do they say is inside?"

"The stuff that dreams are made of. They say it's your heart's desire, whatever you want most in life, just waiting for the first person to open it up and reach on in. All you have to do is figure out how it unlocks and everything you ever wanted is yours for the taking. It's like Excalibur in the stone."

I reached up and closed the crate lid. I still felt the casket and its occupant, buried in darkness, listening to us.

"Excalibur," I said flatly.

"That's the story, but who knows? Nobody's ever gotten it to open, and if you ask me, nobody ever will. Some ancient wizard's bad joke. As far as my heart's desire goes, well, you know me. My dream is cold, hard cash. This is the score of a lifetime."

Spengler was bush-league compared to the rest of the regulars at the Garden, just magically aware enough to qualify for entry, but no real talent. Even so, I couldn't believe how casual he was, unable to feel the chill radiating from inside the crate on the wings of a gale-force wind.

"Let's hope you're right about it staying sealed," I said, backing away from it.

"Why's that?"

"Because something is alive inside that casket," I said, "and I think it hates us."

The doorbell chimed.

We looked at each other, then rushed to the security monitors. A pretty girl in her twenties, platinum blond with a California tan, stood on the doorstep and smiled hopefully up at the security camera.

"Candi," Spengler breathed.

I slapped his arm, glaring. "You were supposed to tell her not to come over!"

"I did! I swear I did! She was almost here when I called, and she said she was going to turn around and go home!"

She gave a little wave up at the camera, flashing a perfect smile, and pressed the doorbell again.

"Something's wrong." I paced the safe room.

"Dan, if she's on the doorstep when these guys show up, what will they do to her?"

"Nothing good," I said, eying the screen, "but we have to think about this. Are you sure that's her? Absolutely, one hundred percent certain?"

"That pleated skirt," Spengler said, pointing at the tiny screen. "I asked her to wear that for me. Even if somebody was screwing with the camera feed, projecting an illusion or something, there's no way they'd know what she was going to be wearing. It's her."

If something looks like a trap and smells like a trap, it's a trap, but we'd be safe as long as we hid inside Spengler's armored nook. Staying put offered our best chance of making it to dawn in one piece. On the other hand, if I was wrong, an innocent girl was standing in the line of fire with no idea what kind of horror was heading her way.

Another smile, another ring of the doorbell.

"Shit," I said, drawing my deck of cards from my hip pocket. "We have to risk it. Bring a gun. We grab her off the porch, we drag her back to the safe room, we stop for absolutely *nothing*, got it?"

"Got it," Spengler said, grabbing one of the bulky pistols from the wall rack and checking the clip.

I shuffled my cards as we jogged through the house. The glossy cardboard crackled under my fingertips, pregnant with raw energy and eager to play. I stood back from the front door and nodded to Spengler. He clutched his gun behind his back, reaching for the doorknob with his other hand.

He hauled open the door, reached out and grabbed Candi by her wrist, and roughly yanked her inside. I ran up and slammed the door behind her.

"No time to explain," he said. "I'm sorry, but you've gotta come with us, I'll tell you everything in a second—"

Reaching for the lock, I caught a glimpse of Candi's face in the corner of my eye. Her real face. Heart sinking, I turned.

"Spengler."

"C'mon honey, don't argue, it'll all make sense in a minute—"

"Spengler," I said more firmly.

"—I'm not going to hurt you, you know me, you can trust me—"

"Spengler!"

He looked at me, clutching Candi in his arms, startled. "What?"

I pointed. "Look at her. Take a deep breath, clear your mind, and really *look* at her."

The thing in Spengler's arms was nothing but a life-size mannequin, carved from jointed wood like an artist's posing model, with a crudely painted face. It wore Candi's clothes. A gash in the sweater where her heart would have been, stained with fresh blood, told me what had happened to the real girl.

"Shit," Spengler said, and then the mannequin turned its head toward me.

I didn't have time to shield myself. Its puppet-head lolled back and its mouth opened wide. Golden sigils glittered inside its maw, a glyph-spell primed and ready to fire. A Trojan horse.

The pulse of magic blasted through the room with the force of a flashbang grenade. Spengler fell backward, the mannequin clinging to him like a lamprey as he desperately rubbed at his eyes, reeling. My muscles didn't want to obey me. Chimes in impossible keys rang in my ears in the aftershock. Behind me, a boot kicked the front door in, slamming it into me and sending me sprawling to the carpet. Cards flew from my outstretched hand.

"I told you arts and crafts were kinda my thing, right?" Meadow Brand asked, standing over me. "We didn't buy your reporter routine for a second, by the way. Half an hour after you left my office we had a full dossier on you. Weren't sure you'd put the pieces together, but I figured I should bring out the big guns just to be safe."

Behind her, other forms filed into the room, hazy in my light-flooded vision.

"Silly locals," Lauren Carmichael said, "always having to throw their weight around. You made a mistake, Mr. Faust. You should have sided with us."

"Candi—" Spengler said, finally pushing the mannequin away and crawling back on the carpet. His pistol lay abandoned a few feet away. The mannequin twitched. "Those are her clothes. What did you *do* to her?"

My vision cleared. Tony hovered by the door, looking nervous, and Sheldon Kaufman stood at Lauren's shoulder like the grim reaper come to call. A pair of cards still nestled in my palm. I could take two of these bastards down, if I used them just right, but then I'd have to deal with the other two. I held my move and kept the cards out of sight.

Lauren looked down at him. "Your whore is dead, Mr. Spengler. Necessary for Ms. Brand's little jest to work, I'm afraid, but no great loss to society. You may or may not join her in the next few minutes, depending on how cooperative you are."

"*Fuck you!*" Spengler screamed, lunging for the gun. He grabbed it and swung it up, aiming for Lauren's head. Suddenly he shrieked as his wrist snapped backward, as if twisted in the gears of some horrible invisible machine. Bones cracked like dry twigs. The gun fell from his convulsing fingers, too far away for me to reach.

This all ends tonight, I'd told Caitlin. Somehow this wasn't the ending I'd been hoping for.

26.

"Remember me, lover-boy?" Meadow asked Spengler with a satisfied smile. Clutching his destroyed wrist and biting back another scream, he looked up at her with sudden recognition.

"You—" was all he managed to say, his breath strained.

"We knew he'd gotten to the Box just ahead of our people," Meadow explained, looking down at me, "but not how he was shipping it or where it would be. Your friend and I met at an airport bar in Atlanta the night he came back from Saudi Arabia, thanks to a carefully planned coincidence. He was waiting for a connecting flight. I was waiting for him. We got tipsy, and then I let him 'convince' me to bring him up to my hotel room. Such a pick-up artist."

She showed me the poppet in her hand. Just a tiny wax doll, wrapped in colored threads, a clump of real hair pinned to its head. Just a wax doll with a snapped-off wrist.

"I would have settled for a little hair and a drop of spittle," she said to Spengler, "but by sunrise I had samples of *all* your vital fluids, didn't I? Makes the poppet so much stronger."

I bent my knee back, getting ready to jump up and make a move. Sheldon's gaze darted towards me.

"I'd stay down if I were you," Sheldon advised. Tony just hovered by the broken door, looking like there were a thousand other places he'd rather be.

Lauren circled the room, pausing to admire one of the paintings.

"Is this an original Matisse?" she said, glancing over her shoulder at Spengler. "You have exquisite taste."

He held his wrist, rocking forward and back, groaning. "Why are you doing this? What do you want?"

"Simple," she said, "we want the Etruscan Box. Don't get me wrong, we weren't opposed to the idea of paying for it, but your little auction has three weeks to go, and our time-table is a bit tighter than that. Where is it, please?"

"Screw you. I'm not telling you anyth—"

Spengler's words erupted in a piercing shriek as his leg snapped at the knee, doubling inward, his toes pressing against his hip. Jagged bone jutted from a tear in his kimono, and blood soaked the beige carpet in a spreading ring. Meadow smiled serenely as she slowly ground the wax doll's leg to mush under her fingertips.

"It's in his safe room!" I shouted. "I'll show you, just leave him alone!"

"Damn it, Dan," Spengler whimpered, tears flooding down his cheeks as he writhed on the carpet. "Don't tell them shit."

"It's not worth it. I'm sorry, it's not worth you dying over it." I looked to Lauren. "His safe room is in the study, behind a bookshelf. We left the door open. The box is in a crate against the back wall."

Lauren smiled. "Now you see? That's what I like. Reasonable and succinct. Ms. Brand?"

Meadow shrugged and dropped the poppet to the floor, discarded.

Then she stomped on it.

Spengler died in a spray of blood and splintered bone. I howled like an animal, scrambling to my feet and hurling one of my palmed cards. It whipped through the air, crackling with pale blue lightning, and sliced into Meadow's face. I turned just as Sheldon lunged forward. He threw a punch from five feet away. A shockwave lanced from the end of his fist, streaking toward me and slamming me in the jaw with the force of a phantom heavyweight. The accountant spun his fists in a graceful circle. They trailed shimmering patterns like twin heat mirages.

"Forsaken Hand style," he said. "Learned it in China."

He spun on his heel and lashed out with his foot. I was ready this time. I flipped my other card in the air and cast a shield charm, the jack of diamonds hovering in the path of his oncoming blow. The spells clashed with a grating squeal and a shower of black sparks. Sheldon fell back and clutched his foot like he'd just rammed his toes into a brick wall.

I dove for the fallen cards. Lauren uttered a litany of sibilant words under her breath, a chant that became a literal serpentine hiss as she blazed toward me, leaving the impression of glossy green scales in her wake. A blinding pain seared my neck. My muscles seized up with agonizing cramps that left me convulsing on my back.

Lauren cradled an ornate hairpin in her fingertips. One end was adorned with a cluster of pearls, and the other glistened with a drop of my blood. A warm, wet trickle ran down my neck.

"Sheldon, Tony, please retrieve the Box," she said, crouching over me. Meadow whimpered in the corner, clutching her face, blood leaking out between her fingers.

Lauren showed me the pin, wiping it clean with a silk handkerchief before fixing it in her auburn hair.

"A paralytic of my own design, Mr. Faust. No worries, the effects are only temporary. Now, my preferred flavor of venom, on the other hand..."

Her hands, glowing with amber light, came down on my chest like a pair of defibrillator pads. Indescribable pain erupted along my spine, a blowtorch charring muscle and bone. I raised every psychic shield I knew, used every trick my frantic mind could muster, but she forced her energy inside me one writhing inch at a time. Finally, it ended. She pulled away with a gasp of pleasure. Something squirmed in my guts, feral and sick.

She took a bundle of hand towels from Spengler's bathroom and tended to Meadow, gently pulling her hands away and pressing the cloth to her wounds.

"Fucker," Meadow spat, her words slurred. "My face, what he did to my fucking face—"

"I know, I know," Lauren said. "It's all right."

Tony and Sheldon trundled up the hall, lugging the crate. My vision blurred, my head pounding and stomach churning like the world's worst hangover. I wanted to throw up, but my stomach seized, trying to keep the sickness in.

"Get it in the van," Lauren told them, helping Meadow to her feet.

"Want me to finish him?" Sheldon asked.

"No. Meadow's losing too much blood. We need to get her to a hospital. He'll be dead in an hour anyway."

"An hour?" Sheldon said with a casual laugh as they hauled the crate out the door. "You're losing your touch."

An engine revved in the driveway, then silence. I lay on the blood-soaked carpet next to Spengler's mutilated corpse and willed my limbs back to life. Slowly, a finger curled. Then a fist.

I pushed myself up on my knees. My guts twisted. Wave after wave of brutal nausea washed over me, and my throat and stomach tightened in response, my own body working against me.

What did she DO to me? I thought, feeling cut off from the currents of magic. My soul lagged behind my skin, body and spirit out of sync, crumbling around the edges.

First things first. I got to my feet, leaning against the wall as I took a few hesitant steps. So far, so good. I stumbled out onto Spengler's porch, weaving like a drunk on a five-day bender. Streetlights bloomed in the dark, burning white phosphorus trails across my vision as I staggered toward my car. No telling if the neighbors had heard Spengler's screams. I had to get away before the cops showed up. It took five tries to get my keys in the ignition.

The car lurched onto the street, jolted forward, stopped, then jolted again. I didn't have enough coordination to work the pedals, couldn't even remember what they were for. Lauren's venom wriggled through my intestines like an eel covered in razor blades, knotting and slicing and twisting.

I pulled over to the side of the road, tires scraping the curb. My phone fell out of my hands as I tried to dial, bouncing onto the passenger side floor. I groped for it blindly. My fingers fumbled against the call screen.

"Daniel?" Mama Margaux said. Her Creole-tinged voice sounded a million miles away. Everything did. Sound, sight, touch, my senses eroding eroding into a winter wasteland of pain.

"Mama. I'm fucked up. Don't know...some kind of curse. Never seen it before."

"Slowly, Daniel, slowly," she said, on alert. "Where are you? I'll come and get you."

"Car. Outside Spengler's house. Spengler's dead. She put something inside me. Get Bentley. Something inside me. It's killing me."

"You just sit there! Sit and breathe. I'm coming—"

The phone slipped from my numb fingers, falling to my lap. She kept talking. I was gone.

#

I knew the room from a thousand nightmares. Every scrap of peeling powder-blue wallpaper, the cheap twin beds, and the plastic toy chest with its broken lid—all marked in my mind as indelibly as a backhand slap.

"Dan," my brother whispered from his bed, "I think Dad's gonna kill us."

He was eight. I was twelve.

"I think that's what happened to Mom," Teddy whispered when I didn't answer him.

I was twelve years old, and I kept a butcher knife under my mattress. It lay there untouched, night after night, a sinister artifact that called my name in the dark.

"I know," I said, answering in two voices. Adult and child as one.

I lay on my back, small again, so very small, staring up at the ceiling.

"Teddy," I said, reciting the words from memory, "you know I'll always protect you, right? We're brothers. You can count on me."

That was the blackest lie I ever told, though I believed it at the time. Footsteps tromped up the stairs, rough and irregular, and my breath caught in my throat.

This isn't real, my mind screamed, *it's a memory, a nightmare, I'm not there anymore.*

Teddy whimpered and hid under the covers. I just watched the door. The knob jiggled and the door flew open, slamming against the wall. My father stood silhouetted in the doorway, a bear of a man with frazzled hair and a bloated gut.

"Why the fuck was this door locked?" he shouted. It wasn't locked. It couldn't have been. He'd gone on a rampage the summer before and drilled out every lock in the house, breaking half the knobs in the process. "There are no locked doors in this house! There are no secrets in this fucking house!"

He charged across the room, ripping the covers away from Teddy's bed, grabbing him by the scruff of the neck.

"What are you doing under there? Are you talking to the neighbors about me? Do you have a radio? Do you have a radio!"

In my father's world, radios were spies and electrical lines mocked him in the middle of the night. In my father's world, holding an eight-year-old by the neck while backhanding him hard enough to split his lip and loosen his teeth was rational behavior.

He's going to kill him, I remembered thinking. *He won't stop this time.*

I jumped from my bed and ran at him, throwing myself on his back. He flung me off like I was weightless, then turned and threw a punch. I lived the blossoming agony all over again, the cartilage in my nose crunching, breaking under his fist.

you're not really here you're not really here you're not really here

He went back to beating Teddy, turning his back on me, my brother's panicked cries drowning out my pain and painting my world blood red.

I reached under the mattress and pulled out the butcher knife.

27.

I writhed on a cold metal table, clawing my way up from the vision like a drowning man reaching for sunlight, naked and soaked in sweat. Flickers of candlelight danced in my vision. My sweat-drenched skin was marked in swirling white paint. Droning, sing-song chanting all around me.

"Hold him down!" a voice echoed, distorted and far away.

"We need to do something about his fever!"

"—working on it," a third voice snapped. "I don't understand the—"

Silence.

A clock ticked on the office wall, counting away meaningless minutes. I sat in a chair too big for me, looking up at a kindly man in a shabby suit on the other side of the desk. A wall of folders lay between us, each stuffed with a rumpled rainbow of papers and memos.

"—I don't understand," I said.

"It's a lot of legal mumbo-jumbo, but the important thing is that you aren't going to juvenile hall. After the hearing, and reviewing your assessments, the judge thinks you'd be better off in an environment, um, better suited to someone with your challenges. A place where you can get the help you need."

"I'm not the one who needs help!"

"Daniel," the man said, "come now. You stabbed your father seven times with a butcher knife. He lost a kidney and four feet of intestine. He nearly died."

"He should have. I was trying to kill him."

My father had looked so smug the day of the hearing, showing up with his hair slicked back and trousers pressed, wearing a suit I didn't even know he owned. He spun a hell of a story. In his version, he tried to stop me from beating Teddy, and I retaliated by stabbing him. I got the broken nose when he defended himself. What else could he do? The kid was nuts. When it was my turn to talk, I was enraged and scared and about as eloquent as your average twelve-year-old, with a public-aid lawyer who didn't know his ass from a hole in the ground. It didn't help that Teddy sided with my father. He saw which way the wind was blowing, and he was too afraid to stand against it. I never blamed him for that. Never once.

The lawyer talked like he was reading out of a travel brochure. "Once you complete your course of therapy, you'll spend some time in a halfway house, learning valuable life skills—"

"What about my brother?" I demanded. "I don't care about any of that. What about my brother?"

"What about him?" He looked puzzled. "He's back at home, with your father."

I was twelve years old, and I had just discovered the meaning of pain. Pain was knowing that you'd failed the people who needed you most. Knowing that they were suffering, you were powerless to save them, and it was all your fault.

"Do you see the trend here?" the lawyer asked, sending a jolt down my spine. I'd been sucked into the memory, reliving the past.

But the lawyer had never said that. In real life I'd gone berserk, demanding they let me go, let me save my brother, and I'd ended up hauled out in handcuffs.

"You ruin everything you touch," he said. "It's in your blood."

Outside the office window, a cloud passed over the sun. The sky turned gray, darkening fast, a storm on the horizon.

"What's going on here?" I said aloud, my young and old voices speaking in tandem.

The lawyer shrugged, standing up. "At least they took good care of you at the funny farm. And then that halfway house! Pity about what they did to you there, but you can't say you didn't deserve it."

You did *deserve it,* I told myself. *What you put Teddy through...you deserved everything that happened.*

The lawyer loomed over me, his body elongating, casting a wavering shadow as the sky outside went black.

"That's right," he said. "Your father was an insane, abusive alcoholic. His father was an insane, abusive alcoholic. With odds like that, how could you have ever thought you had a chance at a normal life? The poison is in your blood, Daniel. Under the circumstances, don't you think the fairest thing you can do for everyone is to just give up and die? Isn't it the right thing to do? It's the only way to break the cycle."

Spengler died because of me.

The lawyer's skin rippled, turning serpentine, a cruel shade of muddy green. "He did, you know. You tried to save him, and he suffered and died because of it. How many times has that happened? How many more times does it have to happen before you embrace the truth?"

I deserve to die, I thought, and the snake on the other side of the desk bobbed its head with gleeful approval.

#

Hands hauled me up into a world of light and pain. My skin burned, like lying under the spark-shower of an acetylene torch. Chanting voices filled my head, droning as I struggled and tried to see past the the blurred lights that scarred my vision.

"Damn it all," a woman shouted, "he's buckin' like a bronco! Get over here and help me!"

"We're losing him!"

Bony fingers touched lightly on my brow, another hand on my shoulder.

"Daniel," a voice whispered in my ear, a soothing sound in the maelstrom, "you have to fight. Remember what we taught you, son. Remember!"

I smelled books. Musty old books, well loved and dog-eared. That smell meant sanctuary to me. I was eighteen years old and learning what the word "home" meant for the first time.

"—might not believe it," Bentley said, standing behind the antique register at the Scrivener's Nook, "but I was a bit of a scrapper back in my day."

He threw some punches at the air, dancing on his feet like a prizefighter. I laughed, perched on a ladder, stocking a row of moldering hardcovers fresh from an estate sale. Corman trundled out of the back room, lugging a cardboard box, and nodded.

"It's true, kiddo. Of course, he's lucky I came along when I did. Damn biker nearly stomped him into a mud puddle. This was the seventies, remember. He's talking about a two-hundred-pound outlaw, not some suburban dad with his midlife-crisis Harley."

"I was," Bentley mused, "a bit outclassed. Still, I knew that when I threw the first blow. The ending was a foregone conclusion."

I looked over at him. "So why'd you start a fight if you knew you were going to lose?"

"Well, someone had to defend that girl's honor." Bentley paused, his smile fleeting. "I think Cormie will agree when I say this, Daniel. I've always felt that the mark of a man is his willingness to fight for his principles. It doesn't matter if you win or lose. It doesn't matter if you ever had a chance to win in the first place. Even if the deck is rigged and the game's against you, you keep fighting until the bitter end."

Corman chuckled, setting his box on a cluttered table. "We come into this world screaming, covered in blood and throwing punches. When all else is lost, it's not a bad strategy."

"Of course, we do most of our fighting at the ballot box and with strongly worded letters these days," Bentley said, "but it's not about violence; it's about doing what you can, whenever you can, to stand up for what you believe. You fight and you never, ever give up. That's what makes a man."

The memory shattered like a broken mirror, shards tumbling and clattering into a million glittering pieces, leaving me in darkness.

#

The serpent reared up before me, ten feet tall and twice as long now. Its cobra hood flared and its tail rattled, a hybrid monster out of a child's nightmares.

I looked up at it. Calm, now.

"I know what you are," I said.

"I am the manifestation of what lies within your corrupt heart," the serpent hissed, "the truth you fear to face."

I shook my head and smiled. "No. You're a cheap party trick."

The tail shook furiously. "I am your judgment, the mirror of your soul!"

"You're the venom Lauren Carmichael spewed into my stomach," I said, "the curse she left behind. You're trying to make me give up, to stop fighting so you can finish me off. Let me tell you something, you piece of shit. I didn't deserve what happened to me. No kid does. I spent years learning that. Sometimes I still forget, but it's going to take a better class of phantom than you to make me put a noose around my own neck."

The snake let out a rasping chuckle, swaying hypnotically from side to side.

"It doesn't matter," it said. "Your body is weak. Dying. I can finish you off myself."

I held up two fingers. "You made two big mistakes invading my mind."

"Oh? Do tell."

Walls rose up around us, flagstones forming under my feet. We faced one another in a shadowed cathedral. Thin fingers of sunlight streamed in through towering stained-glass windows.

"Number one—you pissed me off. Number two—the inside of my mind is a seriously fucked-up place, and I've got home court advantage."

The serpent glanced around, suddenly uncertain. I strolled to one of the windows. Like the others, it depicted a version of St. Patrick driving the snakes from Ireland. On this one, Patrick had a sword. I reached up and peeled it away from the image. The weapon took on depth and form in my hand.

I turned to face the serpent, brandishing a blade of stained glass in hues of ocean and bottle green.

"Let's dance, motherfucker."

28.

The serpent lunged with a furious roar. I dove left, hit the ground rolling, came up, and sliced into its flank. Black blood sprayed across the flagstones. Its tail whipped at me, rattling a staccato beat, ruffling my hair as I ducked underneath. I repaid the move with another wild slash, laying its tail open.

"You'll die here!" it shrieked, coming around again with its jaws wide enough to swallow me whole. "Die, die, di—"

I crouched and brought the sword up in one swift, brutal thrust. The glass blade punched through the serpent's lower jaw and jutted out the top of its head. Streams of black blood flooded its eyes as it screamed, its lacerated tail slamming the cathedral walls.

Light. Candlelight. Cold. Too many sensations, too many images flooded me at once, the mindscape torn away like ripping a painting from its frame.

I was awake.

Candles burned on the stainless-steel tables of a morgue. Red and white wax dripped down mirrored cabinets. I lay naked on a hospital gurney, sweating, skin covered in glyphs in flowing white paint. Unspeakable nausea seized my stomach and I rolled, the gurney tipping, sending me sprawling on all fours on the frigid tile floor.

My throat filled, something cutting off my air. Panic rose as my stomach heaved against the blockage. Pain tore through my esophagus. I clutched my neck, trying to force it up. Then I heard the frenzied hiss of a snake.

The head was the first thing to emerge. It whipped against my teeth and tongue, squeezing its way out between my lips. Then it slid free, launching out of my throat and spilling onto the floor, a swamp-green serpent nearly a foot long and covered in a sheen of bile and slime.

It darted away, slithering across the tile toward a floor drain, intent on escape. A machete came down with a jolting clang, slicing the snake in half and spattering the morgue floor with steaming black blood.

Mama Margaux held up her blade to the light and frowned. "Never seen that happen before."

I gasped for breath, panting, slowly coming back to my senses. I looked around the room. Bentley, Corman, and Jennifer stood around the morgue, staring at me with various looks of astonishment and relief.

"Hi guys," I said, my throat raw and raspy. "Can I... Get some clothes, maybe?"

Jennifer handed me my shirt. The sweat and smeared body paint made it cling to my skin. My muscles ached like I'd just run a marathon.

"Let's face it, sugar," Jennifer drawled, "I think we've all seen you naked one time or another."

"I hadn't," Margaux said as she wiped off her machete with a towel, then added with a mutter, "not that I'm complainin'."

They'd pulled out all the stops. A binding circle around the gurney, etched with Celtic runes, was Jennifer's style mixed with Corman's ritualistic sensibilities. Bentley's alchemy lab took up an entire run of shelves, pale steam still trickling from a neglected alembic, and the tracings on my hands were pure Haitian vodou. I only had one question.

"Why a morgue?" I finished getting dressed. A glimpse of my face and tangled hair in a stainless-steel reflection made me wince. I looked like ten miles of bad road.

"Closest place we could all get to, fast," Margaux said. "Antoine said he'd keep everyone out of our hair while we worked. That boy stood me up on our last date. He owes me."

"So do I," I said, getting to my feet. "I owe all of you. I wouldn't have survived without your help."

"Horsefeathers," Corman said, "you would have done the same for any of us. It's what we do."

"It's who we are," Bentley added.

My family of choice. I waved the four of them close. A morgue might be a weird place for a group hug, but it sure as hell felt good.

"They killed Spengler," I said. "I couldn't stop them. Tried my damnedest but—"

Corman shook his head. "We'll get some payback. Just tell us what we're up against, kiddo."

I gave them the rundown, sparing the grisly details of Spengler's murder. They got the gist of it.

"The Etruscan Box?" Bentley said. "He'd been chasing that old thing for years. A testament to the power of imagination and greed. The Box's refusal to open is the only interesting thing about it, but that hasn't stopped people from imagining all kinds of treasures just waiting to be found inside."

I shook my head. "There's something inside, but I don't think it's treasure. It felt sentient. Alien. Malevolent. Whatever is in that box, I think we're all better off if it stays in there."

"*Ti moun fwonte grandi devan Baron,*" Margaux said. "Some people just can't keep themselves out of the frying pan. Baron Samedi had one eye on Spengler since the day he was born. Give that boy a nuclear bomb, he would've tried to sell it."

Jennifer hopped up on a patch of open counter, her legs swinging. "These cowboys don't seem to understand how we do things around here. Spengler was one of ours. I don't rightly care what's in the box or why they took it, but Spengler was one of ours, and there's gotta be a reckonin' for that."

Nobody disagreed. A washbasin stood near the refrigerator racks, and I splashed handfuls of cold water across my face, trying to jump-start my exhausted brain. All the pieces of the puzzle were right in front of me. I just had to weave them together.

"Nicky's seer said Lauren Carmichael's been working on this for a long time," I told them. "Whatever the Box is hiding, it's big time, and she knows—or believes she knows—how to open it. She's not worried about consequences or who she steps on, either. Whatever's coming, it'll make everything else irrelevant."

"That sounds rather apocalyptic," Bentley said.

I nodded. "That's the impression I got, too. Let's look at what we know. Lauren Carmichael has the power to bind demons, to force them into slavery without any kind of bargain—"

"That's impossible." Jennifer cut me off. "There's always a price for a demon's service. Always."

"I thought so too, but I saw the proof. Caitlin's contract was a hundred percent one-sided. She was forced to sign it against her will."

"Caitlin?" Margaux said, and I caught the hard look in Bentley's eyes.

"You're on a first-name basis with it?" he asked, his voice tight.

"The succubus Lauren bound," I said, pushing ahead, "and subsequently gave to Artie Kaufman for safekeeping. We know why she did it: to enslave a detective named Holt and keep him in line. Holt was doing some dirty work for Carmichael-Sterling Nevada, and the demon was there to ensure his ongoing loyalty. Artie murdered Stacy Pankow, used a soul-trap on her, and forced Holt to help him cover it up."

"So Artie was working for Lauren?" Jennifer said.

"Only to babysit Cai—the succubus, and report on Holt. I get the impression that Artie was never in the inner circle and never would be. They just patted him on the head and fed him cookies to shut him up. Sheldon, Artie's brother, gave him a soul-trap but didn't seem to care that he botched the job. At the golf game, Meadow Brand said they didn't need Stacy's soul in the first place."

"Implying they needed other souls," Corman rumbled.

"I think that was why they needed Detective Holt," I said. "He made sure the case jackets on everyone they murdered ended up on his desk so he could stall the investigation, just like he did with Stacy Pankow. As long as he stayed happy and addicted, he was their get-out-of-jail-free card."

Bentley paced, thinking aloud. "The natural connection is the souls and the Box. One opens the other, somehow."

"They had almost everything they needed, just one—" I paused, grimacing as I remembered. "Damn it, we have to move. The guy they called Tony, he was going to claim the last soul they needed, and it was all set to go down tomorrow night. That doesn't give us a lot of time."

I frowned, catching the looks on their faces. "What?"

"Daniel," Bentley said, "you were unconscious for over sixteen hours. It *is* tomorrow."

#

Trying to organize a group of magicians was usually a battle akin to herding cats. When times were dire, though, we managed to get things done. Jennifer and Corman stayed behind to clean up the morgue, wiping away any sign we'd ever been there, while Margaux went to find her sometime-boyfriend and sweet-talk him into twenty minutes of unfettered Internet access. Before long, Bentley and I sat side by side at a pair of computer desks, alone in a dimly lit staff lounge. A Closed for Cleaning sign hung on the outside of the glass door.

I scoured Carmichael-Sterling's website while Bentley hit the online newspaper archives, trying to track down the mysterious Tony. Outside, the sun dripped behind the city skyline, dyeing the clouds blood orange.

"He talked about construction permits," I said, clicking furiously. "Maybe he's a contractor of some kind."

Bentley slipped a pair of silver-rimmed reading glasses from his vest pocket. "But highly placed. An architect, perhaps?"

Sifting through the archive of press releases, I struck gold.

"Not *an* architect," I said, "*the* architect. Tony Vance, golden boy of the Berlin neo-deco movement and sole designer of the Enclave Resort and Casino. The whole damn thing's his baby from the ground up."

Bentley looked over at me. "Curious. You made it sound like he wasn't an enthusiastic participant."

"He wasn't. Meadow Brand tore him a new one for dragging his heels on the soul-collection thing. When we fought at Spengler's place, he didn't even get involved. He just stood on the sidelines and watched. I'm hoping I might be able to talk some sense into the guy, get him to come over to our side."

"It wouldn't hurt. Oh. Oh dear."

I peered over his shoulder to get a look at the screen. "What is it?"

"Two months ago, Lauren Carmichael's husband and son were murdered in a home invasion. She was conveniently working late that night. Sheldon Kaufman's sister died two weeks later, casualty of a convenience store robbery. Just a day after that, Meadow Brand's father was stabbed to death in what's being reported as a mugging gone wrong."

Why don't you just kill your wife? Sheldon had asked Tony back at the golf course.

Because I don't love my wife.

"Christ," I breathed. "It's not just any souls they need. Family members. Blood relations, maybe. Someone they have a personal bond with."

"An intimate sacrifice," Bentley said.

It's Amber, Tony had said. *It has to be Amber—she's the only one who qualifies.*

"A sacrifice to the Box. Or just to the lock that seals it shut. All right, see if you can dig up a home address for Tony Vance. I'm going to find out who Amber is. We've got to get to her before he does."

My head swirled with maybes. Maybe Tony would lose his nerve. Maybe he'd drag his heels just a little longer. Maybe he'd show his hand too soon, and Amber would fight him off or get away from him in time. There was still a chance.

I love social media and the people who are careless with it. Tony had an open Facebook profile. I rummaged through his pictures and posts, looking for a clue. Then I found one, and wished I hadn't.

"Bentley."

"Did you find her?" he asked, peering over his bifocals.

"Amber's his daughter, Bentley. She's eight years old."

29.

I paced a hole in the staff lounge's cheap blue carpet, trying to focus. We needed Tony Vance's home address, and fast. While Bentley searched the net, coming up empty, I contemplated a dozen angles and discarded them all. My watch read a quarter after seven; even if I could sweet-talk somebody at the company office into giving me what I needed, there wouldn't be anyone there at this hour to answer the phone. Then I looked back to my screen, still showing Tony's profile, and snapped my fingers.

The last picture in the album was a shot of little Amber, cherub-cheeked and triumphant, at an elementary school gymnastics competition. A brightly painted sign in the background told me what I needed to know.

"Bentley, look up an address for Springlake Montessori."

"She won't be at school. It's far too late—"

"No," I said, sitting down beside him. "I just need to know where it is. The founders of Carmichael-Sterling Nevada, Lauren and her inner circle, are all transplants from the company's Seattle office. They bought Sheldon Kaufman a house—that's how I connected the Kaufmans with Carmichael-Sterling in the first place. I'm betting everybody got one. I can get a list of all of the company's properties from the Clark County assessor's office, but not who lives there."

Bentley nodded, typing away. "And Tony Vance's home will probably be the property nearest his daughter's school."

"Exactly. It's the best lead we're going to get."

"What are you going to do?" he said, furrowing his brow.

"Stop him. That girl isn't dying tonight. Not on my watch."

Ten minutes later we had an address. I jotted it down on a scrap of paper and pushed my chair back.

"I need you to round up whoever you can," I told Bentley, "and get over to Spengler's house. Someone's going to come looking for him sooner or later, and the cops won't be far behind. Do a locust job."

A locust job was the magician's equivalent of erasing the porn from your dead buddy's hard drive before his mom sees it. They'd scour Spengler's house for any enchanted relics, journals, grimoires, and occult ciphers, anything that could raise a citizen's eyebrow. It was never hard to enlist folks for that kind of work—and not just to protect our shared secrets. In a locust job, you keep what you take.

I drove to the address I hoped was Tony Vance's house. I didn't pray, as a rule. If there was a God, we weren't on speaking terms, and I didn't think either of us cared what the other had to say. Still, pushing the pedal hard enough to make the engine whine, streetlights strobing across the dirty windshield, I was tempted. Then I remembered God's track record when it comes to helping out little kids.

I was the only person fighting for Amber Vance's life tonight. Succeed or fail, what happened was on my shoulders
alone.

#

Judging from the size of Tony's house, being Lauren
Carmichael's lackey paid well. A low brick wall, more orna-
mental than protective, encircled his estate and its emerald
green lawn. I ditched my car on a side street and came in
from the back, hopping the wall and staying low as I skirted
a playground. A swing dangled from rusty chains, listlessly
rocking in the wake of a chill night breeze.

I peered into the garage. A new Mercedes sat on the other side of a small window, but the garage was big enough
for two cars. No way to tell if Tony was home or not.
Worse, since he'd sat out the fight at Spengler's place, I had
no idea what he was capable of. I'd just have to improvise.

A place this nice would have an alarm system on the
front door, especially if Tony was hiding some of Lauren's
dirty little secrets inside. I wasn't prepared to deal with that
kind of security. My best bet was the door connecting the
attached garage to the rest of the house. Most people don't
think to alarm those, and even fewer are in the habit of
locking up when they come and go because they think their
rolling garage door can keep them safe. Bad assumption.

I scavenged a fist-sized rock from the yard, one that came
to a blunt point, and wrapped my coat around it to help
muffle the noise. A few firm taps broke out a corner of the
garage window. I paused, listening for the whine of an
alarm. Nothing stirred but the wind. A few minutes later,
methodically busting out the glass and clearing the broken

window one shard at a time, I'd made an opening big enough to climb through.

I slipped through the window and onto the garage floor, crouching in the puddle of broken glass. Ears perked, I crept to the inside door and gave the knob a slow turn. Bingo. Light streamed from a silver wall sconce in the inside hallway, casting a warm glow against the blue Victorian wallpaper.

Drifting from room to room like a ghost, I searched for signs of life. The plan was simple. If I found Amber first, I'd get her to safety any way I could and deal with the consequences later. If I found Tony first...well, I still hoped I could reason with him. He'd trudged along with the rest of the group, showing none of their enthusiasm or their bloodthirstiness, to the point that I wondered if Lauren had some kind of leverage over him. If I could turn him around, he'd be our best chance at shutting this whole thing down.

I jiggled a doorknob in my hand. It was firmly locked. Odd, when the rest of the house lay wide open. Curious, I crouched and dug my lockpick case out of my pocket. The antique tumblers rolled over like a dog doing tricks. I let myself in. Shelves, drafting tables, and cluttered cubbyholes lined the walls of the octagonal study beyond the door, lit by a frosted-glass ceiling globe. The centerpiece of the room stood upon a wooden table, a scale model of the Enclave some four feet tall and built to exacting precision.

I circled the model warily. Something about the scalloping spear of its tower, the reproduction so pristine I could see my warped reflection in the curve of its windows, set my teeth on edge. Little smiling people, refugees from a model train set, streamed into the black maw of the casino's front doors. None were walking back out.

A chrome thermos sat on the edge of a messy desk next to a half-finished mug of coffee. I touched the side of the mug. Still warm. If Tony and Amber were both gone, I needed to figure out where he'd taken her. Rummaging through the documents and clutter, leafing through bid bonds, construction reports, and tattered memos, my sense of uneasiness grew. I was no architect, but even I could see something was inherently wrong with the tacked-up blueprints. Stairwells leading to nowhere. Curving halls doubling back on themselves. Most of the plans were perfectly mundane, but the more I looked, the more the little details stood out, the incongruities that had no reason to exist.

The corner of a book poked out from under a stack of drafts. The title caught my eye: *Torments of the Inquisition.* Most of the book was a dry history, the pages as pristine as the day they were printed. A fat chapter on torture methods though, illustrated with woodcuts and diagrams, had more highlights and margin notations than a college calculus textbook.

"Reproduce w/16v electric motor, connect to pneumatic tube system."

"Plexiglas again—Meadow always wants Plexiglas."

"Hold design until L. does final work-up of the Throne. Still need de Rais' help to finish the connecting patterns."

Tucked in next to the depiction of a ferocious, spike-lined chair for heretics was a sketch on engineer's graph paper. Tony's twenty-first-century version was lined with hypodermic needles and connected, at the back, to a cluster of rubber hoses. Flowery script on a yellow sticky note read, "Love the design, but can we make the whole thing transparent? -M."

I looked back at the scale model of the Enclave.

What the hell are you people building? I thought, rummaging through Tony's cubbyholes and shelves. I grabbed anything that looked relevant. Blueprint scraps, notes, their little catalog of torture, stacking it all up to take with me. Then I tugged open a drawer, and everything went wrong.

It felt like that sickening stomach lurch as your car slides toward a collision, when you pump the brakes even though you know nothing is going to stop the impact. The drawer pulled out stiffly, too stiffly, and I looked down and saw the cord on the inside of the empty wooden nook just a second too late.

The cord sprang free, slithering back into the wall. The study door slammed closed. I ran over and yanked on the knob, but a hydraulic arm at the top of the doorframe kept it wedged firmly shut. Tony's mechanical genius extended to his own home: there were worse ways to trap a would-be thief. Taking a few steps back, getting ready to throw my weight at the door, I froze. From behind me came a soft, relentless hissing.

I had snakes on the brain after Lauren's death-curse, but the pungent scent rising in the room alerted me to a more dangerous threat.

Gas!

The lid of Tony's thermos sat slightly open and off-center. I pulled at the flask and found it bolted to the table, nothing but a piece of clever camouflage. I lifted the lid to reveal a brass-tipped nozzle connected to a tube. It looked like he'd rigged an extension of the house's natural gas line to pipe into the study. Inhaling natural gas isn't fatal right away, but I needed to find a way out before the sheer amount of it choked the breathable air out of the sealed room.

Shick, echoed a faint but insistent sound. *Shick*. A grating rasp every ten seconds or so, like the hammer of a gun falling on an empty chamber.

Or the striker on a spark ignition, I realized, horror dawning as the entirety of the design became clear. Tony Vance was serious about protecting Carmichael-Sterling's secrets. Serious enough to destroy his entire life's work with a raging inferno, along with anyone locked in the room when his trap went off.

Shick.

30.

I had to find that striker. I started to tear the room apart, trying to find the source of the sound, pulling out drawers and yanking down shelves, a whirlwind of paper around me as—

Shick.

I looked up. Inside the frosted globe on the ceiling, a black shadow slid sharply forward, the glass softly rattling. I climbed up on the table, balanced precariously next to the casino model, and strained toward it on my tiptoes. My fingertips slid feebly off the bottom curve of the glass. It was just too far to reach.

One wing of the Enclave model, linked to the spear-like tower, sported a roof with a gentle slope. I put one experimental foot on it, adding a little weight. The model quivered but didn't collapse. Delicately, moving as fast as I dared, I settled both feet on the tiny rooftop and gained a few inches of height. I held my breath as I unscrewed the frosted-glass sphere.

The sphere came free. It slipped from my strained fingers and plummeted, smashing and sending shards of snowy glass skidding across the floor. A naked light bulb glared in my eyes as I studied the mechanism mounted beside it. It was simple, a chunk of flint mounted on a short iron rail across from a striking pad that resembled a thumb-sized match head. A timer rattled as the flint pulled back again to strike, riding the rail like the sole passenger on a roller coaster to hell.

I grabbed the rail, feeling the mechanism jerk in my hand, just as the model roof caved in with a plastic crunch. Off balance, I shoved against the model, tipping the entire table and leaving me dangling one-handed with my feet kicking over empty space. If I let go of the rail, if I let the flint strike one more time, I was a dead man.

With the muscles of my left arm burning for relief, I pulled myself up then dropped down hard, trying to use my weight to break the rail free. The mechanism bucked under my hand. Gears pinched my palm and threatened my failing grip. Seconds from letting go, I lifted myself up one more time and dropped. The rail came with me, breaking away from the device. It landed in the model's crumpled remains as we both fell down.

The smell of gas was overpowering now. I smeared tears from my eyes and rubbed my aching arm as I looked for a way out. With the trap disarmed, I was still far from safe. One spark, no matter how tiny, and this room would turn into a blast furnace. The hydraulic arm holding the door shut had regular, unshielded screws, but I didn't have a screwdriver and ramming metal objects together didn't seem like a smart move right now.

The fallen model of the Enclave gave me an idea. I crouched over the section I'd stood on, the plastic roof caved in, and grabbed hold of a glossy wedge. It broke free in my hand, an improvised shiv with a killing edge. I gently slid the triangle of plastic against the first screw's head, gripping it with both hands as I gave it a careful turn. The plastic bent but didn't break. Gradually, slowly, the screw swiveled and rose from its housing.

Three more screws and it was done. I took hold of the arm with a feather-light grip and pulled it away from the door. I held my breath. The study door whined on its hinges as it drifted open a crack.

I left the papers behind. Out in the hallway, my eyes and throat burning, every instinct screamed at me to run. With the gas flooding free it wouldn't take much to engulf the entire house in a screaming fireball. Still, I couldn't leave yet. Tony and Amber were gone. If I hoped for the slightest chance of saving the girl, I had to find out where he'd taken her.

The bedrooms lay empty, lived in but tidy. A lump tightened in my throat as I poked my head into Amber's room, a swirl of white and pink. A well-loved teddy bear nestled between fluffy pillows. *Hang on, kid,* I thought, *I'm coming.* Down in the kitchen, a light flashed on the base of a wireless phone. One new message. I pressed the play button.

"Hey hon," said a tired-sounding woman, "it's me. I'm stuck at JFK for another two hours. Worst airport, swear to God. Mom and Dad said they'd pick Amber up from school so, as promised, you have a nice long weekend all to yourself. No wild parties, young man, and by parties I mean working. Civilization will survive if the world's best architect takes a couple of days off, I promise."

The rest of the words drifted past me like nonsensical syllables, blocked out as I scoured the drawers and cabinets looking for a clue. It was the perfect setup. With Amber staying at her grandparents' house, Tony could strike at his leisure and have plenty of time to cover his tracks. I just hoped he planned to do it late tonight, when everyone would be asleep.

The kitchen's rummage drawer by the phone yielded a spiral-bound notebook filled with names, addresses, and phone numbers. On the first page, one neatly penned entry read "Mom & Dad." Whose parents, though? Tony's or his wife's? I picked up the kitchen phone and dialed from there, so they'd see a familiar name on the caller ID.

It rang once, twice, three times, each ring squeezing the breath from my lungs in an invisible fist. Come on, come on, pick up...

"Jill?" an elderly woman said, answering the phone on the fifth ring. A television blared in the background, a laugh track underscoring a drum riff.

"No ma'am," I said, putting on a faint Southern drawl. "This is Officer Crosby with the police department. Now, don't get alarmed, everything's fine, but we're responding to a break-in at this residence and we're just calling to find the property owner. I understand you're Jill Vance's mother, is that correct?"

"That's right," she said, her voice rising. "Oh, oh my, is everything all right? Is Tony there? Was he hurt?"

"No, no, we think it was just some local kids. They got scared off by the alarm. We're trying to get ahold of Tony. Now, according to our records, there's a little girl named Amber who lives at this residence. We're concerned because she isn't here. Do you know if she would have come straight home after school?"

"Oh, bless your heart for asking," the woman said. "She's staying with her grandfather and me for the weekend. She's sitting on the couch right next to me, safe and sound."

My heart soared. *I'm not too late. I'm not too late.* I tore the page out of the address book, sticking it in my pocket.

"Well, that's great," I said. "You just make sure to lock your doors and windows tight tonight. Thank you, ma'am."

I hung up, tossed the phone to the counter, and opened the sliding glass door leading to the back deck. I froze with my hand on the latch. I couldn't leave the place like this, flooding with gas and ready to blow. Sooner or later somebody would come around, maybe a neighbor or another innocent bystander, and get a lethal surprise.

Out on the deck, next to a high-end grill, I scavenged a couple of bottles of lighter fluid from a cardboard box. Good enough. I laid a trail from the hallway, through the kitchen and outside, snaking it along the grass until the final bottle gave its last sputtering spurt. The trail blazed to life with a touch of my lighter and streaked through the grass toward the house like a bullet from hell.

I didn't stay for the fireworks. I'd already lost too much time. The sky flashed yellow at my back as I got into my car. House windows shattered and doors blew out with an eardrum-pounding explosion. A car alarm went off, howling in the dark. I drove away.

I hit the highway doing eighty, swerving up the ramp and redlining the engine the second I had a straight shot of clear road. I didn't have a plan, just a mission. Priority one was grabbing Amber and stashing her someplace safe until I had a word with her father. He'd switch sides or I'd put him in the ground. Either way, he wasn't laying a hand on that girl, not while I was still breathing.

#

Amber's grandparents lived in a tract house on the outskirts of Vegas, a sleepy little neighborhood where retirees gathered to soak up the sun. Inside lights warmed the flimsy white curtains in the living-room window, and the faint flicker of a television set filled me with hope as I ran up the driveway. I pressed the doorbell, pressed it again, then hammered the heel of my hand on the door. I didn't know what I'd tell them. I wasn't thinking that far ahead.

Nobody answered. I jogged around to the back of the house, to the kitchen door, and hammered on that one too.

They're old, I told myself. *Maybe they can't hear you, or they've got the television up too loud.* I fished out my picks and went to work on the lock. If I stumbled in on them, I'd just have to keep them from calling the cops until I explained myself.

Your son-in-law is on his way over. He's going to murder your granddaughter unless I can talk him out of it. Yeah, they'll believe that.

The door opened with a faint squeal, drowned out by the television blaring in the next room. An audience went into hysterics as David Letterman riffed on the week's news. I crept across the yellowed linoleum, ears perked, edging toward the open doorway. A tin of cocoa mix sat beside a still-wet spoon. A trail of spilled powder dusted the countertop.

I rounded the corner and found Amber's grandparents. Her grandfather slumped on the sofa, his head lolling over the armrest and his arms and legs sprawled at haphazard angles. Her grandmother lay on the carpet between the sofa and the coffee table, unmoving.

I ran over to them, feeling for a pulse. They were both alive, their breathing shallow, but out cold as I snapped my fingers next to their ears and shook their shoulders. A porcelain cup lay on its side, inches from the grandmother's outstretched fingers. Spilled cocoa stained the shag carpet. Another cup sat on the end table, half-finished and still warm. I picked it up and gave it a sniff. Chocolate, but something underneath, concealed by the strong scent. Something chemical.

He drugged them, I thought, picturing it my mind. Tony came by for a visit, offered to make hot chocolate for everyone, then went into the kitchen alone to add a little something special to the drinks. As soon as the narcotics kicked in he'd have the house under his total control, which meant—

No!

"Amber!" I shouted as I ran through the house, slamming open doors, not stopping to think or even breathe. "Amber? I'm a friend of your mom's! If you're hiding, come out, okay? *Amber!*"

I flung open the bathroom door at the end of the hall.

Amber lay face-down at the bottom of the bathtub. Her golden hair spread out in the water like streamers, like tiny fingers reaching for help that never came.

31.

Water spots smeared the wallpaper. Puddles pooled on the cold tile floor. Even drugged, she'd fought him. I plunged my arms into the lukewarm water and hauled her out. Water drenched my clothes, but I couldn't feel it, couldn't even think. I laid her out on the floor, on her back. Her limp hand slapped against the tile. No pulse. I felt her blue lips, her clammy skin, frantic. I'd taken a CPR class years ago, but everything I'd learned was just a mishmash of half-remembered facts. I tried compressions, my hands engulfing her tiny chest as I pressed down against her rib cage, counting, breathing into her lifeless mouth. I knew even before I started that it was a lost cause.

I caressed the little girl's cheek.

"I'm so sorry," I whispered, and left her dead on the bathroom floor.

I shut the door and stood in the hallway, feeling the world quietly fall apart. I took a slow, deep breath.

"*Fuck!*" I screamed, slamming my fist into the wall. A mirror hung at the end of the hallway. I tore it down, threw it to the carpet, and stomped it again and again, glass shattering under my heel, just for the sake of breaking something.

Monsters are real. I'd known that since I was a child. Every day people abuse, hurt, and kill each other for the pettiest of reasons. Somebody gets blown away for a pair of shoes or a new iPod and I just shrug. But Tony Vance murdered his own daughter. He took an innocent eight-year-old girl, drowned her in a bathtub, and sucked out her soul. For what? What could possibly justify that kind of evil? What reward was worth a ticket price that steep?

Lauren Carmichael and her inner circle had to be stopped. Tonight, though, I only had one name on my list. Only one face filled my mind's eye as I walked out of that house of horrors with ice water flooding my veins. Tony Vance was going to answer for what he'd done. Not to the cops, not to God.

He was going to answer to me.

\#

The lights of the Vegas Strip blazed. Any other night they would have put a smile on my face. Tonight, I only had one destination. One target. I concentrated on the slow-moving traffic, my focus sharp as a diamond scalpel.

I knew Tony, or at least I thought I did. He'd possessed just enough humanity to resist joining the others in their bloodthirsty fun, but not enough to walk away. He'd be feeling it now, in the aftermath of the kill. Feeling the weight. Where does an award-winning architect go to reflect and be alone after murdering his daughter? I wasn't certain, but I had a pretty good hunch.

The skeleton of the Enclave stood at the far south end of Las Vegas Boulevard, a mammoth spire of girders and rebar surrounded by a chain link barricade. A cheerful painting plastered to the fence showed an artist's rendition of the finished resort, standing proud under a blue sky as an eager father, his daughter riding on his shoulders, pointed the way to the front doors.

"A New Adventure. A New Las Vegas. The Enclave. Coming Soon."

A construction gate hung open, an open padlock dangling lazily from a length of chain. Next to the foreman's trailer, in a patch of asphalt littered with bundled rebar and pyramids of steel girders, a black Lexus sat empty. I parked behind it. I strode across the construction site, not bothering to mask my footsteps. I wanted Tony to know I was coming for him.

The open cage of a temporary elevator waited for me, lit by a dangling bulb. The cage whirred as it jerked to life at the press of a button, lurching upward, the ground falling away. Ten stories up, twenty, thirty, the traffic on the Strip just a smear of yellow light below. A gust of wind rattled the cage. Gears clanked in the dark.

The elevator ground to a halt on the thirty-sixth floor. End of the line.

Girders speared the open sky. A chill breeze ruffled my hair as I stepped onto bare concrete, the floor marked with splats of white spray-paint—arrows and lines in the secret language of engineers. Fresh barricades of drywall marked the odd room or hallway, but most of the floor was a blank slate waiting to be filled in. A scattering of tools lay out on gallon drums and makeshift sawhorse tables, waiting for tomorrow's shift.

I found Tony at the tower's edge, staring out over the Vegas night. He clutched a fat bottle in his hand, leaning with his other palm pressed against a standing girder.

"I knew you'd find me," he said, not turning around.

I stood about five feet back, a ghost in the shadows. I didn't say anything. I didn't have the words.

"I must have showed up maybe three minutes after you called Jill's folks," he said. "They told me about the break-in. Then they said you'd asked about Amber, and I knew it was you. I just knew. You never would have made it in time, if that's any consolation."

I watched him. Motionless. Something ugly and black burned in the pit of my stomach, like a monster pacing in a thin-barred cage.

"If you're looking for the soul-trap, you're too late. Already gave it to Lauren." He looked at the bottle in his hand, shook his head, and tossed back a swig. "She handed me this. Veuve Clicquot Yellow Label. Don't get me wrong, it's a good fuckin' champagne, thirty-five hundred a bottle, but...yeah, that's our Lauren. It came wrapped with a little bow. Good dog. Here's your bone."

I found my voice.

"Why did you do it?"

He turned to face me. Tears glistened on his cheeks.

"The lockmaker," he said, "was clever. You need five souls to open the Box. Five sacrifices. The trick is, they have to be someone you love. Someone you truly, genuinely love. We found a loophole, though. One person doesn't have to take all that pain. We split it up between the four of us."

He choked up for a second. I waited. Patient.

"Let me tell you a story about Lauren Carmichael," he said. "Maybe twenty years ago, she starts hunting for the

Box. She knew the cost. So what does she do? She goes out and starts dating. Finds the man of her dreams. Raises a happy, healthy son. Genuinely loved them. Devoted wife, loving mom. All the while, all those years, knowing that one day she'd butcher them both to get what she wants. That's just the kind of person she is. How can you fight someone like that?"

I took a step toward him.

"Tell me why."

Tony shook his head. "Do you believe that the end justifies the means?"

"Depends on the end."

"Hypothetical question." He sucked down another pull from the bottle. "A time traveler tells you that a random stranger is destined to start World War III. Boom, nukes drop, end of the human race. He puts a gun in your hand and says the only way to stop it is to shoot the poor bastard dead. What do you do?"

"You murdered your daughter," I said, my voice flat. "Don't waste my time with—"

He waved a hand, interrupting me. "Let's expand it. Let's say the only way to stop the bombs is to wipe out a classroom full of kindergartners. Thirty rosy-cheeked little cherubs against the survival of everyone on Earth. Do you do it? I mean, you'd be immoral not to do it, wouldn't you?"

"Real life is never that simple." I clenched my fists. "There's always another way. Another choice. A better choice than some stupid, made-up 'damned if you do, damned if you don't' mind game."

"You think so?" Tony asked, waggling the champagne bottle. "See, you don't get it. You don't understand what's happening here. The world's dying, Faust. We're killing each other, killing the planet, and it won't stop until the human race wipes itself out or somebody makes it stop. That's Lauren's plan. We're going to save humanity from itself. We're going to make things right. See, we're the good guys. You're the bad guy."

"You murdered your daughter," I said. "You drowned her in a bathtub—"

"*I made hard decisions!*" he roared. He squeezed his eyes shut, shaking his head. When he spoke again, his voice was faint. Broken. "The things we've done, Faust. Christ, the things we're going to do. If you knew the entire plan, the scope of it, you'd never sleep again. It's all for the greater good, though. When our work is done, we'll be heroes. Legends. We're going to save the world."

He offered me the bottle. I just stared at him and imagined what my fingers might feel like clenched around his throat. He shrugged and drank some more.

"It's only right," he said. "All the sacrifice we're demanding of others, how could I not bear part of the pain? What I did tonight...it was monstrous. I know that. Unforgivable. But it was necessary."

"And what happens when Amber's grandparents wake up? Do you really think you're going to get away with this?"

"They're in a Rohypnol dreamland. Good chance of memory loss. Might not even remember I was there. If they do, well, worst-case scenario is I get picked up for questioning. New moon's in two days. After that, nothing matters. That's why we had Holt running interference for us with the police. We didn't need to bury the murder investigations forever. We just needed to stall them until our work is done."

Tony leaned his head back and tilted the champagne bottle, draining the last drops like it was a can of cheap beer. He wiped the back of his hand across his mouth.

"You don't get it," he said. "You can't stop Lauren Carmichael. Anything you might do, anything you might throw at her, she already prepared for years ago. Back in college, she went on this expedition to India. Came back with a plan to save the world."

I remembered what Nicky's fear-deranged seer had babbled, right before the gunshot. *She went to India. She went to India, but it wasn't her who came back.*

"She's got wheels turning inside wheels," Tony said, "and everything's a part of her master plan. Anything that doesn't fit, she annihilates. You can't beat her."

"You're forgetting something," I told him.

"Yeah?"

"She already tried to kill me once. I'm still standing."

Tony sighed, leaning against a standing girder. A gust of wind rippled through the skeletal tower. A car horn blared far below, somewhere in the neon mists.

He looked at me. "You're not gonna be reasonable about this, are you?"

"I'm feeling pretty unreasonable tonight."

"We can make you rich," he said. "Power, sex, drugs, anything you want, name it. All you have to do is stay out of our way. Easiest job you've ever had."

"Here's my counteroffer. You go to the cops, confess to killing your daughter, and ride the consequences."

"You know that's not gonna happen."

I shrugged. "You won't like the alternative."

"Huh," Tony said, and then he threw the bottle at me.

I turned my shoulder and it bounced off, hit the concrete, and shattered. The distraction bought him the second he needed to rush for a plank set up between a pair of sawhorses. His flailing arm knocked aside an abandoned hard hat, and he snatched up a circular saw.

He turned to face me, clutching the cordless saw in his hands like a battle-ax. The machine whined to life, the blade's teeth spinning into a lethal blur, and he moved in for the kill.

32.

Tony charged at me, swinging the screaming saw with long, heavy sweeps. I jumped back once, twice, looking for something to give me an edge. A toolbox, heavy and pitted with age, sat in the shadow of a stack of drywall. I dodged to the right and went for it. The second I did, I knew I'd misjudged the distance. Tony lunged and the saw blade glanced against my forearm, chewing fabric and skin and spattering his face with my blood.

With my teeth gritted against the sudden, searing pain I stumbled out of his reach, sweeping up the heavy toolbox by the handle. I turned just as he made another charge; then I brought up the box and slammed it against the blade. White-hot sparks flew, and the saw screamed. The recoil sent Tony staggering back a step. Before he could recover I ran in swinging and smashed the toolbox against the side of his head.

He reeled back. The saw flew from his grip and skidded across the bare concrete. He teetered toward the building's edge. His face was a bloody mask of terror as he went over the side and caught the ledge at the last second. He dangled from the tower's lip, his legs kicking helplessly.

I dropped the toolbox. Crimson rivulets ran down my arm to the fingertips, the pain almost blinding. I gathered together the torn fabric as best I could and pressed it to the cut. It wasn't that deep—he hadn't sliced into muscle or bone—but it bled like a slaughtered sheep.

"Help," Tony gasped. He clung to the side of the building, one hand and one forearm upon the ledge. "Please, gimme your hand, pull me up."

I stood over him, watching, but all I could see now was a little girl dead in a bathtub.

"I'll turn myself in!" he cried, slowly losing his grip. "C'mon, man! I swear it. You can walk me right to the cops! I'll tell them everything! I'll expose Lauren!"

"That offer expired," I told him.

His forearm slipped. He caught the ledge with his hand. He looked up at me, eyes wet with tears, pleading.

"Please," he begged, "c'mon, you know I'm worth more alive than dead. I can help you! I can help you! Please, please, I don't wanna die, I don't wanna fucking die—"

I felt strangely calm. I was realizing something about myself, and I felt okay with it.

"You were right about one thing," I said softly. "See, I fooled myself. Thought I was some crusading hero for a while there. But that's not who I am at all, is it?"

Tony looked up at me, mouth agape. His fingers, white from the pressure, began to slip.

"I'm the bad guy," I told him, and kicked his fingers away.

Tony screamed as he fell. I stood at the Enclave's edge and watched him go. His flailing arms waved the way down to the pavement. Just another long goodbye.

I found a couple of dirty rags among the construction equipment and knotted them around my forearm. They kept the bleeding under control. The elevator seemed slower doing down than it had going up. The sky felt colder. I got off on the ground floor, stepped around the broken remains of Tony Vance, and got into my car.

I didn't move for a while. It wasn't that I felt bad about killing him. I didn't feel bad at all. That's what scared me.

I took out my phone. Caitlin answered on the third ring.

"Yes?"

"Can I come over?" I asked, then listened to the sound of her breath as she made up her mind.

"Yes."

#

I didn't have far to travel. The address she gave me was just a few blocks up the Strip, a penthouse apartment in the Taipei Tower. I ignored the looks I got in the lobby, trudging across a chrysanthemum-patterned carpet as red as the tattered rags on my arm. A sharp-eyed man in a black suit made a beeline for me, and I braced for an argument.

"Sir—" he started to say.

"I know, I'm bringing down real estate values. Don't worry, I'm just passing through."

"Exactly, sir," he said, gesturing toward an elevator bank down a short hallway. "Miss Brody is expecting you. You'll want to take the express elevator up to fifty-six. It's already unlocked and keyed for you."

She stood in her doorway at the top of the world, dressed in a pencil skirt and a fluffy gray sweater that fell

off one pale shoulder. I stood in front of her like a suppli-
cant at the temple gate, looking for something to say.

"I think I'm broken," I told her.

"I'll open a bottle of wine," she said and took me by the
hand.

Caitlin marked her territory with decor from an '80s music video. Track lighting cast spotlights across hardwood
floors and museum-white walls, with fixtures in chrome
and stainless steel. She sat me down in a plush black leather
sofa under the watchful eye of a Nagel painting as she
slipped into the kitchen. She came back with a bottle of
merlot and two glasses.

"I killed a man tonight," I said while she poured.

She offered me a glass. "I'm sure he had it coming."

"I'm serious."

"And I'm a demon," she said, leaning back on the sofa
and crossing her legs. She regarded me with eyes the color
of molten copper. One blink and they were back to their
normal green. "Don't come to me looking for absolution. I
won't give it to you. What's really got you upset?"

"Yesterday, these people murdered a friend of mine,
right in front of me. He was a nice guy, but he had something they wanted, so they tortured him and they killed
him. Tonight, this guy Tony...he drowned his daughter.
Drowned her and sucked the soul out of her body. She was
only eight years old. I asked him why he did it. He said I
had it all wrong, that they're the good guys. They're trying
to save the world, he told me."

"Everyone," Caitlin said, cradling her wine glass, "is the
hero of his own story. That goes double for fanatics. Some
of the greatest horrors in history were perpetrated by people who insisted, all the way to damnation's door, that they

fought on the side of the angels. I hope you didn't think you could reason with him."

I sipped the wine. It had a strong, musky scent, peppery and ripe. "At first? Yeah. I kinda did."

"How'd that work out for you?"

"Badly."

Caitlin got up and walked over to her stereo, a sleek Bose perched on a glass table. Soft synthesizer strains rose up as she returned to the couch. It sounded like a Duran Duran song.

"There are two answers to evil," she said. "The first is to justify it. The evil that you do is for a good cause, you'll be validated in the end, it needed to be done, etcetera, etcetera. Of course, once you start walking that road, it's all downhill. I'm sure this Tony person didn't start by drowning children. You have to work your way up to that kind of atrocity."

"And the second answer?"

"You own it. Be truthful and accept your own nature."

I leaned back, a line from Shakespeare crossing my mind.

"'It must not be denied that I am a plain-dealing villain,'" I quoted.

Caitlin beamed. "You know the Bard! 'If I had my mouth, I would bite; if I had my liberty, I would do my liking. In the meantime, let me be that I am, and seek not to alter me.'"

"I never would," I said on an impulse, regretting my words as her smile faded.

"Pretty words I've heard before. Always empty in the end. Daniel, why did you call me tonight? Of all the places you could have sought shelter, why here?"

I hadn't figured that out myself. Only that calling her was the first impulse I had, that her voice was the first I wanted to hear.

"I wanted to see you," I said.

She rose, cradling her glass as she slowly paced the floor, looking up to the ceiling.

"I told you at the restaurant," she said, "it doesn't work. We can't be...anything. I shouldn't even be talking to you."

"I don't see why."

She whirled to face me, suddenly furious, her eyes blazing copper. "And I don't see why you don't run! Why you don't lay awake in dread of the ruin I could bring upon you and everyone you hold dear! I could use my magic on you. Bind you to me, reduce you to a mindless slave. I could do it right now and you couldn't stop me. I could do it *right now.*"

The smell of sulfur and jasmine filled the room. I sat very, very still.

"I've done it to other humans," she said, seething with rage. "For the rest of your days, you wouldn't have a single thought in your head that I didn't put there, and you'd *love* it. You'd *thank* me for it. You'd be anything I wanted, and you'd never betray me and you'd never, ever leave!"

I heard the pain on the edge of her anger. I knew that song by heart.

I set my glass on the end table and stood up. She watched me, her hands hooked into claws and her fingernails gleaming like razors, shuddering as if she could barely restrain herself from tearing me apart.

I walked up to her, heart thudding against my rib cage, and met her gaze. Then I reached up and brushed my fingertips against her cheek.

"I'm not going anywhere," I whispered.

Caitlin turned her face away. When she looked back, her moist eyes were forest green once more. She started to say something then stopped, her voice hitching. She looked at my arm and touched the bloody rags.

"We need to do something about this," she said softly. "You're going to get an infection."

She led me into her bathroom. Her shower, a glass-walled stall sporting two facing showerheads and a long bench of polished marble, sat opposite a free-standing tub big enough for three people. A wide picture window beside it looked out over the Vegas skyline. Caitlin gestured for me to sit on the broad rim of the bathtub while she rummaged through pristine ivory cabinets, digging out some first aid supplies. She laid everything out next to the faucet. Then she straddled my lap.

I opened my mouth, but Caitlin touched a finger to my lips and unbuttoned my shirt. She paused, folds of fabric gripped in her slender hands, and looked at me.

"Are you sure this is what you want?" she asked, and I knew she didn't mean fresh bandages.

"Yes."

She tugged my shirt off, letting it fall to the floor. I winced as the rags peeled away next, the ugly wound stark under the overhead lights.

"I am the prince's hound," she mused, giving the cut an experimental poke. "Most of the people I deal with are either terrified of me, plotting to kill me, or both. I don't have friendships. I don't have relationships. I'm not very good at them."

"I'm game if you are," I said.

She held up a bottle of peroxide and unscrewed the cap, making sure I knew what it was. She curled one arm around my shoulders. With the other, she poised the bottle above my wound.

"This is going to hurt," she said.

I nodded. "I can take it."

The peroxide seared the open cut like a branding iron, bubbling in the wound. Caitlin pressed her lips to mine and swallowed my gasp of pain with a desperate, hungry kiss.

33.

I put my good arm around her waist, holding her close as the burn of the peroxide gave way to the fire in the pit of my stomach. She dropped the bottle, letting it clatter and spill in the basin of the tub, embracing me with mad fervor. We clutched each other like drowning sailors clinging to a life preserver.

Caitlin pulled away to mop at the cut with a pad of gauze. "This really needs stitches," she said. "I can drive you to the ER, or..."

I looked in her eyes. "Or?"

She seemed almost bashful as she shrugged. "I could do it. I mean, if you wanted me to."

She wanted to know how far I'd trust her, maybe, or just how much I could take. The answer was easy.

"You do it," I said.

She smiled with a glimmer of what might have been relief. Still straddling my lap, she opened a small sewing kit and threaded a slender needle, taking her time.

"Relax," she said, holding the needle up to the light and testing the tip against her finger. "I'm good with needles."

Caitlin leaned in for another kiss, gently tracing the tip of the needle down my throat, across the curve of my neck.

"Don't suppose you've got a local in that kit?" I asked with a nervous laugh. She grinned and touched her forehead to mine, murmuring softly.

"No anesthetic in my home. I don't believe in it. I think I do have a way to make the procedure easier to bear, though."

I felt her hand on my belt, slipping it through the loops with a sharp tug. I gasped as her fingers slid over my hardness, her touch teasing, feather-light.

"Now then," she whispered, hiking up her skirt and taking me in hand. "I'm going to need you to hold very, very still. Are you ready?"

I nodded, breathless. She lowered herself onto me as she lowered the needle toward my cut. We penetrated one another in the same instant, a wash of sensation that drew a strangled gasp from my throat. She rose up as the surgical thread tugged the ragged flesh closed and then lowered herself again, her body mirroring the needle, matching every sting with a slow wave of pleasure. I barely noticed when she finished the final stitch, reaching over for a tiny pair of scissors to cut the thread.

"I think," she said, wrapping gauze around my arm and fixing it in place with white surgical tape, "we should adjourn to the bedroom."

She laughed as I stood up with her still in my lap, her legs clenching tight around my waist. I nearly tripped over my own fallen pants, and she held out a hand to steady us against a wall as she guided me toward her bed. It was awkward and fumbling, and neither of us could stop gig-gling.

"So much for romance," I laughed, kissing her.

"You're just having balance issues, you poor thing. Feel-ing lightheaded? Did all that blood rush someplace else?" She paused, reaching down as we fell together onto her gray satin comforter. "Oh, it *did*."

Her bed felt like silk feathers under my back as she rolled me over, sitting astride me. Her pace was slow, lan-guid. She pressed her palms to my chest and tossed her curly hair as she rode to the beat of some unheard rhythm. My pulse rising, I tried to hasten her only to have her firm-ly hold my hips in place.

"Do you remember what you said when you freed me?" she said, her eyes gleaming in the dark. "When you thought I was going to kill you?"

"I said I wasn't going to beg."

She leaned down, almost nose to nose with me, flashing a wolf-like smile.

"I want to play a game with you, Daniel Faust."

"What did you have in mind?" I asked, biting back a groan as she moved her body against mine, so slowly I could barely stand it. She whispered her answer, flicking the tip of her tongue against my earlobe.

"You don't get to come. Not until you beg for it," she purred. "Let's see how long you can hold out, hmm? *Impress me*."

Then she held me in an unyielding grip as she played my body like a finely tuned instrument, taking me to the very brink of ecstasy and then dragging me away from release again and again. The digital alarm clock by her bedside read 3:43 A.M. by the time I finally broke, the floating scarlet

numbers bearing mute witness as I promised Caitlin the
moon and the stars if she'd show a heartbeat of mercy. She
giggled, listening to my pleas, then gave me everything I
begged for and more.

#

I woke in the satin embrace of Caitlin's bed, warm and
tranquil. Morning sunlight filtered in through half-closed
venetian blinds. I reached over, wanting to touch her, but
my hand fell on an empty swirl of sheets. Sudden panic
welled up and my eyes shot open, and then I heard her
voice.

"I'm still here."

I looked over. Caitlin sat in a chair in the corner of the
room, draped in a gray silk robe, legs crossed.

"I'm not going anywhere," she said, recognizing my fear.

I nodded, leaning back on the pillow.

"Neither am I," I told her. "What's wrong, couldn't
sleep?"

"I need very little sleep. It's more like what you'd call
meditation. I got up, read a little, did some digging. Decided
to watch you until you woke up. You talk in your sleep, you
know."

"Oh? Did I say anything interesting?"

She smiled. "More like happy little murmurs. But I found
something interesting, reading up on our Ms. Carmichael,
and you still need to update me on everything you've
learned."

"I want to hear all about it," I said, pushing the covers
back and rubbing the sleep from my eyes. "But can I catch a
quick shower first?"

Caitlin arched an eyebrow, rising and walking toward the bathroom. "Time is of the essence. Let's combine the two."

I soaped her back while I brought her up to speed, walking her through the assassination of Nicky Agnelli's seer and the bloody attack on Spengler's house. The twin showerheads filled the glass-walled stall with swirling steam as near-scalding water against my weary skin. Caitlin liked her showers hot.

"The only way to put Nicky's father on my prince's throne," she mused, "is to remove Prince Sitri from power. That cannot happen."

"Depends on what's in the Box," I said, "or what these people think is in the Box, anyway. Maybe they want to make him step down of his own free will? Could it be a blackmail thing?"

She laughed, high and merry. "Blackmail my prince? I think if anyone actually managed that, he'd reward them for their cleverness. Then destroy them. No, it must be an attack of some kind. Troubling, though. It sounds like this is just another side effect of Lauren Carmichael's plan, not her real goal. A bone they're tossing Nicky in order to secure his cooperation."

"What could dethrone a demon prince as a *side effect?*" I said. "It would have to be something..."

Caitlin turned, pressing herself against me, our bodies glistening in the pulsating spray. "Apocalyptic," she murmured, kissing me. "I may have a lead. You've mentioned that India keeps coming up, in regards to Carmichael's past."

"A couple of times, yeah."

She turned me around and traced the curve of my shoulders with a bar of soap.

"My nocturnal ramblings led me to some old news stories about her alma mater, Stanford. Many years ago a young Lauren, undertaking her freshman studies of archeology, talked her way onto a field expedition to southern Nepal, near Chitwan. The team intended to explore and document a recently-excavated temple complex dating back to the Maurya Empire."

I closed my eyes, savoring her touch. "And how did that go?"

"Badly. Two weeks into the expedition, their camp was attacked by murderous bandits. By some miracle, Lauren survived."

"Miracle, huh?" I shook my head. "She's not the kind of person who depends on miracles. Did anybody else make it out?"

"One man. Her professor and mentor, Dr. Eugene Planck. Upon his return he was immediately hospitalized with a nervous breakdown, which quickly progressed into full-blown psychosis. He tried to kill himself by drinking muriatic acid. He wanted, according to witnesses, to 'burn the parasite.' His family had him committed."

Burn the parasite. I thought about Lauren's death-curse, the snake creature she'd forced into my stomach, and shuddered. Was that where she had learned the trick?

"Did he die?" I asked.

"No, and as far as I can tell he's still languishing in a padded room at Napa State Hospital."

"He knows what happened on that expedition. Dr. Planck is probably the only person who can tell us what Lauren's become and what she really wants. Are you thinking what I'm thinking?"

"I'm thinking San Francisco is an hour and a half away by plane, and from there it's a short drive to Napa," Caitlin said. "We can be there and back in time for a late dinner. Speaking of, how do you feel about scrambled eggs and sausage?"

My stomach gave an involuntary grumble. With all the chaos, I couldn't remember the last time I sat down for a decent meal.

"Sounds great," I said.

"Fantastic." She turned off the shower and reached for a towel. "You'll find my kitchen is well stocked. You cook while I go online and buy our tickets. Oh, don't use any of the meat in the red Tupperware."

"Why not?"

"You wouldn't like it. It's...not for you."

She hummed a happy tune as she wrapped a towel around her hair and strolled off. Alone for a moment, I studied my reflection in the bathroom mirror.

"So," I said to myself, "now you're dating a creature from hell. That's new."

I was okay with that.

No, better than okay. Being with Caitlin felt...natural, in a way I couldn't find words for. Like her hand was made to fit in mine. I dreaded the inevitable conversation with Bentley and Corman about it, but for now I was happy just to see where this road would take us. In a week marred by death and pain, I'd found a single red rose growing in the ruins.

I'd take the thorns as they came.

34.

Two hours later we leaned back in stiff chairs as our plane roared down the runway, lifting off for California skies. Caitlin had bought us tickets for business class, and we were sitting toward the back on a half-empty flight.

"Normally I prefer first class," she told me, "but I felt a low profile would be wise. We don't know how many eyes Lauren has, and I imagine she wouldn't want us talking to her dear old professor."

"I'm wondering why she let him live," I said. "And on the note of paying for things, I'm reimbursing you for the tickets."

"No you aren't," Caitlin said. "It's a business expense. I am investigating a potential threat to my prince's safety. I just have to fill out an expense report when we get back."

The plane leveled out. Wisps of cloud slithered past my window. I tilted my head, looking at her.

"Expense report? It just seems a little modern for, well, who you work for."

She fished in her handbag, a slender black Louis Vuitton, and handed me her business card.

"Southern Tropics Import/Export Company
Caitlin Brody, Regional Manager"

"We believe in keeping up with the times," she said. "It's not all backward Latin and slaughtered goats."

The drink cart trundled down the aisle. Caitlin promptly ordered a pair of ginger ales for us. I stared at her.

"Are you going to keep doing that?" I asked.

"Doing what?"

"Ordering for me."

"Oh," she said, putting her hand to her mouth in mock surprise. "Do you mean you *weren't* just feeling slightly air-sick, and a bottle of ginger ale *wouldn't* help your stomach feel better?"

"I suppose," I said, unscrewing the cap, "you may kinda sorta have a point."

"Besides, you get the most adorably consternated look on your face."

I had to smile at that. She was right about the ginger ale, anyway. I waited until the stewardess pushing the drink cart was farther up the aisle, leaving us alone in our little pocket of empty seats. I wasn't looking forward to this, but it was time we laid all our cards on the table.

"Tell me about the ring," I said and tried not to shrink under the sudden, ferocious weight of Caitlin's glare. I held up a hand. "Nicky's seer babbled about a ring Lauren has, something she uses as a tool. She's also got the ability to bind demons with nothing but her own willpower, which is supposed to be impossible. I put two and two together."

"You shouldn't have. I told you, that knowledge is worth—"

"My life, right, I know what you said. But that was then and this is now. Cait...I trust you. Can you trust me?"

She stared at me for a long moment, her gaze softening, then finally shook her head with a sigh of resignation. "All right. But this goes no further. I mean that. It stays with you and it dies with you. If word of what she possesses leaked, there would be a bloodbath like you've never imagined."

I leaned closer to her, blinking. "What exactly are we talking about here?"

"Ever read the 1,001 *Arabian Nights*? Do you know the legend of King Solomon's temple?"

"Sure. Solomon was commissioned by angels to build a temple for storing the Ark of the Covenant. He was offered any payment he could imagine, but he only asked for wisdom. To reward his humility, he was granted magic powers and a ring that could..." My voice trailed off as I realized what she was saying. "You have got to be fucking kidding me."

"A ring that could command demons," Caitlin said.

"But that's just a legend, isn't it?"

"Legends take on lives of their own," she said. "Did it actually belong to Solomon? I don't think so. The first reports about it in hell's archives date back to Emperor Constantine's day, far too late. No idea who made it or how, and it has the most damnable habit of slipping in and out of history before we can get our claws on it. The bottom line is, it's here, it works, and Lauren Carmichael has it."

"If word got out to the occult underground," I said, shaking my head. "Christ, it's the ultimate prize. We'd have hexslingers flying in from the other side of the world to take a shot at getting their hands on that thing. Mages would be killing each other in the streets. A bloodbath doesn't begin to describe it."

She nodded. "Now add to that what my people would do in the name of survival. That ring is perhaps the greatest weapon ever placed in humanity's grasp. We have no defense against it, no refuge from enslavement at its owner's hands. Imagine how frightening that is for us. We don't respond well to being frightened, Daniel. Not well at all."

"It's a goddamned weapon of mass destruction is what it is. A nuke in a signet ring." I shook my head. "I hate to say it, but you're right. Nobody can know about this. What really worries me is that Carmichael's playing a long game. She's not drunk on power. The ring's just another tool to her, a means to an end."

"There are few things more dangerous than a zealot with discipline," Caitlin mused, sipping her ginger ale.

#

My hands clenched against the wheel of our rental car as I pulled into the visitor parking lot past a polished granite sign reading Napa State Hospital. It looked like a college campus with a splash of barbed wire.

"You all right?" Caitlin asked as we walked toward the entrance. I hadn't realized my tension was showing.

"When I was a kid," I started to say, then shook my head. "I just don't like places like this."

Inside, it could have been any hospital in the world, with attentive orderlies and wide, clean halls. Still, a sense of lingering sadness clung to the bricks, the strange sick smell of frustration and mental decay. I wasn't sure if it was the weight of over a century of madness, festering and breeding in the shadows, or just my own personal demons reminding me they were never far away.

We'd called ahead. I thought we might have to pull some kind of a scam, talk our way past the front desk or worse, break in under cover of night, but Dr. Planck was on the "approved for visitors" list. All we had to do was ask. There was still the chance that he'd refuse to see us, but something told me he'd want an audience.

The visitor center reminded me of a nicer county jail. Warm colors, sunny windows, and the constant reminder that your every move was being watched. Caitlin stored her handbag in a locker, along with my wallet and keys, and we walked through a metal detector. We waited in pensive silence until an orderly brought Planck in to see us.

Draped in a beige gown, his snowy-white hair cascading over his bloodshot eyes, Eugene Planck was a dead man walking. His heavily lined face turned curiously toward us as he hobbled over to the table. At first I thought they'd brought us the wrong patient. According to what Caitlin had dug up, he should have been in his fifties, but this man had to have been pushing eighty. Caitlin and I shared a glance, thinking the same thing: he looked like someone had sucked years of his life out through his pores, leaving nothing but a withered husk behind.

"Dr. Planck," I said, rising to my feet. "Thank you for seeing us."

He favored us with a tired smile, sitting down on the other side of the table. "Nobody's called me doctor in a very long time," he rasped. His voice was raw and his words forced their way out on a strangled wheeze. I remembered what Caitlin had told me about his first suicide attempt—

guzzling down acid to burn the parasite in his stomach. "Nobody's come to visit me, either. A rare surprise."

I rested my palms on the table, casting a quick look at the orderly loitering by the door and keeping my voice low.

"I'll lay it on the line for you, Doctor. We need to know everything you can tell us about Lauren Carmichael and the expedition to Nepal."

A pained look crossed his face and he shook his head. "Oh, no, it was so long ago. So very long ago. I'm sure I can't remember."

He was a lousy liar, but I didn't blame him. The haunted look in his eyes told me to go easy.

"Please," I said. "I know you've seen some bad stuff. I know it left scars. You don't want to go back there, and I don't want to make you. Thing is, she's hurting people, innocent people. She's gotta be stopped."

He laughed, a wheezing choke that turned into a wet, hacking cough. He put his hand to his mouth, catching his breath.

"You'll just end up like me," he said.

"You tried to stop her?"

"Didn't try hard enough," Eugene said, his gaze going distant. "If I'd known, if I'd known what she was capable of...no. I still would have been too late. I was delusional and in love."

"She was your student," Caitlin said, and he nodded.

"It happens on every campus, I suppose. Usually lecherous old professors and nubile coeds looking for an easy A. Lauren and I, though, that was different. She was brilliant, the brightest student I'd ever had, and the most ambitious. I tutored her late into the night, and soon she was sharing my bed."

"So she was using you," Caitlin said.

"No, no," he said. "Well, not entirely. She did have feelings for me. I have proof of that."

"How do you know?" she asked.

"Because she let me live."

"Doctor," I said, "what happened in Nepal?"

He sighed. "You don't understand. I can't talk about it. She won't let me."

"She's not here. We are. We can protect you."

He laughed again, giving me an incredulous lopsided smile. "You can't protect me, son. No one can. She's inside of me. She buried a monster in my guts, and it listens to every word I say. I have to keep her secrets for her."

"Please, try," I said. "I wouldn't ask if it wasn't important."

Eugene sighed. He smoothed down the front of his hospital gown, pulling it tight across his emaciated stomach.

"We went to Nepal in nineteen—" he started to say, then let out a pained groan. His stomach bulged. Under the gown, flesh stretched and rippled as something fat and wormlike writhed in his abdomen. He fell silent and it slithered back into the depths of his body, its warning delivered.

My breath caught in my throat. I remembered the feeling of Lauren's snake-curse all too well.

"You can see it. Good. These fellows," he said, giving a nod of his head to the orderly at the door, "they can't see a thing. They just say I'm hallucinating. I'm sorry. I'd help you if I could, I really would. I just can't. This...this is what Lauren Carmichael did to me. She showed me horrors and then she took away my voice. I've been waiting twenty years just to scream."

Caitlin drummed her fingernails on the table, her brow furrowed.

"If there's one thing I know," she said, "it's that every contract has a loophole. You can't speak of what happened in Nepal. Fine. I think we can accommodate that."

He shook his head. "I can't write it down either, or draw pictures. I tried once. Oh, that went badly."

"No, I'm envisioning something a bit more elegant than that," she said, then looked to me. "Dreamwalk. He can just remember it for us."

I guess I didn't have to wonder anymore whether Caitlin's appearance in my dreams was real or a flight of fantasy. "Is it safe?"

"Not remotely. And it doesn't work on the unwilling. He has to open himself to me, give permission."

"Wait, I didn't give permission and you did it to me," I said.

She chuckled, brushing the back of my hand with her fingernails. "Not in words, but you sent an invitation and left your front door wide open. Don't you dare deny it."

"So there's a way?" Eugene said, sudden urgency rasping in his acid-scarred throat. "There's really a way?"

"You could die," Caitlin said, matter-of-factly. "You aren't trained in the occult arts, and you don't know how to manage the energies involved. If anything goes wrong, the process could induce a brain embolism or leave you a vegetable."

He shook his head firmly. "I don't care. I don't care what happens to me. I want to tell my story. I want my voice back."

35.

We needed to stay close for the dreamwalk to work, and a sleepover at the mental hospital wasn't in the cards. We drove until we found a Motel 6 a couple of miles down the road and rented the room at the end. Caitlin went out again to do some shopping, leaving me with orders to lie in bed, watch the grainy television, and try to relax. We all needed to be asleep for this to work, but nothing's harder than getting sleepy on command. The more I tried to rest the less tired I felt, and the sunlight streaming in around the thick curtains didn't help.

Caitlin came back an hour later with a plastic bag from a local grocery store and a sack of cheeseburgers from Wendy's. "Let's get some red meat in your stomach," she said cheerfully. "That'll help."

I got up and ambled to the table by the window. "Don't suppose you got me a Coke with that?"

"Yes," she said, rolling her eyes, "you should absolutely have caffeine right now."

"Oh. Right."

"You can, however, wash it down with a few shots of this," she said, digging in the grocery bag and setting a bottle of Nyquil on the table.

I groaned, shaking my head. "Seriously?"

"Short of knocking over a pharmacy to get the really good stuff, I know of no better aid in the pursuit of short-term unconsciousness."

I sat next to her, my fingertips brushing her thigh. "I'm sure I could think of an idea or two."

"That," she said with a smile, "is exactly what you said when I came back to the motel. You're a bit disoriented."

"Huh? You just came back now."

Caitlin whistled tunelessly and spun her finger, gesturing for me to turn around. I looked over my shoulder. Our bodies, naked and entwined on sweat-soaked sheets, slept peacefully in the double bed.

"We're already asleep," I said flatly.

"Mm-hmm. Your short-term memories are muddled. It happens."

I pointed at the bed. "But I missed the good part!"

"I think," she said, touching my shoulder as she rose from her chair, "an encore can be arranged. Come now. Let's find the good Dr. Planck. It shouldn't be hard. I can feel him yearning for us. He wants to be heard."

I looked around the motel room, concentrating. I couldn't hear the echoes of Planck's soul, not like Caitlin, but I knew a message needed a medium.

"Let's try this." I turned on the television set.

Sunlight filtered through the canopy of a lush tropical jungle, woodshrikes chittering in the branches. I didn't recognize Eugene at first. The man on the television screen, frowning as he studied a crumbling stone slab under a magnifying glass, was young and vibrant. So was the girl beside him, dressed in an explorer's khakis, her eyes wide and bright.

"Lauren," Caitlin hissed.

The stone might have been a doorway, submerged into the loam by tremors and time, choked by centuries of vines and weeds. Something about it, the shape of it, the curious lean of the arch and the glistening sheen of the rock, set my teeth on edge.

"This is all wrong," Planck said on the screen, echoing my thoughts exactly. "These symbols aren't Hindu, and this style is far too old to date from the Maurya Empire. I can't even read this part; it's not Sanskrit or any of the Prakrit languages. This temple shouldn't be here."

Lauren traced a twisting symbol with her finger, following the ragged cut. "We should go in! Come on, where's your sense of adventure? There could be anything inside!"

Planck shook his head, taking a step back.

"Not without the entire team, and not without the right tools to clear the passage without risking any damage to the walls. Not a scratch. You know my motto."

Lauren sighed, but she favored him with the smile of an indulgent lover. "'Proper archeology takes its proper time,'" she recited.

"She didn't listen," Planck said from behind us. He stood in the corner of the room, young again, watching the screen with a look of abject misery. "She went back under the cover of the stars with a machete and sheer stubbornness. The next morning, she had a new ring on her finger, an old pewter thing that looked like something her grandmother might wear. That's when things started to change."

A young Indian trembled on a cot in an army-surplus tent, his terrified eyes bulging and his lips flecked with white foam. We stood next to Planck, the motel room suddenly gone. Oppressive summer heat baked into my bones and sucked the breath from my lungs.

"Snakebite," a stout man with an Australian accent told Eugene, "third bloody case this week. Been seeing 'em all over the camp, bold brown bastards with a nasty bite. The porters are finding 'em in their bedsheets. They're about to take a hike, and I don't blame 'em a damn bit."

"Where are they all coming from? The site was clear when we struck camp."

"Your guess is as good as mine, mate. They're saying this place is cursed."

The outside light slipped away as we plunged into nightfall. Insects droned in the jasmine-scented dark. Eugene opened the tent flap and stepped outside.

Lauren stood with her back to him, facing the jungle, the temple ruin. Whispering.

"Who are you talking to?" he asked cautiously.

"My new friends," she said, turning to face him with a jubilant smile.

"Lauren," Eugene said, hesitant, "nobody's out here but us."

"They're on their way. You'll see them. Not everyone will. Certain sacrifices have to be made for progress. But you? You're special."

She leaned in to kiss his cheek and froze. The trees stopped their swaying, the insects silenced, the world gone rigid and still. Eugene shook his head at us.

"I didn't understand what she meant. More porters died. Snakebite. One of our other interns went missing. We found her body the next morning in the brush, savaged by a pack of feral beasts. Then I sent my assistant on a run to the nearest village to buy food and medical supplies."

The world shifted around us again, canvas flaps dropping over the sky and a card table laden with maps boiling up from the dirt. The Australian paced the tent, wild-eyed, barely able to control himself.

"Just take it slow," Eugene told him. "One thing at a time."

"We can't leave," the Australian said, squeezing his hands at his sides. "I'm telling you, I took the road out of camp and drove for fifteen minutes through the jungle. Ended up coming back into camp. I didn't turn, not once. Did it again. Ended up back in camp. I spent eight hours driving the *same five miles of road*. I'm telling you, Doctor, something is keeping us penned in here. It's killing us off one by one, and it won't let us go!"

"It's impossible. The jungle must have confused you. It's easy to get turned around—"

The Australian slammed his fist against the table. "We're going to die here. You *know* why. That bird of yours. You've heard the whispers. You know what people've seen, what that girl's been doing at night. You just don't want to believe it. We're all going to die here, and it'll be your damn fault."

Eugene's shoulders shook. I stepped closer and saw the tears on his cheeks.

"He's right," he told us. "It was my fault."

"No," Caitlin said. "It was hers."

Night again, and we followed Eugene out of the tent. Half the camp lay barren now, the wind blowing ragged tent flaps wide. Fat brown snakes coiled on empty cots.

They hissed lazily as we walked by. In the distance, a man's shrill scream pierced the night and, just as suddenly, fell silent.

At the edge of the clearing stood a small pavilion built from the scavenged bits and pieces of half a dozen tents. The pavilion was sprawling and shapeless, and a faint droning sound echoed from inside like a tuneless chant in a long-dead tongue. An oriental rug lined the floor at the entrance, caked with sand and dirt. As we followed Eugene inside, we heard the clinking of glasses and faint, conversational laughter.

A human torso, crudely butchered, lay across a glass table with its innards still wet and glistening. Lauren sat beside it, dressed in her Sunday best and sipping tea from a delicate porcelain cup. A man in a dapper black suit sat across from her. His face was a featureless black void, a smudge of frozen smoke.

"Eugene!" Lauren said. "You're just in time for high tea."

"Abelard," Eugene gasped, obviously in shock, "says he can't leave the camp. He says the road—"

"Right, we can't let anyone leave. Obviously. Mr. Gray, would you please do something about that pesky man?"

The black void buzzed, and the suited man hoisted his teacup emphatically. He spoke in the droning voice of a thousand flies' wings.

"Fanciful! I will snatch his nails!"

The man's words sounded like a parody of English, strings of text run through a computer translator and back again. Still, nonsensical as it was, there was no mistaking his gleefully malicious tone.

"Can't you remember his face?" Caitlin asked. Halfway submerged in the memory, Planck looked at us and shook his head.

"I do remember," he said. "That *was* his face."

Another faceless man, garbed in the sash and gown of an old-time British boarding-school teacher, stood beside a chalkboard. He rapped his pointer against a sketch, drawing attention to a chalk drawing of what could only be the Etruscan Box. Runes surrounded the Box, a swirling chaos of incomprehensible letters that tugged at my eyes.

"To open the Box without the requisite sacrifice," buzzed the faceless teacher, "invites the wrath of its guardians."

The seated man waved his teacup, splashing amber droplets on the rug. "They are lean and athirst! They chew on gumption!"

"The number of souls is five, no more and no less. This is the key and the cost to open Belephaia's prison. The ring will render her docile and pliant."

Caitlin's jaw dropped. She grabbed Planck's shoulder.

"Repeat that! What did he say? Are you sure you remember it correctly?"

The room flickered and skipped as time ran in reverse. My stomach lurched.

"—is the key and the cost to open Belephaia's prison," the teacher said again, and Caitlin spat an oath in her native tongue. I touched the small of her back, frowning.

"What is it?"

She shook her head. "Hold on. This is bad. I need to think."

The teacher rapped his pointer against the chalkboard for emphasis. "It will not be long before her brother, the demon prince Sitri, comes to her rescue. You must bind them both, quickly. Only then shall your desires be made flesh."

"Lauren," Eugene pleaded, lost in his memory, "what are you doing? This is wrong, it has to stop."

She shook her head, rising slowly from her chair.

"Oh, Eugene. There's a new day coming, love. A bright and shining new day, and it's all because of me. I should get rid of you, but...it just wouldn't be the same without you there to see it. I want you to share my triumph."

"This is insane!" he stammered.

"No. The world as you know it is insane. What you see here is just a glimpse of the sanity to come. We have a problem now, love. I won't kill you—I can't—but I can't let you talk about this either."

"If we might suggest," the faceless teacher droned, "it poses an excellent opportunity to bond with your children."

The seated man tilted his smoky void toward Planck. "Your lover is a mother, yet you are not a father. Cuckold."

Lauren raised her hands. The skin of her arms pulsed and rippled, a dozen fat worms burrowing and digging under her flesh.

"It will be over quickly, love. I'm just going to put something inside of you. The less you struggle, the easier it will be."

Planck stumbled backward, tripped, and landed flat on his back. I felt his surging fear in my own chest, the memory feeding upon itself and intensifying. The buzzing laughter of the faceless men echoed in my ears, louder and louder, driving out everything but sheer animal panic.

"Caitlin!" I shouted. "Cut him loose. It's too much! *End it!*"

Light, brilliant and agonizing, flared behind my eyelids and the world exploded. I woke, jerking bolt upright in the motel bed, caked in a sheen of ice-cold sweat. Caitlin tugged on jeans and a silk blouse as she hissed tangled words under her breath. She moved like a hurricane on a mission.

"What is it?" I said. "That name, you recognized it."

"I know what she's after now. I know what Lauren's trying to pull off, even if she doesn't. She has no idea what they've tricked her into doing."

"What?"

Caitlin turned to look at me, her face a mask etched in steel.

"Jump-start the apocalypse."

36.

"The universe has laws. Immutable, undebatable," Caitlin said as she finished getting dressed. "You drop an apple, it falls down, not up. Drop a million, a million fall."

"Right," I said, "physics. I get that."

"The occult world is no less legalistic. Names have power. Contracts bind. A web of pacts and treaties, ancient beyond measure, thread their way through the universe."

"You're gonna have to help me out here."

"Long story short," Caitlin said, her voice fierce, "that creature last walked the Earth when your kind were still living in caves and figuring out that fire is hot. It couldn't be destroyed, so my prince, along with his compatriots, bound it in a prison. It shouldn't have been left in this world for humans to find. It *couldn't* have been."

I thought back to my first glimpse of the Box, how utterly sinister and alien it had felt. I remembered my sudden and sure knowledge that the creature inside utterly despised me and had all eternity to stew in its own hatred.

Caitlin turned on her phone and hit the speed dial. After a short pause she rattled off the motel's address and growled into the receiver, "It's me. Send a car. Now. I'll need a conduit and an audience with the prince within the hour. One minute later and I'll feed you your own skin one ragged strip at a time."

She hung up without another word and said, "Those creatures, the smoke-faced men, whatever they were, they lied to Lauren. Prince Sitri is *not* Belephaia's brother. The two of them are bound by ancient vows of Nemesis. If Belephaia is freed, if she sets one toe on Earth, my prince is obligated to travel here and face her in mortal combat. Even he, powerful as he is, must abide by the laws of the universe. If she emerges from that casket, he *has* to come and fight."

"But why lie? Lauren's going to use the ring to bind both of them under her power, so what difference does it make why Sitri is coming?"

Caitlin shook her head, pacing the room.

"No, no, no. Daniel, you don't understand. The ring won't work on her. Belephaia isn't a demon. She's *an angel.*"

My mouth went dry as the Mohave at high noon.

"There's an angel," I said, "in the Box? Wait, isn't that a good thing?"

"If there's a glimmer of hope in your heart," Caitlin snapped, "I suggest you extinguish it. Better yet, allow me the pleasure. Belephaia is a scourge. A firebrand. A destroyer of the wicked and sinful."

"A war angel."

"All angels are war angels. She, though, is one of a kind. Destruction is her only purpose, her only thought and desire. Oh, and her benchmarks for 'naughty' and 'nice' aren't exactly calibrated to human standards. There isn't a soul on this planet who isn't guilty and deserving of annihilation in her eyes. No woman, no man, no child."

I rubbed my forehead, the implications setting in.

"And Lauren is going to unleash this thing in the heart of Sin City," I groaned. "And then Sitri's going to show up looking for a brawl. How much damage are we talking about here? What's the best-case scenario?"

"Best case would be a swift victory for my prince, and even then, he'll be celebrating in the heart of a nuclear storm. When their powers clash, nothing will be left standing. We'll be lucky if they don't turn the entire western seaboard into glass."

"They're that powerful?"

"You can't even imagine." Caitlin paced the floor, shaking her head. "Oh, but that's just the beginning. There are compacts. Treaties that must never be broken. This world is...what's the best way to put it? A demilitarized zone. Everyone protects their interests in a quiet, low-key sort of way, but open conflict on the scale those two would bring? All bets are off."

"Like a giant bar fight," I said. "Right now it's just a bunch of mean drunks poking at each other, but nobody wants to throw the first real punch. As soon as Sitri and Belephaia get into it, everyone with a hunger for power will jump in, and pretty soon it's..."

"Armageddon," Caitlin said. "Nobody is ready for that. We are not ready for that. Oh, we'll take this planet, Daniel, but on our schedule."

"It's a long con. It's brilliant, is what it is."

She arched her eyebrow at me. "Hrm?"

I buttoned my shirt, sketching out the scam in my mind. The pieces fell together in perfect symmetry. Everything fit. I just couldn't see it before now.

"The smoke-faced men. They set Lauren up. Juiced her up somehow, gave her magic and a messiah complex to go with it. Her entire plan is centered around building the Enclave. No idea what she's trying to do with it or why, some part of her mission to save the world, but that's the thing: the faceless men don't give a damn. The Enclave was *never* going to be built. It's the bait, the mission they made up to string her along. As far as Lauren's concerned, opening the box is just going to put a couple of ancient demons under her control. Another tool, more resources, more power. The faceless men gave her twenty years to study, to practice, to gather cash and influence and the will to use it.

"Now the timing is perfect and Lauren has a little cult of followers who are just as driven as she is, guaranteeing the job will get done right. The Box suddenly pops up in the Middle East, off the radar for centuries, but somehow both Lauren's agents and a tomb raider like Spengler catch wind of it in the same week? I'd bet hard cash they weren't the only people who heard the news. They were just the first to get there. Spengler only won the race by dumb luck. He was in the wrong place at the wrong time."

"The faceless men planted it and spread rumors to make sure it'd be found," Caitlin said, nodding. "They dropped it right in Lauren's path when they felt she was ready to pay the price to unlock it. After two decades of slow corruption, she'd be eating right out of their hands."

I nodded. "Damn right. Not just anybody could murder their families in the name of power and still think they were on the side of the just. That takes some hardcore mental dissonance. All this time they've been grooming Lauren and her pals for the big show."

"My prince," Caitlin sighed. "That lock has his fingerprints all over it, one of his black jokes. People have come up with all kinds of fantasies about what's in the Box, but they'd never get near it. Only the ones who knew what was really inside could lay hands on the thing, and the only people who would want to free an angel from its chains are the very sort of people who could never slaughter their loved ones and pluck out their souls for a sacrifice. It's ingenious. He just didn't account for it falling in the hands of the manipulated and misguided."

"Guess he's not as smart as you think," I said, then immediately regretted it. I waved a hand, backing off under the weight of her glare. "So who are the smoke-headed nutjobs pulling the strings? They don't work for hell, so what's their angle?"

Caitlin shook her head. "There are other forces in the universe. The question will keep. For now, I want you to fly back without me. I need to talk to my prince, to warn him and assess our options."

"Don't you want me to stay with you?"

"No, the car won't even arrive for another three hours at least, and you wouldn't be welcome where they're taking me."

"Um, what about the, uh..." I gestured at her phone.

"What?"

"The, uh, you know. What you said on the phone? The car has to be here in an hour or you'll make them eat their own skin?"

"Oh!" she said, blinking with surprise. "Oh, no, I only punish willful disobedience. Still, if I didn't make the threat, they wouldn't grasp the urgency. It's a cultural thing."

#

I felt strange sitting next to an empty seat, waiting for my plane to take off. I hadn't been far from Caitlin's side since last night. The sensation of our first kiss was still ripe in my imagination. I missed her already.

It was crazy, the idea of me and her, but sometimes life goes better with a little craziness. The future came with its own pile of worries, but for now I'd play it like I had a fat stack of chips on the table and Lady Luck blessing my hand: let it ride.

Of course, that assumed there would be a future to share with her.

With ten minutes to takeoff, I took out my phone. I had an idea. It was a long shot, but I had to try.

"Carmichael-Sterling Nevada, how may I direct your call?"

"Lauren Carmichael please," I said.

"I'm sorry, she's in meetings all day and can't be disturbed. Can I take a message?"

"Tell her it's Daniel Faust on the line. She'll want to talk to me."

Their hold music was soft jazz. I stared out the window at the tarmac, feeling the seconds slip away.

"You're not dead," Lauren said. From her tone I couldn't tell if she was disappointed or impressed.

"Can't say the same for your boy Tony Vance."

She hesitated. "That was you? I assumed he committed suicide."

"You don't sound broken up about it."

"He was a soldier. He did his duty."

"Meaning he handed off his daughter's soul before taking the permanent high dive."

"You've figured it out," she said.

"More than you. I've been doing some digging. The thing in the Box, it's not what you think it is. The ring won't work on it."

"Of course it will. This has been in the planning for decades."

"Planned by who? You're being played, Lauren. You can't imagine the size of the shitstorm you're about to unleash."

"Some collateral damage is expected, but my assistants and I will be well protected, I assure you. We have everything under control."

I sighed. It was the answer I expected, but I had to try reasoning with her. Plan B was a lot more violent. The speaker over my head chimed, and the gentle voice of the stewardess called for everyone to turn off their electronics.

"You hear that?" I said, taking the opportunity to toss up a smoke screen. "I'm sitting on a plane at McCarran International, bound for Miami. I want to be on the other side of the country when this goes down. Think about that."

"Meadow's going to be disappointed. She wants to kill you for what you did to her face."

"She murdered a buddy of mine. I think I've got the bigger grievance."

"I agree with you," Lauren said, "but life is rarely just or kind, is it? I'm a rational woman, Mr. Faust, and I believe you're a rational man. Go to Miami and stay there. If you'll keep out of my affairs, I'll keep out of yours. We'll both sleep much easier that way. Do we have a deal?"

Not a chance in hell.

"Deal," I said and hung up the phone.

Lauren and her pals wanted to do things the hard way. I was fine with that. For Caitlin, for Stacy Pankow, for Spengler, for Amber Vance...I'd make sure they got exactly what they had coming to them. Every last bit of it.

37.

I flew home, went back to my apartment and paced in the dark. I'd had enough sleep. My brain tugged at the problem like a kitten with a ball of twine, tossing it around and getting nowhere fast. Lauren had the Box and her harvest of souls, but there had to be a way to get close to her, to track her down and put a stop to this.

I laughed out loud when I figured it out.

My phone rang at half past sunrise. Caitlin sounded worn down, like she'd run a marathon and lost.

"I just landed at McCarran. Come pick me up?"

I pulled up curbside and she got in, leaning her head back and closing her eyes.

"Something tells me you don't have good news," I said.

"The Box," she said, "until last month, was kept in a place of honor in Prince Sitri's personal trophy room. He never even knew it was gone until last night because someone not only stole it out from under his nose, they replaced it with a cunning counterfeit."

I merged into traffic, my brow furrowed. "Sounds like an inside job."

"We concur. There's going to be an inquisition, but that doesn't help us right now. It just confirms that the faceless men orchestrated this entire charade from the beginning. They spread ridiculous myths about the Box around the world for decades, stole it from hell, and dropped it in Lauren's path. They groomed her for twenty years just to be sure she'd be ready to unlock it. Bloody thing's not even Etruscan."

"So what's Sitri going to do?" I asked. "I mean, if Lauren opens it."

"Wage war. As he is bound to do, even knowing he'll herald the apocalypse. Making sure that doesn't happen is on my shoulders."

"And mine."

She smiled, reaching over and touching my arm.

"Our shoulders," she said. "Take me home? I need a shower and a change of clothes. Then we can plan our next move."

"I think I know who can help us. It's a gamble, but if you're up for it, we might have an inside line on finding Lauren."

"What do you have in mind?" Caitlin said, tilting her head curiously.

When I told her, she laughed louder than I had.

#

The Gentlemen's Bet was a dive strip club in a stretch of town where the tourists didn't go. The noonday sun baked down on a couple of battered cars and a semi tractor in the litter-strewn parking lot. The neon silhouette of a naked woman perched on a pair of dice sat lifeless over the front door, looking down over a tattered red carpet made of painted AstroTurf.

I'd suited up for the occasion with a forest green shirt and a metallic tie. Caitlin opted for a slender black dress with a short, cropped jacket. The throwing knives sewn into the jacket's lining didn't even make a whisper as we walked to the door.

"You clean up nicely," she said.

"I can't go making you look bad, now can I?"

"So what do you think our odds are?"

I opened the door for her, thinking it over.

"Fifty-fifty. In this town, that's not a bad proposition."

A lethargic, barrel-chested bouncer gave us a casual once-over and nodded over his shoulder. The sun vanished, replaced by stuffy darkness and the stink of cheap beer. A few patrons loitered in the near-empty club, each of them alone, watching a bored-looking stripper gyrate out of time to a hair metal song. We made a beeline for the hallway at the back of the room.

The bartender jumped out from behind the bar to get in our way, holding up his hands. "Sorry folks, no admittance. Bathrooms are over—"

He froze, taking a stumbling step back as Caitlin flashed molten copper eyes at him. When she spoke, her teeth were too many, too sharp, for any human mouth.

"*Move*," she hissed. She gave him a charming smile as we passed, wearing her human mask once more.

I'd been here enough times on business to know that we wanted the door at the end, the one with the placard reading Private and the best lock in the building. I gestured to the knob.

"Want me to pick that?"

Caitlin thought about it for a moment and shrugged.

"Nah."

The door blasted open under the heel of her calf-high boot, swinging wide and slamming against the inner wall. Nicky, sitting behind an army-surplus metal desk and eating lunch, froze with a forkful of steak halfway to his mouth. Justine and Juliette leaped up from their chairs. The cambion twins flashed fangs as they hissed and crouched.

"Bitches leave," Caitlin growled.

I stared at her. "Did...did you just quote *Robocop*?"

She gave me a wink before looking back across the office. Nicky nodded slowly.

"Do as she says, ladies," he said. "I'll be fine."

"I don't know if you can back that up," I said, taking one of the chairs and dragging it over to the other side of his desk. The decor in Nicky's office hadn't changed since the seventies, just a cheap little hole-in-the-wall. You'd never know half the rackets in Vegas were run out of this room.

The twins slunk out the door. Justine paused on the threshold. Suddenly she leaped at Caitlin, fingernails hooked into claws, going for her eyes. Caitlin spun and grabbed Justine's wrist in one hand and her hair in the other, using the cambion's own momentum to force her down on her knees. Justine's wrist bent back at a bone-grinding angle.

"Yield!" Justine gasped, gritting her teeth. "I yield!"

Caitlin kept the pressure on for a few more agonizing seconds before letting her go. Justine pushed herself up to her feet, rubbing her wrist, hovering on the verge of tears.

"I was just playing," Justine whined. Juliette met her at the door, taking her sister in her arms and glaring daggers at Caitlin.

"She's so *mean*," Juliette said. "Why do you have to be so mean all the time?"

Caitlin shut the door in their faces. Dusting off her hands, she walked over to join us at Nicky's desk.

"You have to excuse the girls," Nicky said. "They're a little, uh—"

"Sociopathic?" I offered.

"I was gonna say high-spirited, but sure, that works too."

"Do you know why we're here?" Caitlin asked.

"I know that when a cop asks you that, they want you to do their job for them. Pardon me if I don't fall all over myself bein' helpful. And what are you doing, Danny? You and the Wingtaker here, that's a team-up I didn't see coming."

"I'll tell you what I'm here for," I said. "I'm here to save your ass."

Nicky chewed a bite of steak, taking his time.

"That's nice. You'd wanna do that why, exactly?"

"Because Lauren Carmichael is using you, and somebody else is playing her. There's only one way this ends if you don't listen to us. Badly."

"Don't know what you're talking about," Nicky said flatly, his gaze drifting toward Caitlin. "Don't know any Lauren anybody. Never met her."

"I'm going to say two magic words," Caitlin said. She loomed over his desk with murder in her eyes. "I've never said them in my life, and you'll likely never hear them again. Listening?"

"I'm all ears," Nicky said.

"Transactional immunity."

That got his attention.

"I'm still listening," he told her, "but I'm maybe not entirely sure what you're offering me immunity for."

I leaned back in my chair. "Let me paint you a picture. Lauren needed help setting up Carmichael-Sterling Nevada. She was an out-of-towner with big ambitions, and you were the guy who could pull the strings and secure the permits to make the Enclave happen."

"I help lots of people," he said, "in exchange for a nominal commission fee of course. What's wrong with that?"

"Nothing. But while you were greasing her wheels, she figured out what you really are. She brought you in on her real scheme. Problem is, how do you stall five murder investigations? There's always blackmail, but that's so messy, and payback's always a risk. Lauren figured it out, or maybe you did. Why not use the ring to snare a succubus? And you knew just the target, somebody who's been a thorn in your side for a long, long time."

Nicky gave Caitlin a nervous glance, but he held his tongue.

"You used Caitlin's powers to turn Detective Holt into a pleasure junkie," I said. "He danced to your tune so long as he got his daily fix. It was the perfect setup. Sitri's hound was out of your way, you had a homicide cop on a leash, and Lauren's crew was free to open the Etruscan Box. A ceremony which, I'm sure you know, would drag Prince Sitri out of hell and give Lauren the chance to enslave him. Coincidentally leaving his throne vacant and your father primed and ready for a power grab."

"And if you could prove any of that," Nicky said, "we wouldn't be having a nice chat like this."

"You're right," Caitlin said. Nicky stared at her. It wasn't the response he'd been expecting. "I can't prove a single thing. Can't do anything to you or about you."

I nodded. "Only problem with the whole scheme, really, is that Lauren's about to blow up the planet. See, that's the part you aren't in on. The thing in the Box? It's an angel. And it's really old and really pissed off."

"You're bluffing," Nicky said.

"Are we?" Caitlin shrugged. "We're keeping things under wraps to avoid a panic, but a full report's been delivered to the prince and his inner council. A council which, last time I checked, includes your father. Why don't you get in touch with him? Ask him who Belephaia is."

He looked from her to me and back again, resting his hand on his desk phone. His brow furrowed as he worked out the implications. "Why don't you two go out to the bar for a few minutes? I gotta make a couple of calls. Tell the bartender I said anything you want; it's on the house."

I stayed close to Caitlin as we stepped back into the club, taking seats at the end of the bar. She ordered a Manhattan, and I asked for a martini with top-shelf vodka. It was on Nicky's dime, and seeing as he had tried to feed me to a pack of feral cambion I figured he owed me a little something. A Rolling Stones song played over the house speakers as a new dancer took the stage.

"He can't actually call his dad, can he?" I asked. "Like, on the phone?"

Caitlin smiled. "No, but he can call my office and they'll arrange a conduit. That's how I spoke with my prince last night."

"Conduit?"

"You take a human and—" She paused. Maybe she saw something in my eyes, or maybe she just remembered my history when it came to demonic possession. She waved it off. "There are ways."

Her hand rested lightly on the bar. I placed mine over it. She turned her hand, our fingers twining.

"We will stop them," I said. "I promise. I'm not letting anything or anyone take you away from me now. Not a chance."

She chuckled, shaking her head. "I forgot what it felt like to care about anything but my duty. To have something worth fighting to hold on to. I like this feeling." She traced a fingernail over the back of my hand. "I like this feeling too."

I started to say something, cut short by a voice at our backs.

"Oh. My. Light," Juliette said. We turned to look at her. She pointed at our hands. "Are you two *rutting*?"

"That is so gross." Justine stood next to her with her mouth agape. "You are so gross."

"No," Caitlin said, grinning. "We're holding hands. What I did with your father, that was rutting."

Justine made a strangled squeaking noise, like a cat had lodged in her throat and was trying to kick its way out. Juliette stammered incoherently as she dragged her sister away by the arm. I let go of Caitlin's hand just long enough to hold up my open palm.

"High-five me."

She slapped her palm against mine. We settled into a comfortable silence.

"You didn't actually—" I eventually asked, and Caitlin arched an eyebrow.

"They'll always wonder," she said. "I do hope you're not the jealous type, Daniel. I *am* a succubus. If you want me to list my lovers, we're going to be here a while."

I shook my head. "Not even a little bit."

"Good. But for the record? Never. You don't rut with a pride demon; you hold up a mirror for him to stare into while he pleasures himself. I'm only slightly exaggerating."

Nicky appeared in the hallway, pale as a sheet. Beads of sweat pooled at his hairline. He looked like a middle manager who'd just gotten called on the carpet by his CEO.

"C'mon back," he said. "Let's talk."

38.

"The first thing I want," Nicky said, pouring himself a splash of whiskey from a bottle in his desk drawer, "is immunity for my dad, too. He didn't know anything about this, and that's the honest truth."

"You set up a coup attempt without telling him?" I asked, sitting on the other side of the desk and cradling my martini.

"You gotta understand, Danny, how it is for people like me. My old man's a big shot back home. Me, I'm nothing but his big mistake. I thought I could prove to him, y'know, that I can roll like he does, like a fullblood. Maybe if I did, I thought...maybe he'd like me."

"You conspired against your lawful prince," Caitlin said, "and that's not even considering what you did to *me*. If I had my way, I'd teach you exactly how we fullbloods respond to insolence. Your usefulness is the only thing sparing you, for the moment, from an eternity of pain."

"Of course," I said, playing the good cop, "anybody who helps take Carmichael and her buddies down, well, I gotta think Sitri's gonna remember that in a favorable light."

"You think so?" he asked, and I looked to Caitlin.

"Your name will be mentioned in my final report. Favorably," she said.

Nicky folded his hands behind his head, obviously liking the sound of that. He thought it over for a moment. "I got good news and bad news. Good news is, I can tell you exactly where Lauren and the Box are. Bad news is, they're opening it tonight, so you've only got a few hours. You know the Silverlode, over on Fremont?"

I nodded. "Sure. It's been closed for what, three years now?"

"Closed, but not abandoned," Nicky said. "Carmichael-Sterling Nevada bought it up as soon as they hit town, thanks to a little help from yours truly. Officially, they're renovating it for a summer opening. That's just a smoke screen for the press, though. The only renovations going on in there are courtesy of that creepy chick Meadow."

"Puppets?" I remembered her attack on Spengler's house.

Nicky snorted and tossed back a swig of whiskey. "Try buzz saws and booby traps. She's like that guy from the *Saw* movies, but without the sense of humor. They fortified the place just for tonight's main event. You aren't getting in there without a small army."

"Fortunately," I said, "I've got one. Any idea where in the building they'll be?"

"Top floor. The old Klondike Room. The hotel elevator or the emergency stairs will take you straight to it, but it's a suicide run."

"We can manage it," Caitlin said.

"I can manage it," I told her. "As long as Lauren has that ring, I don't want you getting within a mile of her."

She frowned. "You're not going in there alone."

"Don't worry, I won't be. I'll have the best backup in the business."

"What else do you want from me?" Nicky asked.

"You've got friends on the force," I said. "Things could get loud. It'd be nice if the police kinda forgot the Silverlode existed for a few hours tonight."

"Done and done. And hey, one other thing. Lauren couldn't use this. She tossed it my way like some sorta tip for good service. I figure you might want it."

Nicky dug around in his desk drawer and dropped his find on the blotter between us. A leather pouch fringed with turquoise beads. Its dulled pewter clasp seemed to absorb the light. I could feel the raw enchantment from here, a hungry, sucking void, only half-satisfied with the partial meal it had already devoured.

Stacy Pankow's soul.

I took the pouch. Tiny psychic needles bristled against my palm.

"I've been looking for this," I said, then turned to Caitlin. "Shall we?"

She rose and walked with me. I was halfway out the door when Nicky called out.

"Hey, Dan?"

I looked back at him.

"We good?" he asked, wringing his hands and giving me puppy-dog eyes. I had to think about that.

"I don't know, Nicky, are we? You told those feral cambion where to find me."

He shrugged, biting his bottom lip. "You pissed me off. I mean, you know me—I get irrational sometimes. Besides, I knew you could handle those punks. I figured they'd just scare you a little. And I was right. Right?" He sighed. "Look, I'm sorry, okay? I shouldn't have done that, and I won't do it again. We've known each other since old times, Danny. It bothers me, us being at odds like this."

Nicky and I would never be friends again—we had too much bad blood for that, too much wreckage between us, but I didn't need any more enemies.

"Yeah," I said, not feeling the words. "Yeah, Nicky. We're good."

I pined for air-conditioning the second we left the club. Taking out my phone as we crossed the parking lot, I squinted against the sudden return of the sun.

"I'm texting everyone, calling for an emergency meet-up. We're gonna need all the help we can get."

"Go," Caitlin said. "Call me when you're done and let me know what the plan is."

"Huh? You aren't coming?"

She stopped next to the car, turning to look at me, her gaze unreadable.

"Daniel, introducing me to your friends, your community, would raise some very uncomfortable questions for you. I don't need to put you in that position."

I had thought about that. Yeah, it wasn't going to make me very popular, and Bentley would hit the roof. I might have a hard time feeling welcome at the Tiger's Garden for a while. Maybe ever again.

I put my phone away and rested my hands on her hips. Holding her close.

"We both knew," I said, "this wasn't going to be easy, you and me being together. This isn't the first challenge we've faced, and it sure as hell won't be the last. But I've got nothing to be ashamed of. My friends will stand by me, and if they don't, then fuck 'em because they weren't really my friends to start with."

She leaned in. Our lips brushed, soft as petals. She smelled like the ocean.

"All right," she said, "let's go meet the family then."

#

I decided to skip our usual haunt. While its entrances move on a regular basis, the Tiger's Garden usually hovers somewhere about a block away from the Silverlode. Lauren's people would be watching the street like hawks, and I didn't want to give them any sign that the Vegas occult underground was mobilizing for war.

"leave it 2 me," Jennifer's text read, and fifteen minutes later she sent over an address. We found parking in a garage off Las Vegas Boulevard and went a couple of blocks on foot, blending in with the tourist crowds.

"Really? Margaritaville?" Caitlin said, staring up at the sign. Calypso music bubbled out of an open doorway. Caribbean-style seating spread out under the wings of a dangling seaplane.

"Well, it is five o'clock somewhere," I said, leading her inside. "And Lauren won't be looking for us here."

"Indeed. No one would ever look for magicians in a place that serves copious amounts of alcohol."

Touché. I worried about the number of solid citizens milling around the place, considering what we had to discuss, but Jennifer had thought of everything. We found the whole crew up on the open terrace, where she'd evidently booked tables for a group three times our size. The tropical music, the noise from the street below, and a few empty tables for a buffer all worked together to give us a bit of much-needed privacy.

A rainbow of drinks decorated the table, garnished with springs of mint and wedges of pineapple carved to look like shark fins. The one holdout was Mama Margaux, sipping a layered milkshake topped with a volcano of whipped cream. Jennifer sat next to her, with a long flower box wrapped in gold ribbon taking up the chair on her other side. Bentley and Corman, each halfway through a frosted margarita, leaned against one another and watched the traffic go by. The gang was all here.

Except for Spengler, I thought, swallowing a momentary stab of guilt. Caitlin stood behind me as we approached, and I caught a glimpse of her wringing her hands. I didn't think anything could make her nervous.

They all fell silent as we walked up to the table. Their eyes had weight, questioning, roving. I reached behind Caitlin, resting a reassuring hand on the small of her back.

"Everybody," I said, "I want you to meet someone. This is Caitlin."

If any of the tourists a few tables away had looked in our direction, they wouldn't have seen a thing. Just a pack of people sitting in sudden silence, waiting for someone to talk. If they could see like we did, though, attuned to the currents of magic, it would have been a totally different story. Psychic tendrils took to the wind like a sea anemone's tentacles, rippling in the air, testing, probing. Some jerked back in sudden shock while others curved around, sniffing at Caitlin's spirit-body with dark curiosity.

I could feel Bentley and Corman's minds, their presence a warm pressure on my sinuses, and I realized what they were doing. They wanted to know if I'd been corrupted. Poisoned, addicted, like Caitlin had done to Detective Holt.

"No," I said firmly, and the pressure receded.

"Is that what I—" Jennifer started to say, then leaned over to Margaux and whispered, "Is that what I think it is?"

"Mm-hmm," she murmured, her face a blank slate.

Bentley's hands dropped under the table, and I knew him well enough to know what that meant. My own hand drifted toward my pocket, the weight of my cards reassuring against my hip. Mama pushed back her chair, just half an inch. Corman's eyes narrowed. I felt the situation slipping out of control, like a ball of yarn tumbling down a flight of stairs, one useless end clutched in my fingertips.

"You're my family," I said, and the movement stopped dead. I looked at them and shook my head. "Growing up, I didn't really have one worth a damn. You all know where I came from, where I've been. Your stories are a lot like mine. We aren't just friends. What we have is deeper than that. The lengths we've gone for each other are farther than that. We chose each other, as family. Because we needed each other."

Corman's eyes widened. Margaux nodded almost imperceptibly.

"When times are hard," I said, "we have each other's backs. We trust each other. I know it goes against everything in your gut, but right now, I want you—I need you—to trust me. Trust me when I tell you that Caitlin...Caitlin's okay. This woman saved my life. I hope you can respect that. I hope you can respect me."

Now the pensive silence was palpable. I looked across the table, my heart pounding. If they turned me away, cast me out...

Caitlin put her arm around my waist. Now it was her turn to give a reassuring touch. Bentley's gaze flitted to her hand, to the way she looked at me. His expression softened and he took a deep breath, nodding to himself.

"I think we've been terribly rude," he said softly. "We need two more chairs at this table."

Jennifer moved the flower box, patting the empty chair. "C'mere, Cait, you can sit next to me. Y'know, I dated Daniel for a coupla months once—"

"Too soon," I groaned, pulling over a chair and looking for the drink menu.

"Oh, no," Caitlin said. "I want to hear all about it."

Corman just smiled, patting Bentley on the back and whispering in his ear. I felt tears in my eyes and a kind of relief I hadn't known existed.

There was no guarantee any of us would live to see the morning, but whatever Lauren had in store for us, we'd face it together.

39.

With a frozen margarita in hand and the waitress out of earshot, I got down to business.

"Tonight, Lauren Carmichael and her followers are going to open the Etruscan Box. If she succeeds, it's pretty much game over for the entire planet. Not that we'll be around to worry about it, because Las Vegas will be a smoking crater."

Caitlin and I ran them through the high points of the story. We skirted around the parts about Solomon's ring. I meant what I had said to Caitlin back on the plane: the fewer people who knew it existed, the safer we all were. I felt bad, holding out on everybody right after they'd gone out on a limb for me, but then I imagined the consequences if word got out. I knew I was making the right call.

"These smoke-faced men," Corman grumbled, "I've never heard of anything like 'em. You sure this professor had all his marbles in one bag, kiddo? I mean, he *has* spent the last twenty years in a rubber room."

Mama Margaux mused over her drink. She had swapped her shake for a rum hurricane once we started talking. The apocalypse always goes better with booze.

"I've seen some of the Loa pictured a little like that, but the deed doesn't fit. The spirits get up to grim mischief sometimes, but not that grim."

"Mama's right," Jennifer drawled. "Whoever these boys are, they're into delivering doom on an epic scale. Patient critters, too."

I looked around the table and said, "Whoever they are, we'll settle up with them soon enough. Priority one, tonight, is to get the Box and take down Lauren and her crew."

"Got any ideas?" Corman asked.

"Well, etiquette and tradition dictate that I challenge them to a formal duel of sorcery refereed by an elder scholar of the art. All things considered, though, I'm leaning toward just shooting them. Everyone in favor of the just-shoot-them plan?"

Everyone held up their hands.

"Getting in, that's the hard part," I said. "The entrance is on Fremont, in the pedestrian mall. Big crowds, lots of attention. We can't just kick in the front door without being noticed."

Jennifer rubbed her chin. "They gotta have a cargo entrance, don't they? I mean, when the place was open for business, they weren't bringin' delivery trucks up that street."

Bentley slid a fountain pen from his shirt pocket and reached for a spare napkin. He sketched as he spoke, outlining the building.

"There is indeed. The Silverlode's quite the historical artifact. The casino, here, and the hotel tower were originally separate, adjoining buildings. Benny Binion bought them both in the early fifties and remodeled them as a single venue, Binion's Silverlode. The old girl had a good run. Finally closed its doors about ten years ago. An investment firm tried their hand at reopening for a couple of years after that, but they never got the magic back."

I pointed at a thin line. "So what's this? An alley?"

"An alley from a street one block over," Bentley said. "There's a service entrance to the casino along with a loading-bay door. Quite private. Here's your problem, though. The Klondike Room is here, on the twelfth floor. To get to the stairs, you'll have to cross the casino and the hotel lobby."

I thought back to Nicky's warning about Meadow Brand's traps, and my jaw tightened. "Nicky said the hotel elevator will take me right up to the Klondike. That right?"

Corman snorted. "Sure, if you're in a hurry to get killed. Think about it, kiddo. Elevator that opens right into the room where they're camping out? They'll cut you down the second the doors open, and they'll see the car coming up five minutes before it gets there. Same problem with the emergency stairwell."

Margaux frowned at the sketch. "What kind of place was the Klondike? Bar or a restaurant?"

"Full service," Bentley said. "Had the best steak and martini special in town, and for peanuts too. Cormie and I used to be regular fixtures there."

"They didn't squeeze slabs of beef into the elevator with the dinner guests," she said. "Had to be a way for the workin' folks to go up top, too, and supply the kitchen. Bet you there's a service elevator."

"What kind of opposition are we looking at?" Corman asked.

"Three sorcerers," I said. "They're good, and I mean good. First up is Sheldon Kaufman. He's a brawler, does this thing he calls Forsaken Hand style—"

Bentley scrunched his nose. "Ugh. I'd thought that school went extinct a long time ago. Dreadful people. I'll not put you off your drinks by describing their teaching techniques."

I nodded. "Least of our worries, I think. Number two is Meadow Brand. She builds things. I'm not sure if she can do any spontaneous, impromptu magic, but the Silverlode's her house and she's had plenty of time to prepare surprises for us. Finally, there's Lauren. You've all seen what she's capable of."

"So how do you want to play it?" Jennifer asked.

I sat back and sipped my margarita, watching the slow traffic on the boulevard. So many happy, innocent people, not knowing they could be headed for their last sunset on Earth. I'd botched this thing from start to finish. Spengler died in front of me because I couldn't save him. I was too late to rescue Amber Vance. Now, all eyes were on me, and they expected me to come up with a plan to stop Armageddon. No pressure.

"We hit them hard and fast. Not just because we're on a deadline—the longer it takes me to climb that tower, the longer they have to prepare a welcoming party. I need to know what I'm running into, before I run into it. Corman, you're the best remote viewer in the business. If you're up for it, I want you on astral overwatch."

Corman nodded firmly. "Been a long time since I was the best, kiddo, but I've still got the juice where it counts. I'm in."

"I'll translate for Cormie," Bentley said. "He doesn't have much breath when he's in a trance state. You wear an earpiece, and I'll relay everything he says over the telephone."

I turned to Margaux. "Mama, I'm expecting heavy wards. Keep-out-or-die kinda stuff. I seem to recall your spirit buddies are good at dismantling those."

"Good? Hah! Those wards will crack like eggshells in a blender. Give me a couple hours, maybe three, to make the sacrifices and butter them up. My spirits'll dance with you, Danny boy. No barrier built by mortal hands will stand in your way."

"And for everything else," Jennifer said, "you got me. Oh, I am going in with you. You know me, I'm a hands-on kinda witch, and I don't mind the rough stuff."

Caitlin cleared her throat. "I'll be in communication with...my people. Preparing for the worst, in the event that they open the Box and my prince is summoned forth."

I studied the napkin sketch. No way to tell what we'd face once we got inside. On astral overwatch, Corman's disembodied eyes should be able to scout ahead and offer a few seconds of warning, but that was all the help we'd get. Once we hit the door, it'd be a twelve-floor sprint through everything they could throw at us.

"They'll anticipate someone jimmying the door at the service entrance," I said. "Good place for a nasty trap. I'd love to get in through the loading bay instead, but I'm not sure how. Any suggestions?"

"Boom-boom. Clump of C-4 the size of a butter stick," Jennifer said.

"Loud," Bentley said, "but they'll almost certainly be alerted to your presence as soon as the assault begins, no matter how you go in. Loud and disorienting might be to our advantage."

"Wait," I said, "plastic explosives? You can get that?"

"Darlin', I deal in mass quantities of recreational substances for a living. Outlaw bikers are some of my best customers. When I say I can get some boom-boom, I mean I can *get* some boom-boom. Lemme make some calls, I'll have it by tonight."

It made sense. Nicky had said he could keep the cops at bay, at least for a little while, and hopefully the back lot was secluded enough that the blast would sound more like fireworks or a backfiring car to the crowds a block away.

"I think we're ready." I pushed back my chair, offering my hand to Caitlin. "Let's meet up at eight tonight. We'll get the job done."

It wasn't much of a speech. I felt like I should say something to rally the troops, considering what was on the line, but then again I didn't need to. Looking around the table at the resolve in their eyes, I could see that everybody knew the stakes. They'd follow me into hell if they had to.

I hoped that saying didn't turn literal.

"One thing," Jennifer said, handing me the long flower box. I took it in my hands, surprised by its weight. "I saved that for you, from the locust job we pulled on Spengler's house. I think he'd want you to have it. Don't open it here."

Bentley held up a finger. "Daniel? A word?"

I nodded and walked with him to the opposite edge of the patio deck. He fumbled for words, and I waited patiently while he found them. I already knew what he was going to say.

"I'm not okay with this," he said.

"I know."

"No, please, hear me out. When Cormie and I found you, you were...a ruin. What that cult did to you, what those demons did inside of you, was unspeakable. Your spirit was in tatters, scarred, torn. Most people would have died from that kind of abuse, but you survived. You survived and grew into a vibrant, strong man who we are so very, very proud of."

"You think it's going to happen again. Is that it? You think Caitlin's going to hurt me?"

Bentley shook his head, the wrinkles at the corners of his eyes tightening.

"She's a demon, Daniel. I'm not convinced she's *capable* of not hurting you. I know what she is, and it scares me to death. But then...I saw how she looked at you."

I nodded, holding my silence.

"It's the way Cormie looked at me, when we were young. That's what he whispered to me, when you sat down together. That the two of you reminded him of us."

"This isn't going to be easy," I told him. "Not for any of us. I just need to know you've got my back."

He pulled me into a hug, his bottom lip quivering. His shoulders felt frail in my arms, like a bird's bones.

"Always, son," he whispered. "Always."

40.

Caitlin and I didn't say much on our walk back to the parking garage. She settled into the passenger seat while I put the flower box in the trunk. When I got in, she looked over at me, an unspoken word on her parted lips.

"You okay?" I asked.

"I'm processing," she said. "This is all very new for me. They...they seem nice."

She was looking for something. I could see it in her eyes, a strange uncertainty, a hunger she didn't know how to deal with. I wasn't certain what it was, but I had a hunch.

"Yeah, I think they liked you."

She smiled, relief in her eyes. "I'm not used to caring about that. I mean, if I'm dealing with a human and I need them to want me, I can *make* them want me. I can make them feel whatever I need them to feel."

"But it's not the real thing."

"No. It's not."

I started the engine and backed out of the parking space.

"I want to be there with you tonight," Caitlin said. "I hate that I can't, but that damned ring—"

"I know. Don't worry, I'll get it away from her. Even if I have to take her finger off with it."

"Meanwhile, I'll be playing politics. Ever since my prince advised his inner council on the Box situation, word's spread like wildfire. There's a gallery of potential usurpers sharpening their knives as we speak."

I squinted as we pulled out of the garage, the golden afternoon light splashing across my dusty windshield. "Why'd he do it, then? He had to have known people would talk."

"Exactly. What better time than a crisis to find out how your confidants really feel? The disloyal make themselves obvious, drooling over the thought of an empty throne. Once tonight is over and done, I suspect there will be some vigorous housecleaning in my prince's court."

"You sound like you're enjoying this."

"That part? I am. Some traitorous would-be conquerors are going to be very surprised when they wake up in chains tomorrow. There will be punishment. Severe. Merciless. Punishment. Pain is so much more enjoyable when it's inflicted on the truly deserving." She paused, quirking an eyebrow. "Does that bother you?"

I thought about it for a second and shrugged.

"You're a career woman. I respect that."

We drove to her place. Sitting in the car, the radio turned off, we listened to the engine idle and stared at the bloody sky.

"So what now?" she said softly.

I took the fringed pouch from my pocket and stared at it, feeling the weight of Stacy's half-soul in my fingertips.

"Now I go to the storm tunnels and have a chat with a dead girl. Then I'm gonna go save the world. After that, my evening's pretty much free. Want to get together for drinks?"

Caitlin turned in her seat. She stroked my neck with the tips of her fingernails, sending shivers down my spine.

"You come back to me," she said.

"That's a promise," I told her, pulling her close. We kissed, and she rested her head on my shoulder.

#

Even by the afternoon light, the culvert leading down to the storm tunnels was a treacherous abyss. With my flashlight fixed to my shirt pocket, I slowly climbed down the cutout rungs. My beam flashed across broken glass and concrete. Over in a patch of weeds, a rat's beady scarlet eyes glowed in the reflected light. It turned and ran, scampering past the wall of tribal graffiti and disappearing into the tunnel. I followed it down.

Past the first bend, snoring echoed off the tunnel walls. Eric slept like a log with the battery-powered lamp glowing behind the ramshackle walls of his lean-to. He'd apparently taken my advice about staying clear of Tunnel C. I crept past as quietly as I could, trying not to wake him.

The trail of enchanted dust was just as I had left it, stretched from end to end across the tunnel mouth. I stood at the edge of the line and squinted into the inky gloom.

"Stacy," I whispered. "Stacy."

Stacy Pankow's mangled wraith loomed out of the darkness, a broken vision in gossamer white. One useless foot trailed behind her as she glided toward me. Her jaw gaped wide in a soundless scream. She stretched out her remaining arm, clawing at the air, but couldn't cross the dust.

I held up the pouch so she could see it. Her frosted eyes widened. Some part of her, buried under the confusion and pain, recognized what was missing.

"Stacy," I said, "we need to talk."

#

When I emerged from the tunnel, storm clouds choked the darkening sky. The forecast had called for clear and dry.

Dammit, I thought, running for the culvert ladder, *they're already starting.* I jumped into my car and gunned the engine. In the distance, a finger of white lightning licked the sky, crackling between the clouds, mirroring the neon streets below.

Jennifer waited for me down the back alley leading to the Silverlode, rummaging in the trunk of her little blue hatchback. The casino stood cold and silent, but to our magic-attuned eyes it flared like a beacon of black gold. Wards and death-hexes bristled at every window and door. Purple ribbons of energy coiled like serpents around the bricks, wreathing the tower in their rippling runic coils. I pulled up behind Jennifer and got out of the car, cupping a hand over my eyes as I stared at the monstrosity.

"They really don't want to be disturbed," I said.

I got the flower box out of my back seat. Jennifer tossed me a Bluetooth earpiece.

"I'd say we've seen worse," she said, "but I hate lyin'."

She pulled on a shoulder holster. While I linked up the earpiece with my phone and tried to get Bentley on the line,

Jennifer handloaded a chrome revolver with a barrel big enough to intimidate a rhinoceros.

"What?" she said, catching my look. "Girl's gotta protect herself."

"We're here," Bentley said on the other end of the line.

"Good," I told him. "I'm putting us on a conference call. Dialing up Mama now."

Margaux came on the line to the tune of distant drumbeats, a cacophony that swirled across the phone line and abruptly fell silent.

"Five minutes," she said, her voice strained, and put her line on mute.

"Cormie's meditating," Bentley said. "He'll be in a trance in no time, just a little rusty."

"Don't want to pressure anybody, but time's not on our side here," I said. I leaned against my car. We waited.

Jennifer looked over at me after a minute of pensive silence.

"So. Datin' a succubus, huh?"

"Oh, we are *not* having this conversation right now," I said.

"I'm just saying. I might've started looking for love on the fairer side of the street after we broke up, but at least I stayed inside my own species."

"It just sort of happened."

"Well," she said, looking up at the Silverlode, "she seems all right. So far. Fair warning, if she messes with your head I'm gonna claw her eyes out."

"Fairly noted," I said. "And thanks."

She looked at me with a smirk. "So, her lady parts, are they just like—"

Margaux's return to the conference call saved me. She put us on speaker, the line crackling with staccato drumbeats and a strange, high-pitched and chaotic melody, like a flute playing inside a blender.

"The cause is true," Margaux panted, "and the spirits have been paid. They're gonna help."

A wind blew across the parking lot, hot as steam, feeling like the breath of God on my back.

"Cormie's there with you," Bentley said. "He's in the astral. He says the Silverlode—it's like nothing he's ever seen. He can't even get near the edge of the tower, the wards are too thick."

I nodded. "Roger that. We can see it too. Mama, are you sure your spirits can crack this piggy bank?"

"Like nitroglycerin. Don't you doubt it, boy."

The wind swirled around us. Hungry. Eager to fight.

"All right," I said, "here's how we play it. Jennifer blows the loading bay door. Mama, your boys take out the wards. Tell them to hit the outer layer and just keep plowing through until they come out the other side. Bentley, tell Corman to follow behind them as close as he can and warn us about any traps. Me and Jenny will bring up the rear."

The C-4 really did look like a stick of butter, neatly wrapped in brown paper. So did the next brick she took from her trunk. And the next.

"How much did you get?" I asked.

She shrugged with a smile. "I called in some favors. Figured we might as well go all out on the shock and awe."

Jennifer scrutinized the tall corrugated-metal door, sized for a truck, and stuck the clump of plastic explosive near the left seam. She fiddled with it for a moment, carefully shaping the putty, and stuck what looked like a spark plug into the middle of the mass. She set the next charge on the service door and walked around the corner to split the third brick of explosive between a pair of boarded-up windows.

I set the flower box on the hood of my car and untied the festive ribbon. Inside, nestled in a bed of crepe paper, lay my gift from Spengler's safe room: his Benelli Nova Tactical, a sleek, black, pump-action shotgun with ghost-ring sights. I loaded four cartridges, feeding them in one at a time. I liked the idea of bringing Spengler's gun on the raid. At least in spirit, the whole family would be together one last time.

Jennifer finished setting the charge and ran back to join me behind her car. She held up a detonator with a bright red, plastic squeeze-trigger.

"You ready for this?" She looked halfway between excitement and terror. I knew the feeling, my pulse racing as I readied for the charge. We'd win or we'd die tonight. No other options.

"Ready as I'm gonna be. Mama?"

"Just say the word," Margaux whispered, her voice strained as she concentrated on her ritual. The drumbeats in the background quickened, echoing my pounding heart.

"Bentley and Corman?"

"Cormie's astral body is floating about five feet above your heads," Bentley said. "Says he's fit as a fiddle and ready to go."

I took a deep breath. The Silverlode loomed over us like a living thing, a hungry monster waiting to be fed. Or a dragon waiting to be slain.

"All right," I said. "Let's show these Seattle assholes how we do things in Vegas. Jennifer?"

She held up the detonator. I nodded.

"*Light 'em up!*"

41.

One click of the detonator, so fast her fingers blurred, and the alley erupted in a blast of crumpled metal and flame. Superheated air blew past us, flowing toward the black, billowing smoke like oxygen filling a sudden vacuum. Margaux's horde of disembodied wraiths slammed into the outer wards at a hundred miles an hour. The clashing enchantments screamed inside my head, a discordant howl like iron fingernails on a chalkboard.

"*Go!*" I shouted, charging down the alley, cradling Spengler's shotgun in my hands and keeping my head down. The loading-bay door crumpled inward, punched by a giant's fist, edges of the torn metal blackened and smoking. I jumped through the gap and hit a small storage room. Its shelves were empty and caked with years of dust. The door lay just ahead.

"Wait!" Bentley shouted into my earpiece, just as my foot snagged a length of fishing line.

The trip wire snapped. The ceiling groaned. I hurled myself to the bare concrete floor, landing on my shoulder and rolling just as a scythe blade on a wooden arm swung across my path. Behind me, Jennifer stopped short, the vicious blade sweeping half an inch from her nose.

"Gonna need a little more advance warning than that," I breathed. Jennifer's face was pale.

"Sorry," Bentley said. "Up ahead, just past the door, three more trip wires. Two low, one high."

We didn't have time to catch our breaths. I led the charge, jumping and ducking around the fishing line, emerging onto the silent casino floor. Only the emergency lights were on, casting row after row of dead slot machines in a pale cemetery glow. All we needed to do was cross the room, get through the connecting hallway, and reach the hotel lobby.

A broad avenue of antique scalloped carpet ran through the heart of the casino. Meadow Brand stood there, waiting for us.

"Lauren thought you left town," she said. "I knew better."

I came to a stop about ten feet away from her, Jennifer at my side.

"So you came to greet us?" I said. "Very considerate of you."

Something moved in the shadows. A figure darted past in the corner of my eye, slipping between the slot machines, vanishing from sight. A moment later, something flickered in my peripheral vision on the other side of the room, too quick to catch.

Bentley's worried voice came on the line. "You've got trouble. Cormie says you're not alone in there. He can't tell what they are. They just look like blobs on the astral, blobs of dark heat. They're...artificial."

"Mm-hmm," I murmured for both his and Jennifer's benefit, "and they're flanking us. Also, that's not Meadow Brand."

"How do you know?" Jennifer whispered.

"Because last time I saw her, I carved her face open. Either she got the world's best and fastest plastic surgery, or she's just psychically projecting herself onto one of her puppets."

I took a step closer. There was definitely something wrong with "Meadow." Her movements were too jerky, her expression too uneven, too plastic.

"Last chance," I told her. "I know you're up there with the others. Don't open the Box. It's not what you think."

She laughed. A harsh and bitter sound.

"It's exactly what we think. Power. Raw, beautiful power. All we could ever want. In less than an hour, hell itself will eat out of our hands. And we're just getting started."

"Daniel," Bentley said over the earpiece, insistent, "more of them. At least fifteen, maybe twenty of those things, all around you. She's stalling you while they get ready to attack."

I felt them. Soulless creatures in the dark, closing in but staying just out of sight, their jerky movements like marionettes on a mad puppeteer's strings. I waved Jennifer close and whispered in her ear.

"Get ready to run for it. She's got more pets than we have bullets, so make every shot count." I looked over to the Meadow-thing and shook my head, raising my voice. "You forgot your line, by the way."

"What line?" Meadow demanded.

"When you rant about your master plan for world domination, you're supposed to end with 'but it's too bad you won't live to see it.' I mean, if you're gonna act like an ass-hole pulp villain, at least show some commitment to the part."

Her hands curled at her sides. "Funny. You won't be laughing when—"

I leveled the shotgun and blew her head off.

The illusion ripped away in a spray of steel shot and ma-hogany splinters. The creature before us was nothing but a jointed wooden armature doll, a life-sized version of the ti-ny puppets artists use for anatomy sketches. It collapsed to its knees, its psychic strings cut.

"When I interrupt you like that?" I said. "I don't know, maybe I'm just easily amused, but I think that was pretty funny."

The creatures loomed into view all around us. More mannequins like the first, but their hands were misshapen and melded with metal. Rusted iron hooks, sickles, and wickedly serrated knives glimmered in the dark, ready to rend and tear.

Jennifer took a stainless-steel razor blade from her pock-et and rested it on the tip of her tongue. She clenched it between her teeth as she hissed a garbled, barbaric chant. Energy swirled around us like a slow cyclone, raw and bru-tal. I concentrated, lending my strength to hers, building the embryonic spell into something more powerful than either of us could do alone.

Moving as one, the mannequins attacked.

Jennifer raised her tattooed arm, her revolver clutched in her opposite hand, and viciously ripped the blade in her teeth across her own skin. Blood sprayed out around us, too much blood for the depth of the wound, too much for one human's body, as the gathered magic crystallized and took form. The spray of blood hung frozen in the air, droplets suspended in space like tiny uncut rubies. Almost immediately her torn skin began to reknit itself under the writhing ink of her tattoos.

The first wave of mannequins hit the curtain of blood and exploded. They blasted backward in a fountain of twisted metal and shattered wood. Jennifer spat out the razor. We ran.

She broke left and I headed right, taking the long way around a bank of slot machines with the surviving mannequins hot on our heels. Her fat revolver barked again and again. I turned, feeling a shadow looming, and put the muzzle of my shotgun flush against another mannequin's forehead before pulling the trigger. It flipped backward, tumbling neck over heels, and another two puppets clambered over its body before it even stopped twitching.

"Need some help here!" I shouted. The connecting hallway loomed ahead of us, a shadowy stretch of innocent-looking marble tiles and unlit electric wall sconces.

"Trip wire!" Bentley's voice crackled. "Chest high!"

I hit the cold tiles with the shotgun clutched to my chest, rolling. Jennifer went down on her knees and slid under it, leaning back to fire off another wild shot. The mannequins kept coming in a relentless, silent tide of death.

"Ten feet ahead! Ankle height!" Bentley called. We jumped it as the pursuing mannequins hit the first trip wire behind us. It snapped with an audible twang. Saw blades screamed as they fired from hidden recesses in the walls, slicing the front-runners to kindling. The others didn't hesitate, climbing over their fallen comrades without a trace of survival instinct. Jennifer turned to shoot, but her gun clicked on an empty chamber. I fired off another round, blasting a sprinting mannequin in half at the waist. One cartridge left.

The mannequins snapped the next wire. I looked back as tubes in the ceiling sprayed the horde with a watery mist. Ahead of us, a pair of wall portraits advertising long-dead lounge singers swung out from their frames, exposing a pair of nozzles angled to cover the entire hallway.

I smelled gasoline.

"Down!" I shouted, shoving Jennifer to the floor and covering her with my body just as the nozzles erupted. Gouts of flame streaked over our heads, hitting the gasoline-drenched mannequins and sending them up in a bonfire.

We crawled under the nozzles and crossed the threshold to the hotel lobby. Heavy footprints marred the dust on the floor, most leading to the main elevator beside an abandoned check-in desk. They'd blocked the front doors the crude way, stripping bed frames and desks from the guest rooms and piling them in a makeshift barricade.

Even without mouths, the mannequins screamed behind us. The wordless shrilling throbbed inside my brain as they stumbled over one another. They slammed off the hallway walls, burning and confused and dying. I pointed to the barricade.

"Can you clear enough room for us to get out?"

"Where are you going?" Jennifer said as I vaulted the check-in desk. I threw my shoulder against the door behind it, the flimsy wood cracking under the blow.

"I've gotta get those sprinklers working!"

Respect for an old landmark aside, I wouldn't have minded if the tower went up in flames and took Lauren and her cult with it. It wouldn't burn fast enough to stop them from opening the Box, though, and if we went up to confront them we'd end up trapped at the top of a raging inferno. The hotel had a fire-suppression system—the tiny sprinkler nozzles studding the lobby ceiling were proof of it—but the thick black smoke roiling from the burning hallway wasn't doing a thing besides killing us slowly. Maybe triggering the system by hand would work.

Around the corner, in a utility room the size of a walk-in closet, I discovered why the sprinklers weren't coming on. Metal panels sat propped against the wall, the innards of the hotel's alarm and fire system nothing but a gutted mess of empty fuse slots and bare wires. Since Carmichael-Sterling Nevada's pledge to renovate and reopen the Silverlode was nothing but a sham in the first place, they hadn't put any effort into hooking up more than basic electricity.

Not like they have to worry about the place burning down either, I thought, *considering they believe they're about to enslave a couple of magic genies who can whisk them away to safety.*

The fire would spread. Too fast for the hotel tower to be anything but a death trap, too slow to do our job for us. I figured I'd meet up with Jennifer in the lobby, help clear a path to the front door, and we'd figure out a plan once our escape route was in place.

I was almost to the check-in desk when a burning mannequin, shrieking and thrashing its blazing wooden arms, threw itself at me.

I jumped back, swinging my shotgun like a club. The barrel cracked across the side of its head and dropped it in the open doorway, where it flopped brokenly. The threshold caught fire. Flames spread across the plaster walls and seared them black.

"Daniel!" Jennifer shouted, running over. She stood on the opposite side of a growing wall of fire. Her hands, shimmering mirages in the heat, reached helplessly for me. It was no good. The wild flames took to the narrow hallway like a junkie to a crack vial.

"Forget it!" I said, backing off from the creeping blaze. "Can you get out through the front door?"

She nodded, looking back over her shoulder. "But what about you?"

What about me? I couldn't think about that right now. I still had a job to do.

"I'll find another way, don't worry. I'll be fine! Do me a favor: wait two minutes and send the main elevator up to the top floor. Then get out of here. Go meet up with the others. I'll be in touch."

She gritted her teeth, frustrated, but nodded her assent. I turned and ran.

"Don't know if you're keeping up on current events—" I said, one hand on my earpiece.

"On it," Bentley's voice crackled. "Cormie's looking for fire exits."

"What I need right now is that service elevator. Our deadline just got a little tighter."

I jogged down a maintenance corridor, past a corkboard still displaying yellowed bulletins from ten years ago.

"Take the first left," Bentley said after a moment's pause, "then a short right."

The service elevator was big enough to deliver a grand piano. Dirty canvas padding covered the walls, and a scuffed rubber mat lined the floor. I hit the button for twelve and the doors rumbled shut, the cage springing to life with a wheezing groan.

I thought back to every fire drill I had sat through as a kid, and how they had hammered it into my head that the one thing you never, ever do in a fire is use the elevators. Of course, I was pretty sure "don't pick a fight with a crew of sorcerers who already kicked your ass once this week" was also on the list of things you shouldn't do. I wasn't setting any safety records tonight.

Right about now, Jennifer would be sending the empty main elevator up to the Klondike, giving me the chance to slip around and get the element of surprise. At least, I hoped so. It was the only advantage I was going to get.

I held my breath. The elevator chimed.

Top floor, end of the line.

42.

The doors ground open, too loud for my liking, on a dark and empty kitchen. Fat blending bowls and double-decker ovens gathered dust. They'd been abandoned for years. I dropped low, crawl-walking around the counters with my shotgun held tight to my chest. Light streamed in through a service window to my left. Hearing voices, I slowly peeked up and over, into the lounge beyond.

The Klondike Room really was a marvel of Old Vegas. I could imagine Sinatra singing on the scallop-walled stage with an approving crowd spread among the plush red velvet chairs and low glass cocktail tables. Toward the back, near the great brass doors of the main elevator, tables set with faded white cloth waited for a steak dinner that would never arrive.

Tonight's performance was nothing so elegant. The Etruscan Box sat on a black marble pillar at center stage. Swirls and sigils in bone-white chalk adorned the wooden slats around it. Hundreds of candles flooded the room with flickering light, set out on every table and ledge in patterns

that hinted at some mad geometric design. On the only table without a candle, set up on stage squarely before the
Box, sat five little pouches.

"I can't believe he's this fucking stupid," Meadow said,
planted in front in front of the elevator doors. Tiny glowing
numbers inched their way upward, the empty cage making
its way to the top floor.

"I can't believe he got past your traps," Sheldon said from
the stage, kneeling as he put the final touches on a painted
glyph. "It's almost like you're more interested in torturing
people than building an effective security system."

"Ms. Carmichael," Meadow said, "please tell Sheldon that
if his idiot brother hadn't fucked things up, we wouldn't
even be in this situation. And Tony would still be alive."

"Lauren," Sheldon said as he stood up and brushed the
dust from his slacks, "please tell Little Miss Torquemada
that if she'd spend more time acting like a professional and
less time acting like something out of a horror movie—"

"Both of you, quiet," Lauren said. She stood, imperious
and regal, a step behind Meadow. Her hands wavered in the
candlelight, slow and sinuous, fingertips trailing luminous
green mist.

Meadow turned her head, the light catching her ravaged
face, and I held my breath. A vicious scar ran from her forehead to her jaw, carving off a lop of skin at the side of her
nose. A string of tape and sutures held her raw, red flesh
together.

"He dies slow," she hissed, "him and anyone with him."

Lauren narrowed her eyes, concentrating on the elevator
door. "He dies, period, and we get back to work."

Three against one is a sucker's bet. Odds were I'd be
dead in the next ten minutes. Jennifer and me together, we

might have taken them, but I'm a firm believer in contingency plans. Mine sat snug in my hip pocket, right next to my deck of cards.

If you can't change the odds, you can always change the game.

"Is Jenny safe?" I whispered as loud as I dared, hoping the earpiece would pick it up.

"She's here with me," Margaux said. "Fire department's on the way, and they've cleared Fremont Street. You can see the flames in the windows, up to the third floor and climbing fast."

"You have to leave," Bentley cut in. "*Now*, Daniel. Cormie says there's an old fire escape on the west side of the building, but it stops at the eighth floor. You don't have much time!"

I took the earpiece and stuffed it in my shirt pocket. No distractions. My breath slowed. My pupils dilated, showing me the room in a spray of color, the winds of magic tracing the world in violet and gold. When we had fought at Spengler's house, they got the drop on me. Things were different now.

They'd probably kill me, but I'd make damn sure they bled for their victory.

The elevator let out a merry chime. Before the doors were even halfway open, Lauren unleashed a torrent of bilious green fog, spilling from her hands like a flamethrower's plume and flooding the elevator cage with acidic death. She was just realizing her mistake, looking at the steaming, pitted ruins of an empty elevator, when I burst through the swinging kitchen door and blasted them with the shotgun.

I was fast. Lauren was faster. She spun and threw up her empty palm. The air shimmered, turning to jelly, and a wall of shotgun pellets hung in the web of her makeshift shield before tumbling to the ground. She twirled her other hand in a spinning motion, pointing, and suddenly I wasn't holding a shotgun anymore. A fat rattlesnake nestled in my hands, its head twisting around to bite. On instinct, I threw the snake as far as I could. By the time it landed the illusion was gone, and my weapon clattered against the edge of the stage.

I only had the one cartridge left anyway. I went for my cards, but then I saw Sheldon running up on me, his fists glowing with furious red energy. I couldn't let him get close, not yet. I circled the closest table, a four-seater draped for dinner and displaying a dozen candles in tiny silver cups.

"For my next trick," I announced and grabbed hold of the tablecloth's edge. The cloth whipped away in one smooth movement and left the candles standing on bare wood, untouched. Keeping the momentum, I swung the tablecloth over my head, bringing it around and letting it fly. It hit Sheldon square in the face and wrapped around him like a needy ghost, enveloping his arms and legs and sending him to the ground in a kicking tangle.

A lance of green light flashed past my eyes, striking the wood-paneled wall and leaving a sizzling hole in its wake. I raced across the room, jumping over Sheldon, as my cards leaped from my pocket in a riffling stream to land in the palm of my outstretched hand. I ducked another of Lauren's blasts and offered my retort, sending a pair of luminous poker cards screaming across the room like razor-edged boomerangs. Lauren threw herself behind a potted plant. Meadow ran over to help Sheldon, tugging at the clingy enchanted tablecloth.

"Gimme your gun!" she shrieked at Sheldon as he forced one arm free. "Give me your fucking gun!"

Lauren and I darted from cover to cover like gunfighters at high noon, taking shots where we could, keeping our heads down and our hands fast. I was almost to the stage when Sheldon got loose, shoving Meadow away and charging like an enraged bull. He had his pistol, all right, but he was good and pissed and wanted to finish this fight with his bare hands. Perfect. That's what I was counting on.

I backed up a few steps onto the stage and turned to face him. My timing had to be absolutely flawless, or it was all over. I raised my open hand, invoking the threads of a spell.

He lunged out with a curled fist, sending a shockwave of power that hit me point blank in the stomach from five feet away, knocking the wind out of me and shattering my concentration. Then he leaped, his foot a blur as it whirled toward me. I felt ribs crack as I flew backward, slamming into the table with the soul-trap pouches and sending it clattering to the ground, leaving me prone in a puddle of broken glass. Sheldon crouched over me, grabbed me by my collar, and hoisted me up, his fist drawn back.

I didn't see it land. I just felt the sudden white-hot pain as my nose cracked, painting my vision blood red, and then nothing.

I must have only been out for a couple of minutes. I woke up, propped up against a railing off to the side of the stage. I tasted blood, my upper lip wet and sticky. My nose and ribs throbbed with icy pain.

Meadow Brand stood over me. She had Sheldon's gun now. He and Lauren were working to touch up the stage, fixing the paint I'd smeared and setting the soul-traps in their proper place once more.

"Can't blame a guy for trying," I said with an exhausted smile. Meadow's finger tightened on the trigger.

"Spirited," Lauren said, walking over to join us, "but you're on the wrong side, Mr. Faust. You act like we're trying to destroy the world, when we only want to save it."

"Yeah? I know a dead little girl who probably thinks different."

She looked wounded. "We aren't sociopaths, Mr. Faust. A sociopath is, by definition, incapable of human empathy. Opening the Box requires a sacrifice of loved ones. We have all paid for our work, paid in pain and tears."

"Not nearly enough," I said.

"You'll understand," she said with a faintly condescending smile. "Ms. Brand has requested that you be kept alive, in order to see the glory of our work. And to...make amends for injuring her."

Meadow stared down the sights of the gun with a killer's eyes.

"When our new slaves get here," she snarled, "the things I am gonna make them do to you—you'll wish you'd never been born. And before I let you die? I'm going to make them gather up all your friends, everybody you ever cared about, so you can watch them suffer and die first."

"Oh, yeah," I said to Lauren, ignoring Meadow. "I can tell you're a bunch of real saints. This one's humanitarian of the year material."

"The Enclave project requires a woman of Ms. Brand's unique talents," Lauren said with a long-suffering sigh, then shot her a warning glance. "I tolerate her eccentricities. Within limits."

"Yes ma'am," Meadow hissed, her eyes fixed on mine. She held the pistol in a steel grip.

Sheldon clapped his hands from the stage. "We're ready!"

"Very good," Lauren said, adjusting the signet ring on her left hand. "Sheldon, you have the honor of opening the lock. I will bind Belephaia as soon as she emerges, then Sitri as he arrives."

She ascended the stage, standing in an arcane circle painted in daubs of yellow and white. Sheldon stood before the box, arms outstretched, the tray of pouches at his side. Latin words rumbled from his throat, twisting in the air as they slipped back, regressing to a coarser and more barbarous tongue.

Streamers of pale white light slithered from the soul-traps like snakes' tongues licking the air. The streamers stretched toward the Box, crackling as they made contact with its onyx hasp.

"You really don't want to do this," I told Meadow. "You really don't."

"Shut up," she snarled. "We win, you lose. Simple as that."

The streamers tightened. They were lances now, pulsing and throbbing with pure soul-energy as they spread pools of blazing light in every nook, cranny, and recess of the casket's face. Sheldon's chant grew louder, and louder still, spiraling into a raw-throated ecstatic cry.

The Box opened.

43.

I shouldn't have looked.

I knew I shouldn't have looked, but as the Box slowly opened, swinging on ancient hinges, I sat in the perfect spot to take a peek inside. What I saw would haunt my nightmares forever.

A space bigger than the casket that contained it, infinitely bigger, bathed in blinding light. A feathered wing covered in thousands of blinking, staring eyes, each a different color, each pronouncing a different judgment on my corrupt heart. Knowing every sin I'd ever committed and every sin I ever would commit, my heart nearly bursting under the weight of their raw hatred. I saw the tip of a yellowed and rotting bone spear, long and wickedly curved, then realized I was looking at a fingernail...

One of the streamers of light sputtered. It yanked me from my reverie, hauling me back from the edge of madness and focusing my attention on the soul-traps. Sheldon looked at them, dumbfounded, shaking his head as the errant light crackled and whipped back, recoiling into its pouch as if rejected.

If you can't change the odds, change the game.

I just leaned back and smiled.

"The number of souls is five," I said, echoing what the smoke-faced man had told Lauren so many years ago. "What was it he said? 'To open the Box without the requisite sacrifice invites the wrath of its guardians.' Something like that?"

Lauren looked at me, torn between outrage and sudden terror. "What did you do?"

"It must not be denied that I am a plain-dealing villain," I said, the smile slipping from my face as my eyes went hard. "I fucked you over, that's what."

The storm tunnel stank of mildew and regret. Stacy's pouch rested heavy in my hand. Her half-formed wraith hovered across the line of dust, tortured mouth wide in a soundless wail.

"I know. I'm so sorry. I want to free you, but...I need to hold onto this, just a little while longer. I swear to you, though. I swear to you, I'll be back as soon as I'm done."

"My timing had to be perfect," I told Lauren, "and it was. I *let* Sheldon hit me, so he could knock me right into the tray of soul-traps. Once I went down, palming one of the pouches and switching it with Stacy's half-empty one was easy. Four and a half souls. You opened the box without the proper sacrifice. Gotta think that's going to hurt."

The Box slammed shut. A new light boiled from the ebony casket itself, violent and swirling, the color of orange stained glass. Sheldon looked over, pinned in place, trembling as he called out.

"L-Lauren?"

The other soul-traps snapped closed, their lights whipping back into the pouches, rejected and undevoured.

"*Lauren!*" Sheldon screamed, just before the orange light ate him alive.

It crashed over him like a rogue wave, flooding his mouth, saturating his skin, motes of brilliant fire swirling around him. The motes ate him like a school of piranha feasting on a bleeding calf. Skin tore away in tiny chunks, blood spattering the stage, the light shredding him one nickel-sized bite of flesh at a time.

Meadow lunged at me, pressing the barrel of her gun to my forehead. I'd been waiting. I jerked my head to the side and grabbed the pistol, twisting it hard and yanking it from her grip. She dove out of the way as I fired off two fast shots. The bullets went wide, shattering a glass table and sending burning candles to the floor, a tablecloth igniting.

Sheldon's eyes exploded. Still transfixed by the light, he shrieked endlessly as it chewed him down to ragged muscle and bone. Lauren ran from the stage, throwing up a desperate shield to ripple the air as I snapped off another shot. Meadow waited by the emergency stairwell, holding the door open.

"Lauren!" Meadow shouted. "Let's *go!*"

"You're not leaving," I snarled, giving chase. Then I froze and looked back. The Silverlode was going down in flames, literally. If I abandoned the pouches on the stage, they'd be lost forever. Maybe the souls trapped inside would be freed when the enchanted leather burned, but maybe they wouldn't.

I could settle up with Lauren and Meadow another time. Cursing under my breath, I dove for the stage as hungry tendrils of orange light snapped like whips just above my head. I grabbed the tray, clutched it to my chest, and rolled clear as Sheldon's ravaged corpse collapsed in a bloody heap. I didn't stop running until I hit the emergency stairwell, pausing just long enough to count the pouches and stow them in my pockets.

A few floors down, a metal door rattled and chunked shut. I took the concrete steps two at a time, swinging around the handrails. By the time I hit the eighth floor my heart was pounding like a kettledrum and my breath was ragged, but there wasn't a second to lose. Bentley had said the fire escape topped out on the eighth floor. That must be where Lauren and Meadow were headed, and it'd be my way out too.

The door grip rattled uselessly in my hand. Looking closer, I could see the warped metal in the doorjamb, how it ran like melted wax. They'd destroyed the lock.

I ran down to the seventh floor landing and hauled open the stairwell door. A sudden furnace-blast of heat seared my lungs and stole my breath. Flames licked the walls of the hallway beyond, curling the antique hotel wallpaper and blackening the dusty carpet.

If the fire was this out of control, going any lower would be suicide. I could run back up to nine and hope the flames hadn't reached it yet, then try jumping down to the fire escape, but if the windows didn't line up I'd be trapped. Meanwhile, my window of opportunity on seven closing tighter than a hangman's noose.

I took my last breath of clean air and ran for it, keeping to the middle of the hallway as the fire raged around me. I knew it was a bad idea once I hit the first intersection and suddenly couldn't tell left from right. The billowing smoke stung my watering eyes, spinning me around, leaving me choking and blind.

The hotel rumbled. Somewhere to my side, sparks flew as a chunk of burning wall came crashing down.

I kept low, my sleeve over my mouth, aching for breath as I ran the other way. I couldn't inhale without the air gusting back out in a hacking cough. An open doorway offered a hint of escape, and I took it. Dead end. Just another stripped-down hotel room, the ceiling blanketed in roiling smoke.

I ran to the window. Red and blue lights strobed against the darkness far below. No sign of the fire escape. I'd gotten turned around, confused in the chaos, and now I was trapped. Out in the hallway, another tremor sent timbers crashing down from the ceiling, throwing up walls of flame.

Seven floors. I'd heard of people surviving falls from that high up, miracle cases. Far more likely I'd end up a broken ragdoll on the asphalt, but it was still better than burning to death. I threw my shoulder against the window, gritting my teeth against the jarring pain, but the glass didn't budge. The smoke had stolen my strength and my breath, leaving me weak as a newborn kitten. With my burning eyes squeezed shut I punched the window again and again. I tried to muster the focus for a spell, but constant lung-searing coughs tore my concentration to pieces.

No good. I slumped to the carpet, spent.

I left the earpiece in my pocket. My friends didn't need to listen to me die. That wasn't the memory I wanted to leave them with. I just hoped the smoke would kill me before the fire did.

Fuck it, I thought, bitter. *At least I saved the world.*

Something moved in the hallway. A plank of burning wood, shoved aside. I rubbed my streaming eyes as I struggled to focus.

Caitlin strode through the flames, untouched, her white leather greatcoat billowing behind her. I thought I was hallucinating until she scooped me up in her arms.

"You stupid man," she whispered, cradling my head against her breast. "Hold on tight."

She took a few steps back and ran, leaping for the window, smashing through. For a brief, shining moment we hung suspended over the abyss, trailed by a frozen rain of glass. It felt like we could fly.

Then I fell, clutched in Caitlin's arms.

44.

My memories of the night were hazy. I remembered Caitlin bundling me into the back seat of her car, a ride that turned into a gurney slide under too-bright lights, an oxygen mask over my face. Then nothing.

I spent about a week at Desert Springs Hospital, most of it on a respirator. They bandaged my ribs, set my broken nose, and patched up a dozen other cuts and scrapes I didn't even remember getting. A chubby doctor came by once a day to check my charts and tell me how lucky I was to be alive. He didn't know the half of it.

I was worried about being connected to the Silverlode fire, but I didn't need to be. Hospitals have to report knife and gunshot wounds to the cops. Smoke inhalation, not so much. The official story was that I'd been rescued from a house fire out in the burbs, and nobody challenged it.

Tuesday was my discharge day. I woke from a nap to find Bentley sitting at my bedside, reading an Agatha Christie novel.

"I hear they're letting you go," he said, slipping in a bookmark and resting the paperback on his knee.

"About damn time, too. That's the problem with hospitals. They kill you with boredom."

Out of the corner of my eye, on the grainy television mounted high on the wall, I saw Lauren Carmichael's face. Grabbing the remote, I unmuted the TV and raised the volume.

"—tragedy for this great community," she said, flashbulbs popping around her. "Despite the loss of a classic civic landmark, we can only be thankful that the fire was quickly contained, thanks to the hard work of the Las Vegas Fire Department, and that no one was seriously hurt."

"She's giving a press conference?" I said.

Bentley glared at the screen. "It's been repeating all morning. Everybody loves a catastrophe."

Lauren stared into the camera. I knew it was only a recording, but somehow I could still feel her eyes drilling into mine.

"To the arsonist responsible for this senseless act of destruction, I will say only this. We will find you. And we will bring you to justice."

"Not if I find you first," I muttered.

"What's next for Carmichael-Sterling Nevada?" one reporter called from the audience.

Lauren put on a million-dollar smile. "What's next? Progress. The tragedy at the Silverlode in no way hinders our primary goal, the completion of the Enclave Resort and Casino. We intend to put a new face on Las Vegas. New life, new jobs, new capital and growth. Make no mistake: the Enclave will rise."

I muted the television.

"So what's next for Daniel Faust?" Bentley asked.

"Funny. Normally I'd say, 'The same thing I did last month and the month before that.' You know me, I've never been too purpose-driven. Still..."

"Yes?"

"Feels like maybe I should be," I said. "Don't know. Just feels like I'm missing out on something. Used to be happy just coasting by. Maybe that's not enough anymore."

"You'll figure it out," Bentley said. He patted my shoulder. We both turned, feeling the silhouette in the doorway before we saw it.

"Am I interrupting?" Caitlin asked.

"Not at all," Bentley said, pushing himself up from the chair. "I have to get back to the bookstore. Come by when you can, Daniel. We should have dinner."

He paused in the doorway, talking to Caitlin in a low whisper. She nodded, lightly touching his arm. He gave me a wave and strolled out of sight.

"My hero," I said, smiling at her. "What was that about?"

"He thanked me. Wasn't expecting that. Also wanted to ask about the Box."

My stomach clenched. "We have to get back in there somehow. If Lauren gets her hands on that thing—"

"Relax," she said, walking over to stand by my bedside. She rested her hand on my chest. "It's taken care of. We made a generous campaign donation to a certain public representative. As a result, the city contracted with Blue Valley Waste Management to handle the cleanup and salvage operation at the Silverlode."

"And?"

"And the management at Blue Valley is on Nicky Agnelli's payroll. Nicky's very, very eager to curry favor with my prince and make up for his mischief, as you might imagine. The Box will be retrieved and returned to its proper home." She stroked my forehead. "We can talk shop later. How are you?"

"Alive, thanks to you."

She smiled, shaking her head.

"You saved me too. Now then, I understand you're a free man, so why don't we get you out of that gown and into something a bit more stylish?"

My papers signed and stamped, an intern rolled me to the hospital doors in a wheelchair. After days in bed, the last thing I wanted to do was sit down one minute longer. Caitlin left us at the curb, and pulled up in her Audi a moment later.

A plastic bag filled with my belongings, plus a stack of papers and a prescription for a low-grade painkiller, rested on my lap as she pulled out of the parking lot.

"Where to?" she asked.

"This alley up on the right. That'll do."

She idled the engine, and I got out of the car. It felt good to stretch my legs and breathe the clean desert air. I reached into the plastic bag and set the six soul-traps, one at a time, on the Audi's hood.

"Seems like I should be doing this in a park or a cemetery or someplace serene," I said, fiddling with the latch on the first pouch. "Seems like I should have something profound to say, to send you off with. But I don't. For what it's worth, I'm sorry some crazy fucks murdered you for no good reason. I'm sorry I wasn't good enough to save you. Just...go."

A cloud of faint, glimmering light, like a spray of diamonds, drifted up from the pouch's open mouth. It rose, taken by a gust of wind, and vanished. The next four pouches went the same way, their prisoners released to the open sky. Only one remained. Stacy.

"Don't even think," Caitlin said as I got back in the car, "that I'm not going down there with you."

#

Stacy waited for us in the dark. Her misshapen wraith hovered on the far side of the line of enchanted dust, her mouth wide in a perpetual cry of terror. Finally, after all the chaos, all the bloodshed, I'd set things right. Finally, the job was done.

"Okay," I said to her, holding up the pouch. "This should set you free. It's okay, Stacy. You're going to a better place."

"Um, Daniel?" Caitlin said beside me.

"Yeah?"

She shook her head. "You do know she's going to hell, right?"

I froze, my fingers tight on the pouch's ties. "What?"

"Far be it from me to read off the litany of her sins, but the girl was hardly a beacon of virtue."

"She was a *victim*," I said, my jaw clenched.

"That she was." Caitlin nodded. "I'm not happy about it either, Daniel, and it's not fair, but neither is it subject to appeal."

I never had a chance of saving her. It was a sucker's game all along. I turned on Caitlin, furious.

"This is bullshit. Kaufman abused her—"

"If you don't like how the universe works, take it up with the architects. I just work here. If it's any consolation, this has nothing to do with what she did with Kaufman. Her downward spiral took place long, long before she ever met him. You don't know the girl, Daniel. You don't know anything about her. You never did."

She was right. I only knew Stacy through her grandfather's love, and love is blind. I had never thought to question if the picture he painted, this pristine, innocent girl, was even real. I thought I liked the idea of being the crusading hero out to avenge the fallen damsel. I liked it a little too much.

I'm the bad guy, I had told Tony Vance right before he took the high dive. I should have paid better attention.

"I'm sorry," I told Caitlin. "I just thought...never mind."

I looked at the pouch. At Stacy's hovering form, trapped between worlds.

"I can't open this. I can't damn her."

"It's your choice," Caitlin said, "but think on this. Life goes on. She may not be...happy where she goes, but situations change. There's a spark of hope even in the blackest darkness, the hope that someday, somehow, things can get better. If you leave her like this, that hope is gone. She will spend her eternity frozen. Stagnant. Hopeless."

I had thought I was Stacy's savior. Turned out I was her executioner. Opening the pouch and sending her to hell, that'd be on my head. That was the kind of blood you couldn't scrub clean. Leaving her like this, though...I didn't have the right to do that to her. More than anything, I knew the value of a spark of hope.

"She deserves a fighting chance," I said, staring down at the pouch in my hands, "same as anybody."

Caitlin moved close, touching my shoulder. "Then set her free."

I opened the pouch.

"Goodbye," I whispered as motes of light flew toward Stacy's wraith, joining with her, her body restored in a soft white glow. For a brief moment I saw her there, perfected, whole once more. She opened her mouth as if to say something, starting to smile.

Then she vanished in a blast of acrid air, leaving nothing behind but the faint stench of sulfur.

The empty pouch slipped from my numb fingertips. Caitlin pulled me close, holding me in silence.

After a moment, she said, "I think we should go celebrate."

"I'm not sure what there is to celebrate."

She pulled back, smiling at me, and blinked away a bit of moisture in her eyes.

"Us," she said simply. "Us, and today, and tonight, and tomorrow."

She was right.

I'd won some; I'd lost some. More important, I'd survived. I had choices to make, a life to live. And I had Caitlin.

"You know what?" I said. "Those sound like some pretty good reasons."

I offered her my arm. She slipped hers around mine, walking beside me as we turned back up the winding storm tunnel, back to the waiting light of day.

"How do you feel about sushi?" she asked.

"After a week of hospital food, I'd eat my own shoe and like it. Sushi sounds great."

"I know just the place. I'll call ahead when we get to the car. You're going to love it, trust me..."

This was crazy, Caitlin and me, and I knew our troubles were just getting started. We had a long hard road ahead of us and no maps to guide the way. Still, I wouldn't have given it up for the world.

Trust her? Yeah, I did.

Heaven help me, I did.

Epilogue

The first thing Artie Kaufman felt was cold. Wet, clammy cold like a New England rain, the kind that sinks into your bones and stays there.

The second thing he felt, when he moved his hand, was the leather cuff.

He blinked, head groggy and pounding like the hangover after a three-day bender. He tried to rub his eyes, only to feel his wrist jerk taut against the buckled leather strap that bound it. The rusted metal chair felt like a block of ice against his naked back and legs.

"Hey," he said, voice edged with a note of fear, "what the fuck? Is this some kind of joke?"

Why couldn't he remember how he'd gotten here? Last night was a blur. He'd been rooking that dipshit fanboy at his weekly poker game, then...what? *Okay, Artie, no more tequila before bed. You're getting too old to party like a college kid.*

He tugged against the straps that bound his wrists and ankles. Ahead of him was darkness—no, not darkness. A wall of black glass. He craned his neck to try to figure out where he was. The grimy tile floor looked weirdly familiar, like that truck stop bathroom where he shot most of his movies, but the rest of the room was different. Like a doctor's office at a hospital or a clinic, but everything rusted and falling apart.

"Guys?" he called out. "C'mon, this isn't funny. You're starting to freak me out. Hello?"

"Hello, Artie," Stacy said, walking out where he could see her.

He didn't know where she'd gotten the dress, some kind of renaissance fair thing in crimson and faded white. A bracelet of twined daffodils draped from her wrist, but the once bright flowers were just dried husks. A withered rose, its petals curled and rotten, adorned her blond hair.

Oh thank God, Artie thought. "Hey, baby girl, a little help here? I think the guys are playing a prank on me."

"You're confused. I was confused at first, too. Then I met a pretty lady who explained everything to me. She gave me two messages to deliver to you."

"Stacy," Artie snapped, "I don't have time for this shit, okay—"

"The first message, which she said you'd understand, is that she's one of Caitlin's sisters. She's going to make sure you stay properly entertained until Caitlin comes back to deal with you personally."

Caitlin.

The memories hit him like a fist to the face. The chase through the house. The contract. The fire. Caitlin. *No tears now, Artie. This is just a taste of what's to come.* He stared at Stacy with bulging eyes, horror dawning.

"The second message," Stacy said, "is 'Welcome to hell.'"

Artie flailed at the cuffs, frantic, jerking against the steel chair.

"I was trying to get my life together when you found me," Stacy said. "Did you know that? I did a lot of things I wasn't proud of back home, with some bad people. I ran to Vegas to try to get away from all that. I wanted a new start. I found you instead."

Artie ignored her, consumed with his own terror. "Come on, come on, untie me. Let's get out of here—"

"There was a pretty good chance I'd have done it. Given time, given help. I could have made something of myself. I could have been a better person. I wanted to be. But it turned out that wanting wasn't good enough."

He shook his head wildly at her. "Are you listening, you stupid bitch? *Untie me right fucking now!*"

"I'll never see my grandfather again," Stacy said. "Never see anyone I cared about, anyone I loved. Never see the sun. Not for all eternity. I know that I'm responsible for the choices I made, for the crimes I committed. But you, Artie? You're the reason I'm here."

She pulled a cart, wobbling on one broken wheel, around to the front of the chair so he could see it. Surgical tools, half of them rusted and dull, lined a silver tray.

"Bitch," Artie whispered, too terrified to put any force behind the word, "what do you think you're doing?"

"Do you remember what you told me when you first met me?"

He forced a smile, head bobbing like a puppet. "Yeah! Yeah! I said you had star quality! I meant it, baby girl, meant every word of it!"

"The pretty lady I met, she said the exact same thing. She said it wasn't fair how this all happened, but she had a way I could make things a little bit better for myself. She said Caitlin asked for a very special favor, just for me. Isn't that nice?"

Stacy's hand hovered over the tray. After a moment's indecision she picked up a scalpel, its dark, pitted surface caked with decay.

"What is this?" Artie squirmed helplessly in the chair. "What, you want revenge? Is that what this is all about? You think that's gonna make you feel better?"

Movement caught his eye, beyond the wall of blackened glass. Outlines of figures in the dark, seated, watching intently.

An audience?

"No," Stacy said with a wistful sigh. "No, Artie, you don't understand. Revenge won't make me feel better. Besides, you aren't worth it. This isn't about you at all."

She touched the edge of the scalpel to his cheek.

"This is my audition."

AFTERWORD

Readers familiar with the Vegas Strip will have noted the changing of casino names. This was done to provide a certain amount of legal cover (since the real casinos might not look kindly upon accusations of getting friendly with a guy like Nicky Agnelli...) and allow for certain deviations from reality when necessary. Just assume that Daniel Faust's Vegas is a slightly skewed version of our own, glimpsed through a smoky glass.

That said, every location mentioned in The Long Way Down is a real place you can visit, with the exception of the Tiger's Garden.

Probably.

Special thanks to James T. Egan and Kira Rubenthaler at Bookfly Design for their absolutely top-notch cover design and copy-editing work. Thanks to my friends for indulgently putting up with me while I'm lost in a writing binge, and to the always-awesome staff at Hotel 32, my home away from home when I'm doing field research in Vegas.

Thanks to you, especially, for reading! If you'd like to see more (and get the inside track on Daniel Faust's next adventure), head over to craigschaeferbooks.com and hop onto my mailing list for announcements about new releases. You can also catch me on Facebook (at facebook.com/CraigSchaeferBooks), Twitter (at @craig_schaefer), or just drop me an email at craig@craigschaeferbooks.com. I'd love to hear from you.

14461693R00221

Printed in Poland
by Amazon Fulfillment
Poland Sp. z o.o., Wrocław